M000033060

The
Accidental
Spy

Novels by David Gardner

The Journalist: A Paranormal Thriller

The Last Speaker of Skalwegian

The Accidental Spy

The Accidental *Spy*

DAVID GARDNER

Encircle Publications
Farmington, Maine, U.S.A.

Editor, Encircle Publications: Cynthia Brackett-Vincent

Book design and cover design by Deirdre Wait
Cover images © Getty Images

Published by:

Encircle Publications
PO Box 187
Farmington, ME 04938

info@encirclepub.com
http://encirclepub.com

Two roads diverged in a yellow wood,
And sorry I could not travel both...
—Robert Frost, "The Road Not Taken"

Spy: A person employed by a governmental agency to obtain secret information on a hostile country.
—The Philips Dictionary of Espionage

Accidental Spy: Some poor jerk dragged into a world of trouble.
—Harvey Hudson

Chapter 1

Bunny Ears
Summer, 2019

Harvey Hudson released the steering wheel and swatted at the blue balloon ("Congrats! You Did It!") that was banging against the back of his head.

What was the 'It' for? Someone earned a law degree? Pulled off a bank heist? Successfully underwent potty training? All three?

One day before turning fifty-six, and here he was, delivering balloons. How had he let this happen to himself?

He chewed on the last of the Skittles he'd swiped from a bulky candy basket attached to a red balloon shaped like a birthday cake. Too many sweets for some spoiled kid. He was doing the pudgy brat a favor. The Snickers bar was tempting. Maybe later.

Harvey reached across the front seat, grabbed a handful of candy bars from the Skittle-less basket ($149), and dropped them into its modest neighbor ($39). He often shifted candy from larger baskets to lesser ones. He thought of himself as the Robin Hood of balloon-delivery.

He'd had just $87 in the bank a few weeks ago when he'd shambled past a help-wanted sign in the front window of the Rapid Rabbit Balloon Service. He paused and reread the sign. "Part-time Delivery Person Needed. Become a Rapid Rabbit!"

Yeah, what the hell. He hurried inside before he came to his senses. He would have taken any gig—balloon-delivery specialist, male stripper, or get-away driver for a grizzled bank robber.

With his part-time job delivering balloons and his full-time work as a beginning technical writer, Harvey could just stay afloat. His ex-wife had cleaned him out.

He double-parked on a smart street of brick-front homes on Boston's Beacon Hill. Hesitating, he clamped the hated bunny ears over his head and attached the spongy red nose. Sighing, he grabbed the $149 basket and, head down, ambled up the walkway and rang the bell. The balloon bobbed overhead, taunting him.

The woman who opened the door was a slim and pretty brunette in her fifties. She had a narrow face and large, dark eyes.

She was his boss at his day job.

Also his high school sweetheart.

Harvey wanted to disappear into the ground.

Margo took a step back. "Oh."

Harvey pulled off the bulbous red nose and stuffed it into his shirt pocket. "Uh… this is where you live?"

Margo shook her head. "I'm here with my daughter for a birthday party."

Harvey shifted from one foot to the other. "I'm… um… delivering balloons just for tonight to help out a buddy who had two wisdom teeth pulled this morning, a professor who lost his job the same time I did."

Margo blinked twice.

"A sociologist," Harvey added.

Margo gripped the edge of the door.

"Named Fred," Harvey said.

Margo nodded.

"The guy took the job in desperation because he's broke, recently divorced, and down on his luck," Harvey said and realized he was describing himself.

He handed the basket to Margo.

Did she believe him? Probably not. Did the company have a rule against moonlighting? He'd soon find out.

Margo poked around inside the basket. "There's too much candy in here."

"At least there aren't any Skittles."

Margo selected a Reese's Peanut Butter Cup. "I've moved tomorrow's team meeting up to 10:00 a.m. Did you get my email?"

Harvey nodded.

Was that her way of telling him that moonlighters don't get fired? He hoped so. He was pathetically unqualified as a technical writer, and his job was in jeopardy.

Harvey hated meetings. Sometimes he thought the software engineers asked him questions he couldn't answer just to see him squirm. Many were kids in their twenties, making double his salary.

And he hated lying to Margo. At least he could be honest about one small thing. "Actually, this is my night gig. I've had it for a few weeks."

Margo unwrapped the Reese's, nipped off a corner, chewed and said, "Is that why I caught you asleep at your desk yesterday?"

No, it's because the job is so goddamn boring. He shook his head. "I wasn't sleeping. I have the habit of relaxing and closing my eyes whenever I'm searching for the perfect way to convey a particularly difficult concept to our worthy customers."

"And snoring?"

Margo was smiling now. That same cute smile from high school. He remembered it from the time they'd sneaked a first kiss in the back row of calculus class. The girl he'd loved and lost.

She set the basket down and pulled a twenty from the side pocket of her slacks. "Um… would you… uh… accept a tip?"

"No."

She shoved the bill into his shirt pocket. "Yes, you will."

Harvey shifted his weight to his left foot. A liar doesn't deserve a $20 tip. At most, a few dimes and nickels, couch-cushion change.

Margo finished the peanut butter cup in silence.

He didn't quite know what to say now.

Yes, he did know. He should tell her the truth.

He'd outsourced his job to India.

Was that illegal? Probably not. But highly unethical. Would she protect him after he'd confessed? Unlikely, which meant he would lose his job. But living a lie was exhausting and just plain wrong. She'd hired him and trusted him. She deserved better. He cleared his throat, once, twice, a third time. "Margo, there's something I have to tell you. It seems I—"

"Is that the balloon guy?" a young woman called from inside the house.

"That's my daughter," Margo said and picked up the basket. A blue balloon bobbed on a string attached to the handle. "I'll be right back."

Harvey stood at the open door, trying to think of some way to soften his upcoming confession. Or maybe just blurt it out and get it over with?

"Happy birthday, Dad!"

The daughter's voice again from inside.

"Candy and a kid's balloon again this year! Are you trying to tell me something?"

The daughter laughed.

Harvey recognized the man's voice.

Tucker Aldrich was the CEO of the company where Harvey worked. He was also Margo's ex-husband and a first-class dickhead.

So, it meant the balloon and candy basket were for Tucker and not some child. Harvey was sorry he'd passed on the Snickers bar.

The hell with telling the truth.

Margo came back out, holding a glass of white wine. She leaned against the door frame. "What were you going to say earlier?"

"Uh… that you're an over-tipper."

"Only when the delivery person is a cute, curly-haired guy with a spongy red nose," she said and sipped her wine. "Did I mention that the meeting's moved to 10:00?"

"Yes."

Silence, then Margo said, "Well, I'll see you tomorrow."

She closed the door behind her.

Harvey stared at the bronze horse-head knocker. He wanted to rip it off. The door too. He in fact wanted to tear the whole damn building down on Tucker's head.

Margo hadn't forgotten that she'd told him about the meeting. Margo was incapable of forgetting. She was warning him to show up.

Team meetings were a nightmare. The scruffy programmers spoke computerese, argued over stuff Harvey didn't understand, and gleefully pointed out errors in his documentation.

But way off in New Delhi, lovely Amaya understood, and with luck she might save his job.

Tomorrow's meeting would make or break him.

Harvey shuffled down the walkway, his head lowered, his bunny ears slipping down his forehead. He'd been so shocked to see Margo that he'd forgotten to take them off. One of life's bad moments.

Still, she had called him cute.

Yeah, sure. He was just hours from turning fifty-six, had found additional gray hairs while shaving that morning, and was thickening around the waist from too many Skittles and Snickers.

Harvey climbed into his car and slumped in the driver's seat. He was angry with Tucker for stealing Margo and angry at Margo for not offering him a glass of wine. But most of all, Harvey was angry with himself for letting her see him in bunny ears.

When he'd first started making deliveries a few weeks earlier, he'd refused to wear them, then thought, what the hell? Doesn't everyone at some time want to play the fool? There was no pressure to succeed, to show off, to one-up a colleague.

What if everyone—from a prisoner sitting out a life term to the President of the United States—had to set aside one day a year and play the fool, to go out in public wearing a spongy red nose and bunny ears?

What-Ifs and Whys had obsessed Harvey as a child, who from morning to night had trailed behind his father and mother and pestered them with questions. (What if there was a ladder to the moon? What if everyone had four arms? Why is cousin Alice getting those bumps on her chest?)

Later, he would turn his pestering curiosity into a profession. He thought of himself as a 'speculative historian'. (What if the Allies had lost the Second World War? What if Caesar hadn't crossed the Rubicon? What if no one had invented the computer?)

Harvey started the engine, reached over to tap the next address into the GPS, then leaned back.

Why humiliate himself like this? His ex-wife had always insisted he was punishing himself with guilt over his younger brother. Harvey denied this, but he knew she was right.

Enough. He had reached his lifetime quota of humiliation.

Here's another What-If: What if he quit this goddamn job?

Harvey shut off the engine, climbed out of the car, went around back, and popped the trunk.

A dozen balloons bobbed on basket handles, aching to go free.

Harvey tied the spongy red nose to a balloon that read "Get Well Soon!" He cut it loose. Next, he liberated a black balloon picturing a race car ("Turning Ten!"). Finally, he tied his rabbit ears to a cluster of white orbs trailing a banner that read, "Congrats, New Parents!" and set the bunch free.

He watched until the last of the balloons caught the breeze and disappeared into the night sky.

He slammed the trunk closed, climbed into his car, and right away started to fret. What if a balloon floated to the harbor for some sea creature to swallow (Headline: "Reckless Ex-Professor Kills Orca!").

Just one more reason to be angry with himself.

Chapter 2

Harvey-the-Lion-Slayer

Harvey shuffled into the empty conference room and checked his watch—early, for once. He'd slept badly, drank too much coffee at breakfast, and grouched at a guy in the subway for stepping on his toe. This meeting would decide his future with the company.

Harvey stood at the tall windows that looked fourteen floors down at the rows of Back Bay townhouses, the Charles River, the MIT buildings on the far bank, and the leafy Boston suburbs beyond. It was a warm and cloudless day in July. An eight-person rowing team skimmed gracefully across the Charles, looking to Harvey like a fragile water insect propelled by eight long legs.

The defunct Middlebridge College where he'd taught for so many years didn't have the money for a rowing team. Or even enough to remain open. Harvey ached to be back there teaching. Fifty-six was a tough age to be in the market, but he sure as hell wouldn't give up looking. And his textbook should be a game-changer. He'd almost finished writing it when the college collapsed. Now he could work on the book all day, thanks to lovely Amaya in New Delhi.

What was she doing at this minute? Was she at her desk, working on his documentation? Or brushing her shiny, long black hair? Was she as fetching as he fantasized? Probably not. Anyway, she'd be in bed. It was the middle of the night in New Delhi.

Team members wandered in. Harvey grabbed a seat with a view of the river.

He'd learned his students' names the first day of class, but here he didn't try. He identified his colleagues by characteristics. Across from him slumped the young guy with the red beard down to his chest, who always brought a sticky bun to meetings and chewed with his mouth half open. And two seats to the lad's right was a thin woman who yawned and fidgeted, and next to her sat an ex-basketball star with tiny ears. All knees and elbows.

Most were just kids. When they weren't asking embarrassing questions about his troubled documentation, Harvey found them an agreeable bunch. They reminded him of his former students.

Owen arrived and settled down with a wheeze next to Harvey. Owen was a wheezer, a corpulent man who wore thick, wire-rim glasses and the occasional red bow tie. The guy was Harvey's best—and only—friend at work, aside from Margo. They were the same age, a couple of geezerheads seated side-by-side, surrounded by hyper-caffeinated youngsters who spoke rapid computerese.

Harvey always thought that *Owen* was an outdated and rather uncommon name, as was his own. They'd make a perfect clown team: *Owen and Harvey.* Harvey pictured orange, double-breasted suits, wide pink neckties, spongy red noses, bunny ears, and long flapping shoes. Tumbles and pratfalls.

When did people start using names? Probably just a single name at first, not much more than a grunt. Grok or Snuk or something like that. Did the practice evolve into the bearer's role? Grok-the-Lion-Slayer? Snuk-the-Village-Queen?

Some people change their name, either for legal purposes—marriage, to evade debtors or the law—or just on a whim. What if everyone was required to change their name as they grew older? It would force people to define themselves through their name and make them face up to what they've become. Harvey would have lied. Harvey-the-Former-Balloon-Provider? Not a chance.

He would be Harvey-the-Lion-Slayer.

Margo arrived and gave him a look he couldn't interpret. Had she told Tucker that it was the company's new and pitifully inept tech writer who'd delivered the previous night's Skittles-less candy basket? Or was she troubled by the documentation that Amaya had written and Harvey had handed around for review three days earlier?

Margo's reputation was on the line because she'd hired him, and reputation was everything for Margo. Her job was safe, however, because she co-owned T&M Consultants with her slimeball ex. Harvey knew how much she hated sharing the company with Tucker. Margo wasn't a sharer. What especially angered her was that Tucker had taken over running the company when she'd left to give birth to their daughter and had relinquished little power once she returned. That resulted in muffled shouts behind closed doors.

A dozen team members sat around the table. Only Tucker was missing. He always arrived last, his grand entrance. A few engineers thumbed through the twenty-three pages of the documentation that Amaya had written and that Harvey had photocopied and distributed, his sole contribution. He saw dog-eared pages, others with paper clips, and notes scribbled in the margins.

Harvey's stomach seized. Sweat trickled down his back. Today was the big day.

He shouldn't have quit his night gig. At least he could have kept himself alive on sweets.

He caught Margo's eye. Another uninterpretable nod.

He'd lost track of Margo for many years, then a couple months ago had run into her on the street in downtown Boston. They'd walked to a Starbucks and talked about their divorces, about how she had a daughter in graduate school and he had a daughter in medical school, about what they've been doing over the years. She mentioned the company that she and Tucker had formed early in their marriage. Harvey told her he'd lost his job but was working—just temporarily, you understand, until he found another academic post—as a technical writer for a well-funded and up-and-coming high-tech company.

That wasn't quite true. Harvey couldn't bring himself to admit that he had a one-week writing job for a fellow ex-history professor who ill-advisedly thought he could start a successful online service providing horoscopes for cats and dogs.

A happy coincidence, Margo had said. Her company had just lost its technical writer.

Harvey didn't hesitate to accept her offer.

Sure, he'd inflated his qualifications, but just how hard could technical writing be? He'd written a well-received PhD dissertation, after all, plus dozens of scholarly articles, and he was close to finishing his book, *Big History: The Birth and Death of Everything.*

As it turned out, technical writing was damn hard. He'd let Margo down. He'd let himself down.

And the job bored him from the first day when he and a freckled, pot-scented youth destined for the mailroom were escorted into a darkened room to watch a cheesy video for newcomers: "The Amazing World of Pipeline Pumps."

Harvey hadn't found pipeline pumps all that amazing. Nor had the kid who'd snored through the show. The video opened with a helicopter shot of massive gray pumps spaced evenly along wilderness pipelines. Booster pumps, they were called. T&M Consultants wrote the vital software that controlled them, a deep-voiced man reported. A vital component of the petroleum industry, he added, then said something about the vital role that the pipes and pumps played in the vital U.S. economy, and Harvey drifted off to sleep.

Harvey started to doze off again when Tucker stepped through the door to start today's meeting. His administrative assistant followed, a miniature gray lady with wobbly ankles and a tenuous grip on a massive birthday cake. Tucker made no move to help her. She set the cake on a side table and slipped away.

There was a feeble round of applause for Tucker's having successfully reached his fifty-sixth year.

Today was also Harvey's birthday. His mother would call and invite him over to celebrate it along with Tommy's, which was just two days after his own. She would bake the usual chocolate cake with the white frosting. It was impossible to get out of attending.

Tucker didn't scowl at Harvey or make a snarky remark about the balloon-delivery profession, which Harvey took to mean that Margo hadn't told on him. Loyal Margo.

And disloyal me.

Tucker stood at the head of the table as he always did; he wore a dark suit and dreary tie as he always did. Everyone else had on cotton slacks and jeans and blouses and shirts of a varying degree of grunge. Harvey wore an aging brown sports jacket and a maroon T-shirt, his teaching costume.

Harvey and Tucker not only shared a birthday but a close friendship that had lasted until high school, when they became bitter competitors. They'd vied for quarterback on the football team, which Tucker won, and grades—an easy victory for Harvey—and competed over girls, which was a tie until Tucker stole Margo. At six feet two, Tucker was a little taller than Harvey, from a somewhat wealthier family, and was a little more athletic. But Harvey was better in a fight because his father had been on the Harvard boxing team. Their harmless exchanges of fisticuffs were one of the few father/son things they had done together.

Yeah, Tucker hadn't always been a douchebag. They used to sit in his treehouse, thumb through wrinkled copies of *Playboy,* and peek through a telescope at the woman next door when she showered with the shade up. No, not a complete jerk. But he had stolen Margo.

Tucker gave a short pep talk that no one listened to. Everyone was wolfing down pieces of the cake with the white frosting and "Happy Birthday, Boss!" in red food dye. The team had a collective sweet tooth, the one way Harvey felt he fit in. But no cake today. His stomach churned.

Tucker dropped a copy of the review documentation onto the table. "Who has questions?"

The lanky basketball star went first, one of the worst of the tormentors. "I didn't quite understand what you meant by 'regressive double-derivative code' on page sixteen."

That was said politely. A first. Harvey had no idea what regressive double-derivative code meant, either. Or much of anything else in the paper. Only Amaya did. He remembered the passage because he'd read the twenty-two pages three times, hoping something would stick. Harvey shuffled through his copy, then looked up and said, "Read section 3.2.4 again. It should make everything abundantly clear."

Or not. The basketball player nodded.

Harvey would contact Amaya immediately after the meeting for an explanation that he would email to the lanky point guard.

Then the young woman with the nose ring and green hair asked an equally well-mannered question that Harvey deftly deflected. Then came Charlie's turn—or was he named Sam? He finished his sticky bun, wiped his fingers on his jeans, and said that the documentation looked really solid.

Murmurs of agreement around the table.

Harvey slumped lower in his chair, relieved, exhausted, thankful. Margo gave him a discreet thumbs up.

Tucker didn't compliment Harvey on the documentation, but didn't bitch about it either, which was as close as Tucker ever got to a compliment. He moved on to something about integrating coding modules, or disintegrating coding modules, or modulating disintegrated code—a conversation that left Harvey numb.

So, he'd passed. Sure, he was a fake, a fraud, and a phony. But he'd survived.

He took a deep breath and half-closed his eyes.

Thanks, Amaya.

He pictured her on the window seat of her study, half turned to look out, sunlight reflecting off her shiny black hair as she gazed at a serene garden of weathered stone statues and broad-leafed vegetation, while green-and-red birds vocalized and flitted about. He imagined a polite and modest woman about his age, with a nice smile, a nice voice, a nice face. What would she be wearing? Was she wrapped in a flowing magenta sari? No, not while at home. More likely, she was relaxing in jeans and a pretty white blouse, which was okay, too.

Surprisingly, only one-fifth of his salary went to her.

He'd emailed her huge amounts of background material two weeks earlier, and she'd finished writing the documentation on schedule. What a find: a skilled programmer with a knack for writing. Also, no doubt beautiful.

At a team meeting a few weeks earlier, Tucker had joked that, since Harvey wasn't up to the task, maybe he should outsource his job to India. That got a big laugh around the table.

Afterwards, Harvey hurried back to his cubicle and outsourced his job to India.

He'd been receiving a stream of emails from Lotus Worldwide Consultants in New Delhi, which he'd ignored. But after Tucker put him on probation and then, at the next meeting, joked about outsourcing, Harvey had found one of the Indian company's lingering emails and applied.

They'd taken him on immediately and at a surprisingly low rate. Equally surprising, was why they'd contacted him in the first place. Had they blanketed the Web with millions of emails, or had they simply targeted him as a technical writer? But how would they have known? And did it matter now?

He glanced at the wall clock. Time slowed at Tucker's meetings. Something to do with the effect that acute boredom had on Einsteinian relativity.

Harvey let his thoughts drift to Einstein's effect on Western thinking (covered in a late chapter of the book Harvey was writing), and from there his thoughts winged their way to India, to Amaya, to the desk where she wrote. He wondered about the person who'd designed her desk, who'd built it, driven it to the warehouse, sold it. Going even farther back, he wondered who'd planted the tree and who'd cut it down. What if lightning had hit that particular tree, and it never became a desk? Or if the water buffalo pulling the cart had plunged down a mountainside? In that case, Amaya would now be seated unknowingly and fetchingly before a desk of a different shape and color.

For Harvey, the entire world and all of mankind were connected. He wondered, for example, how many hands had touched his smart phone before he bought it. He thought of the mental energy that went into designing it, of the threads of knowledge that reached back through Einstein and Newton and to the great Arab mathematicians and Greek scientists and philosophers, and beyond that to the clever man or woman who was first to bang two rocks together to start a campfire.

Harvey saw all of history as one humongous ball of twine, of everything and everyone connected and interdependent, living or dead. Sometimes the idea was too heavy to hold in his head, and he had to sit down.

His specialty was Big History, an obscure field that treated everything from the Big Bang to the present. That was the subject of the book he was laboring over. Harvey thought of the Big History courses he had taught at Middlebridge College as a reflection of his soul. He loved teaching it, loved preparing lectures, even loved correcting exams.

He promised himself that he would claw his way back, no

matter how long it took and no matter the setbacks. And he would succeed. After all, he'd been the former president of a prestigious, international history organization, had been named teacher of the year twice in a row, and had published numerous papers. It would just take time.

Harvey returned to earth when Tucker's administrative assistant stumbled through the door with a familiar basket of candy. It seemed the meeting had ended.

"I want everyone to take something when you leave," Tucker said. "I bought this as a special birthday treat for all of you."

Harvey and Margo exchanged glances. She rolled her eyes. Harvey remembered how she had done that the time back in junior high when she'd come around a corner and caught him and a buddy practicing armpit farts, an event which still caused Harvey's cheeks to burn.

Margo stopped rolling her eyes and smiled at Harvey.

He smiled back, then wondered if she was seeing anyone.

And was Amaya?

Chapter 3

If Only…

Harvey sat on his mother's massive white couch with his shins pressed against a coffee table heaped with books on art, architecture, and cats. His mother sat across from him in a padded wooden rocker, her knitting needles flying.

"I didn't know you knitted," Harvey said.

"I just started," she said, holding up her right hand and wiggling her fingers. "It's for my arthritis."

"I'm glad you're taking such good care of yourself."

She complained of aches and pains, but was otherwise the picture of health for a seventy-eight-year-old. She ate right, did stretches in the morning, and walked with friends every day. In winter, the group took an Uber to the mall to get in their steps.

Today, she wore her hair in a tight bun. It was gray now, but was originally red and curly. Harvey had inherited his mother's curls and color, but he got his large eyes and wide, boxer's shoulders from his father.

Harvey worried about his mother, growing old and alone in this big house. He wished he could do more for her. He never felt like a good son. Far from it.

She held her knitting out at arm's length, tipped her head sideways, and gave the piece an up-and-down look.

The start of a scarf? A sweater? Something deep blue, anyway. Her favorite color.

"Any luck with your job search?" she asked.

Harvey shook his head. "No one's tripping over their feet to hire a fifty-six-year-old history professor."

"You should have followed in your father's footsteps."

That again?

"I didn't want to be a doctor."

"You'd still have a job. The world always needs surgeons."

Harvey opened his mouth, hesitated, closed it.

The knitting needles clicked, and an occasional car rumbled by. This was a quiet street in an upscale section of Brookline, snug up against Boston. His mother lived in a grand white colonial perched on a hill that Harvey and Tommy sledded down in winter. She loved the house and never wanted to leave it, the dream home of a girl who'd grown up poor. Harvey had promised her that she would never have to move, a constant source of worry for him. When his father died, he left a surprise mortgage that was keeping Harvey broke and working two jobs.

His mother hooked her wire-rimmed glasses back over her ears and turned to him. "Are you still driving balloons all over town?"

"No."

"Good. That type of job is beneath a member of the Hudson family."

Harvey's father had been a renowned surgeon; his mother had acquired her status from her husband's profession. She'd grown up over a hardware store, and at sixteen she'd had to drop out of high school to work in a cloth mill and help support the family. She'd been a red-haired beauty, however, and at eighteen she'd eloped with a Harvard medical student.

"No more balloons," Harvey added.

Pizzas instead, but he didn't mention this. He'd made his first run the night before, arriving home exhausted and smelling of soggy pizza boxes, but with $108 in tips in his pocket. That matched his best balloon-and-candy-basket night and did not involve bunny ears.

Harvey was pleasantly surprised by his feeling of peace and freedom as he drove around Boston delivering balloons or pizzas. He'd always craved freedom, open spaces, and moving about. His technical-writing job kept him miles from a window, trapped in a tight gray cubicle with a faint chemical smell. At Middlebridge College, he'd had a roomy office with a view of the quadrangle, and he'd been free to move around—fifty minutes teaching here, fifty minutes in another building across campus, with a blanket of crunchy, colored leaves underfoot in the fall, snow during winter, and a soft, rich carpet of grass in spring. Students would call him 'Professor Hudson' or 'Doctor Hudson.' His boss at Pete's Speedy Pizza called him 'Hudson' or sometimes just, "Hey, you!"

Harvey's mother set her knitting on an end table, pulled herself to her feet, and started for the kitchen. "How's the book coming?"

"I'm finishing the section on the French Revolution. I've just beheaded Louis the Sixteenth."

"Good. He had it coming. So did his tart of a wife. Speaking of tarts, how's—"

"Brenda? She's still in Los Angeles, living with a gray-faced insurance executive with a three-legged poodle."

Harvey's mother paused at the kitchen door and looked back. "So, she dumps you, flies off for the sunny West Coast, and she does what? Takes up with an insurance salesman instead of some big-name director with a blond ponytail and a Rolls Royce convertible? That woman has no style. You're better off without her."

The two women had detested each other from their first meeting.

"How's your job going?" she asked. "Last time we talked, you said it wasn't working out."

"It is now. Really well."

"That's nice," his mother said before disappearing into the kitchen. "I hope Tucker is treating you decently," she added, her voice raised. "I liked him as a boy, but he turned into an awful teenager, snobbish and self-involved. Has he gotten any better?"

"Worse."

"Figures. Well, keep looking for a better job. At least you're not in a bad position. I've read that people in high tech earn basketfuls of money."

Not beginning technical writers, especially when a chunk of one's salary goes to a freelancer in New Delhi.

What was Amaya doing now? Was she thinking of him?

Of course not. A foolish thought. Still...

"Your father was a great money-maker."

His father had indeed made bushels of money, and he'd spent it like the proverbial drunken sailor—a yacht, race horses, a summer place in Marblehead, and a series of young lovelies from the nursing staff. He died six years earlier of a massive heart attack in the operating room, not as a patient, but with scalpel in hand while bending over a third-tier golf pro with a defective gall bladder.

His shaky fortune died with him. The horses went, the boat, the summer home, and the curvy nurses, and it turned out he'd secretly remortgaged the Brookline house. Harvey was still married and teaching when his father collapsed and drove his scalpel into the golfer's upper right arm. The resulting lawsuit took all the stocks and bonds. Harvey then started managing his mother's finances, paying the mortgage, taxes, and upkeep. He let her believe she was living on her late husband's investments.

Brenda had complained about the situation constantly and shrilly and—Harvey admitted—with reason. She'd wanted her own six-bedroom house in Brookline rather than a pinched, third-floor apartment across from a boisterous student bar.

Why, Harvey often asked himself, hadn't his dad put aside just one of his millions for a rainy day?

Since losing his professor's salary, Harvey lived from paycheck to paycheck and from tip to tip. He still supported his mother, however. How could he do anything else? He owed her so much. He could never replace her loss, never overcome his guilt.

She came into the living room, taking tiny steps, balancing a large birthday cake in both hands. It was the traditional chocolate with white frosting. The two candles were unlit, as usual, one for Harvey and one for Tommy. She set the cake on the coffee table, went back to the kitchen and returned with plates, forks, napkins, and a large knife. She set a plate in front of Harvey and cut a big slice of cake. "The first one's for you, Tommy."

"I'm Harvey."

"That's what I said. Why would I say 'Tommy'?"

Yes, why.

At least there weren't presents this year for Tommy. For decades, his mother had bought age-appropriate gifts for him.

What happened to them? Given to charity, Harvey supposed.

He forced down a small bite of cake before his throat closed. Tears clouded his eyes.

Harvey's mother settled back in her rocker. She never ate the birthday cake. She said, "If only Tommy were here with us."

Yes, if only.

One of life's big If Onlys.

If only Harvey had taken that job at the University of New Hampshire rather than the higher-paying position at Middlebridge College, then he'd still be a history professor. If he'd gone to medical school, then he wouldn't have to deliver late-night pizzas to stoned college students.

And if as a kid he'd walked Tommy straight to the barbershop that first day of the family vacation forty-eight years ago as he'd been instructed to instead of sneaking off to the ocean, then Tommy would still be alive.

Eating cake, opening presents, laughing.
Tommy.

Chapter 4

The Sunburned Cowboy

Margo popped her head into Harvey's cubicle. "Are you eating lunch at the Public Garden?"

"Yup."

"Want company?"

"Yup."

"I'll meet you at noon. I have calls to make."

Margo smiled and left.

A nice smile.

His mother had liked Margo but always said she was too driven for Harvey. Still, if they'd stayed together, his mother would have accepted Margo into the family and treated her as the daughter she'd never had. His mother had grown up with five brothers and sisters. She'd always wanted a large family of her own. Now there was just him.

Harvey was almost ten when his mother returned from what his father had said was an extended visit to her cousin in Fort Lauderdale. Years later, Harvey figured out that his mother had been institutionalized. He remembered bounding across the lawn that day to hug her after she stepped out of the car. "You've grown so much," she said, ruffling his hair. "You've grown so much, Tommy."

Over the years, she still sometimes called him Tommy.

The body was never found. Harvey's mother fashioned various scenarios for how Tommy had survived: picked up by a fishing boat or washed safely ashore somewhere down the coast and suffering from amnesia from the shock of the cold water. "One of these days he'll remember everything," she would say and point at the front door. "And he'll come walking right in."

The woman who returned after twenty-one months looked like his mother and sounded like his mother but didn't act like her. For the next few years she wandered around the house, talking out loud, sometimes to herself, sometimes to Tommy. Harvey learned much about what was going on inside his mother's head, some of which he wished he hadn't learned.

To her friends, she appeared normal. She was still as sociable, fashionable, well-mannered, and witty as before. That Hazel Hudson sometimes spoke of Tommy as still alive was understandable. Her friends were mothers, after all.

Her belief that Tommy hadn't drowned troubled Harvey as much as his role in Tommy's death. That had been a single event, something that softened as the years passed, but his mother's anguish never diminished. Sometimes Harvey wanted to shake her by the shoulders and tell her that Tommy was dead and gone forever.

But he never had. Would he some day? Would she even listen? If she did, would facing the truth make her even unhappier? It probably would. So let things be.

Lunch bag in hand, Harvey walked the four blocks to the Boston Public Garden, sat on a favorite bench facing the larger of the two conjoined ponds, and munched on a soggy tuna-and-tomato sandwich. It was a lonely guy's lunch. At least Margo would be along today. To save money, he rarely ate in restaurants with Owen or with the rest of the team, who were half his age and went off by themselves, although from time-to-time one or the other would issue a half-hearted invitation.

Harvey tilted his head back and let the sun warm his forehead. He smelled the flowers, felt the breeze on his face, and heard children laughing. He hated his cubicle and longed for space and sunlight. He should have become a farmer. Better, a sunburned cowpoke, riding the range, sweating under a broad-brimmed leather hat, with no houses or cars or high-tech buildings anywhere in sight.

Instead, he worked in a windowless cubicle fourteen stories above ground and breathed filtered and overly air-conditioned air. He'd have preferred the scent of sage brush, red dust, longhorn farts.

But when he worked on his book, he would slip into his happy zone and didn't need the open prairie, cattle to herd, and a sturdy steed beneath him. Bliss.

Life was nevertheless looking up. His day job was safe, so he could make the mortgage payments on his mother's house, and Pete gave him a free pizza at the end of every shift.

Still, Harvey felt guilty about outsourcing his job. He'd never stolen anything—well, there were those Skittles—and here he was, stealing time from his employer.

But mixed in with his guilt was a measure of excitement. For once, he, Harvey Hudson, was on the wrong side of what was right.

Maybe he'd not been cut out to become a cowboy but a bandit instead, an anachronistic train robber in a black hat and a red bandanna tied across his face, waving a silvery, long-barreled six-shooter ("Drop your valuables in the bag, ladies and gentlemen, and no one gets hurt.").

His phone chimed.

It was his daughter. She called often, spoke briefly, and was swamped in her third year at Harvard Med.

"Hi, Dad. Did I catch you at a bad time?"

"Kathy, you never catch me at a bad time."

"I meant to get to Grandma's for the birthday party, but got overwhelmed preparing for an exam. Was it gruesome?"

"No worse than usual."

"Did Grandma point out that you should have gone to medical school?"

"Twice."

Kathy laughed. "How's the day job going?"

"Fine, actually."

"I'm proud of you, Dad, for the way you picked yourself up and moved on."

"Thanks. You've always been supportive of your poor old pop. But I haven't exactly moved on. I'm still trying to find a teaching job."

"I should hope so. Are you... um... still delivering balloons?"

"Pizzas."

"I thought it was balloons. In any case, you should quit. Also, stop sending me money. In a few years, I'll be a disgustingly wealthy surgeon."

"I like sending you money, and I like driving around town delivering tomatoey, high-cholesterol comestibles. It's relaxing. I feel I'm doing a service to the community, and the tips are great. Never once at the end of one of my thought-provoking history lectures did a grateful student rush up and fold a ten-dollar bill into my hand."

Kathy was quiet for a moment. "I think, Dad, that you put yourself into humiliating situations because of... well, you know."

Harvey did know. "Have you switched to psychiatry?"

"No, I'm just saying that you—"

"How's your mother doing?"

"I guess we're changing topics," Kathy said.

"It seems so."

"Actually, I called because Mom's getting married again."

Harvey's stomach tightened. It wasn't from jealousy—he didn't want Brenda back—but it hurt that she'd found someone, and he hadn't. "Is it that pot-bellied insurance geek with the three-legged mutt?"

"Right. And… uh… Mom wants me to ask if you'd like to come to the wedding."

"She's fucking kidding, right?"

"I don't think I've ever heard you use that word before, but no, she really does want you there."

"Tell her I'll tie a big red bow around her and give her away with joy in my heart."

"I'll take that as a no."

"As a fuck no."

Kathy giggled. "I'll reword your reply and pass it on. Oops, I gotta run. My class is getting ready to watch a guy get his appendix yanked out. Loads of fun. Love you a bunch."

"And I love you."

Harvey pocketed his phone. He and Kathy had the same take on the foibles of human nature, and the same things that had made him laugh also made her laugh. Brenda had complained about being left out. She was not a laugher.

Sometimes Harvey actually did miss her. Or at least her female companionship. For five weeks, he'd seen Giselle, a former colleague. She was a transplanted Parisian and a sparrow of a woman with exquisite and expensive tastes in food, wine and couture. Seeing her, Harvey soon learned, meant an hour each Wednesday and Sunday evening for a perfunctory tumble, surrounded by creepy, staring cats, with Giselle yipping in his ear. That had ended two months earlier when, as she escorted him out, she mentioned she was leaving early the next morning for a job in Fresno, then pecked him on the cheek, said goodbye, and closed the door behind him.

Harvey finished his sandwich and a handful of carrot sticks— his doctor-to-be daughter nagged him to eat fresh vegetables and fewer sweets, and she sent him loaves of multi-grained, cardboard-flavored, organic bread that had been baked by grass-fed elves in the tall, green hills of Vermont.

He waited a few more minutes for Margo, gave up, tossed his empty lunch bag into a trash can, and started back to his office.

As he got close to the miniature iron bridge that divided the two ponds, he spotted a pretty brunette in a summery blue dress leaning over the railing and snapping photos of the ducks. She was about his age. He wanted to engage her in talk, say something clever, ask her out on a date.

People often met casually like that, fell in love, married. Those were the accidents of history, the whimsies of What-Ifs. What if he talked to the brunette and something developed? Or what if she started a conversation with him?

But he didn't, and she didn't, and Harvey walked on.

He'd met Brenda at Middlebridge College, him new on the faculty, her visiting a friend. Harvey and Brenda had bumped into each other, literally, in the cafeteria, when they'd banged trays. Her coffee spilled into the saucer. His cheeseburger and French fries slid to the floor. Both said "Sorry," both smiled, and both started talking at the same time.

What if he'd turned left after leaving the cash register instead of turning right? He'd then have avoided a collision and a bad marriage. Or arrived five minutes later after grading one more paper (History 203, "The War of Independence to 1900"). What if she'd paused to talk to someone, or she'd dropped her napkin and been delayed for just a few seconds?

What-Ifs. All of history was a series of What-Ifs.

"Hey, Curly!"

Harvey stopped walking. That had been his nickname in high school. He hadn't heard it in decades.

Margo slid sideways on her bench and gave it a pat. "Sit."

"You're my boss, so I suppose I have to."

"Of course."

Harvey sat down.

"It seems I went to the wrong meeting place," Margo said.

"Yup."

"You looked lost in thought just now. What was it this time?"

"Cafeterias, dropped cheeseburgers, and What-Ifs."

"Of course." Margo said. "Your famous What-Ifs." She held out a bag of Spicy Nacho Doritos, a dietary weakness of hers dating back to high school.

Harvey took one and bit off the end. "What if we hadn't run into each other that day in Boston? I'd still probably be looking for a full-time job." He finished the chip. "I've been wanting to ask this: Was it a pity hire?"

Margo nodded her head back and forth. "Well, somewhat. I figured you'd inflated your qualifications but that you'd come up to speed, which you certainly have. Also, you could always make me laugh, and…"

"And what?"

"And I knew that hiring you would piss off Tucker," Margo said with a smile, then touched Harvey's forearm. "We had some good times."

Yes, they had—the dances, the rock concerts, and the clumsy tumbles in the back seat of his father's ostentatious black Mercedes. "We did have good times until you started having your good times with Tucker. I never understood—"

"Hold that thought," Margo said, her finger raised. She pulled her phone from her purse.

At times, she was good at giving him her full attention and at other times just as good at ignoring him.

A busy and important woman, on the phone half the day.

He wished he could call Amaya in India and chat. He'd given her his number, but she'd ignored his requests for hers. Every time he answered his phone, he hoped it was her. What an idiot, he thought. He was acting like a dreamy sophomore boy who drooled every time he passed the head cheerleader in the hallway.

Margo nodded into her phone, then slipped it back into her

purse, a large blue thing half her size. "You never told me where you're living."

"I've got a nice place in Cambridge," Harvey said, "about halfway between MIT and Harvard."

It was not a nice place, but a cramped, one-bedroom apartment over a poultry store in a downscale neighborhood to which Harvey returned late at night smelling of soggy pizza boxes.

Margo finished her chips, carefully folded the bag, and slipped it into her purse. She was the neatest person Harvey had ever met.

She said, "Back in high school, you could always get me to laugh and think, usually about the oddest things. You were often lost in thought, bumping into walls, forgetting where you were going, misplacing your jacket, brainy and distracted. A proto-professor."

"And I was good at producing armpit farts."

"World class."

Harvey smiled, and Margo smiled, and again she answered her phone.

The pretty lady in the blue dress approached. What if she stopped to adjust her sandal when she got near, accepted a womanly compliment on footwear from Margo, fell into conversation with both, and took an interest in him?

And later, no doubt broke his heart.

Life had good What-Ifs and bad What-Ifs. In his textbook, Harvey discussed both from a historic perspective. Cleverly, he liked to think.

The lady walked on, theirs apparently not a relationship to be, foiled by low-heeled sandals needing no adjustments.

Life was tenuous, both at the microscopic level of blue sandals and at the macro level of the stars.

When Harvey lectured on astronomy, he spoke of the tenuousness of life. Had not a massive asteroid struck the early Earth, we would have no moon. If dark matter didn't exist, then our galaxy might not have formed, at least in its present configuration. Had a celestial body not slammed into the Yucatan Peninsula sixty-five-million years ago and killed off the dinosaurs, then mammals—and later man—would not have emerged to rule the planet.

And if Earth's clouds were as opaque as those on Venus, would anyone have ever guessed there were other planets and stars and galaxies?

Harvey's obsession with What-Ifs had started right after Tommy drowned.

What if Tommy had awakened that morning with a fever and couldn't go to the barbershop? What if it had rained, and they'd stayed inside to play a board game? What if a vacationing lifeguard had plunged into the waves and swum Tommy to safety? What if Tommy hadn't had a disobedient older brother who'd taken him to the beach instead of directly to the barber?

Margo tapped Harvey's wrist. "You're lost in thought again."

"I was thinking of how to come up with a cunning way to explain an excruciatingly complex concept to our more dim-witted clients."

"Bullshit."

Margo liked to swear from time to time. It was unexpected, coming from this neat little woman with the large dark eyes.

Harvey watched the lady in blue stop to talk to a policeman on horseback. She stroked the animal's nose, smiled at the cop, who smiled back. A potential What-If. The lady in blue meets the man in blue. Romance ensues.

Romance. Harvey turned to Margo. "I've wondered for years why you dumped me for Tucker, except that he was tall, dark, handsome, rich and athletic—although I'd like to point out that the football team posted a losing record every year of his tenure as quarterback."

Margo turned away, turned back. "He had ambitions."

That figured. Margo came from a family of high achievers. She would never place him in that category. "Just that?" he said.

"He was hunky."

"In the movies, the hunky athlete—except on film he unfailingly takes his team to the state championship and wins in a nail-biting overtime—steals the perky cheerleader from the nerdy but cute nice guy, but then the quarterback turns out to be a self-centered creep, and the cheerleader falls tearfully into the arms of the nerdy but cute nice guy, often with curly red hair, and they live happily ever after, or at least until the credits roll."

Margo said, "Are you seeing anyone?"

"Are you changing the subject?"

"Of course."

'Of course'—it had always been Margo's favorite expression. Decisive. Final.

Was he seeing anyone? He didn't have the time. He returned late at night to his miserable digs, ate a free but cold pizza (pepperoni if he was lucky, plain cheese if not), and crawled between his lonely sheets. But he wasn't going to admit that to Margo, so he said, "I've got a little something going on with a woman from New Delhi."

Something going on? Was he fourteen again? He'd never met Amaya, never seen a picture of her, knew her only through several dozen highly technical and mind-numbing emails.

Margo said, "Is it that beauty you were with that time I bumped into you many years ago in the Harvard bookstore?"

"No, someone else."

For two-and-a-half dreamy months during graduate school, Harvey had chastely dated Chandra. She was funny, polite, brilliant, and her name meant 'moon' in Hindi. Harvey always thought of her as a celestial body, something shining in the sky, hanging high above his head, and totally out of reach.

"I wasn't in her league," Harvey said. "Amaya got her doctorate, went back to India, and married an orthodontist."

He'd said *Amaya* instead of *Chandra*. He started to correct himself, but Margo wasn't paying attention because she'd was deep in another phone call.

He often thought of Chandra, especially since his divorce. What if they'd married? Harvey pictured himself in exotic New Delhi, teaching history in some pleasant little college, driving home through snarled traffic to a houseful of the world's cutest kids, who would scamper over the moment he stepped through the door and hug his knees.

But where would that leave his daughter? It would leave her in that land where dwelled the never-born, that's where. Harvey couldn't imagine life without Kathy. So his marriage hadn't been a mistake. Still, he couldn't stop thinking about Chandra.

And he couldn't stop himself from transferring her laugh and looks to Amaya.

Both women lived in New Delhi. Had they ever crossed on the sidewalk?

Margo shouted, "Damn it!" and dropped her phone into her purse. "That was Tucker, if you couldn't guess."

It pleased Harvey that Margo was angry with Tucker, but at the same time, he was afraid she'd finally get fed up with the jerk, pull her money out of the company, and depart. If that happened, Tucker would assign him some twenty-four-year-old as boss. Margo had made Harvey her direct report to spare him the humiliation of having to report to a kid less than half his age.

She tapped his forearm. "Let's walk."

They crossed back over the footbridge. Two women leaned over the railing to snap photos, but neither was the lovely lady in blue.

Margo said, "That last batch of documentation was terrific."

"Thanks. I… uh… worked pretty hard on it."

Margo picked up a Popsicle stick and walked it to a trash can. "However, I noticed two places where you spelled 'color' with a 'u,' like the Brits.

"Uh…"

"Also, you sometimes used 'which' the way they do on the other side of the Atlantic and in some of the former British colonies instead of using 'that' in the way we do. And now and then, the word choices and the sentence structuring didn't quite sound American."

Harvey slowed to a shuffle. He hadn't caught all those problems. Margo was a skilled writer. Margo was frighteningly skilled at everything. He said, "I read too many British novels."

Margo gave him a look he couldn't interpret.

Was she suspicious? Have others noticed the same thing? Would Margo take her doubts to Tucker?

Damn, damn, damn.

Chapter 5

The FBI is Calling

Harvey braced his feet against the side of his cubicle, tilted his chair back, and waited for Amaya's email. If he stretched his arms, his fingertips could just reach the opposite sides of his cubby. He had one of the smallest cubicles in the company and, worse, it was next to the coffee room, so all day long he listened to his coworkers bitching about the weather, the boss, and the apartment mate who left dirty socks and underwear lying all over the damn place.

It was 1:45 p.m., which made it night in India. Amaya always emailed exactly at 2:00 p.m., Boston time. She was precise, pretty—Harvey knew that for sure—and a night owl.

He'd spent the last half hour reacquainting himself with how people in India wrote English, which was close to the British system. For the next set of Amaya's documentation, he would have to do a better job of finding the words that ended in 'our' ('colour,' as an example) and find places where 'that' should replace 'which.' It would be a tedious process, even with global search-and-replace, and would take valuable time away from working on his book.

Margo walked by the opening of his cubicle without stopping, but she did smile.

Harvey hoped that meant her curiosity about the Britishness of the documentation hadn't morphed into suspicion. On the walk back to the office from the Public Garden, he'd worried about losing his job, hardly hearing what Margo was saying, and at the same time, he'd also pondered his relationship with her. If there was a relationship.

First loves were the strongest, he'd read somewhere, and they lived in a person forever like a stealth virus. Can a first love be rekindled? Or any type of love? He'd heard of divorced couples remarrying, but that was rare.

Harvey had been crazy about Margo in high school. How had she felt about him? A soft spot at most. He could make her laugh, could help her with her calculus, and would hold hands through sappy movies he would never have gone to on his own, and they'd had sweaty good fun in the rear seat of his father's leathery Mercedes. But that was it—just fun—at least for Margo, anyway. Had she felt the same for him he'd felt for her, she wouldn't have dropped him for that dickhead Tucker.

The image of the first time he'd seen them together had burned itself forever into his brain. School was about to start, and Margo and Tucker were sitting in his red convertible, the top down. She leaned over and kissed him. A second time. A third.

The ground had dropped away.

He and Margo had argued the evening before. She'd wanted him to apply to MIT along with her. He'd resisted. She then proposed Harvard. Again Harvey objected. He didn't want the pressure. State Universities were more fun. She rebuttoned her blouse, hopped out of the car, slammed the door, and walked home.

They'd broken up twice before over the same subject.

Harvey yawned, stretched, and pulled his laptop closer. He was sleeping poorly and was having naked-in-public dreams. They'd started right after he'd outsourced his job. He had no need to consult a mental-health professional for an interpretation.

It hadn't helped that the burglar alarm in the poultry store below had gone off during the night, followed by sirens and squad cars, yelling and door-slamming. Once more someone had broken into the place, reportedly a money-laundering operation. The cops caught the sad culprit every time. Despite the proximity to Harvard and MIT, Cambridge burglars seemed no smarter than elsewhere.

In anticipation of Amaya's email, Harvey transferred his laptop from desk to tummy.

When he'd first started working with Amaya, he'd sent planning documents and early software builds to her from the company's network and, at her request, had given her access to his computer, which streamlined operations. Only later did he realize that someone within his own company might be monitoring his communications with her, and that's when he'd switched to his personal laptop.

Amaya's email popped up exactly at 2:00.

Harvey,

How are you, and what was your team's reaction to our first documentation effort? I hope things went well. If not, please let me know how I can improve. I do not want to lose this contract. Your work is very important to me.

I have attached a long list of questions which I want you to ask your developers for me, plus detailed explanations for you related to each question.

I hope that you and your daughter are happy and well,

Amaya

Harvey looked forward to Amaya's emails, although they were always too crisp and businesslike. But she'd recently asked about his personal life, a first. He'd told her about Kathy and his living alone, which was a way to let her know he was divorced and available.

And an idiot. Why would a fifty-six-year-old man with a

decent education and who was reasonably normal in most areas of his life, fantasize over a woman he'd never met? Was this the first step toward madness? Possibly. Could he stop himself? Probably not.

Harvey opened the attachment and groaned. The list of questions and Amaya's explanations of them went on forever. Her queries were always clear and to the point when he posed them at meetings, but the engineers' follow-ups were troublesome. As they spoke, Harvey would frantically tap their gibberish into his laptop and mutter that he needed a day to ponder the subject (and to send a panicky email to Amaya).

Harvey typed:

> Amaya,
>   Your effort was met with astonishing success. Your ability to explain difficult material and the way you organize the overall documentation are remarkable.
>   I hope you can have the next set of documentation completed in time for me to pass out review copies next Tuesday. But I'm sure you can—you work miracles.

Harvey rested his hands on his lap. Add a bit more praise? Or had he gone too far already? Was 'miracles' over the top?

Move on.

Now came the delicate part:

> I've always wanted to visit India. That is, if I can scrape together the funds.

Harvey stopped typing and leaned back. Guys with money problems were a turnoff. He deleted the line and started over:

> I'm planning a trip to India, a lifetime dream, but have not

yet picked the date. I've been told that New Delhi is a
fascinating place, and I hope to swing by.

Again, Harvey stopped typing. Does one just 'swing by' in a
country as vast as India? Does that sound too forward? Or should
he plunge ahead and ask if he could see her?

He plunged ahead:

Do you have plans to visit the States? If so, it would be
wonderful if we could get together. I could show you
around Boston and maybe drive us down to the beaches
at Cape Cod or up to the mountains of Vermont.

And once more, Harvey stopped. Too much? Of course it was
too much. A drive to the mountains implied an overnight stay.
But before Harvey lost his courage, the fearless cowpoke in him
clicked SEND.

And he immediately wished he hadn't, immediately felt like
an idiot and a desperate middle-aged man who lived in a one-
bedroom apartment and ate stale pizza before climbing into a cold
and lonely bed.

What must this woman think? Would she even reply?

Margo walked past his cubicle again but didn't look in. Her
face was tight and unsmiling. Harvey sensed that something had
been worrying her lately. His buddy Owen, who always had his
ear to the ground, said the FBI was sniffing around the company.
Harvey doubted that. Why would the Bureau take an interest in
petroleum pumps? In fact, why would anyone take an interest in
petroleum pumps?

Finally, Amaya replied. Harvey leaned in close.

The documentation is on schedule.
Best, Amaya

That's all? Nothing about his trip to India? Or hers to Boston? Harvey felt like an idiot.

So, what's new?

Chapter 6

Chimpanzees with iPads

Harvey stepped into Tucker's office and dropped into the chair across from the desk. It held a photo of Tucker's daughter in her high school graduation robe, a stapler, stacks of manila folders, and a transparent plastic cube containing a golf ball autographed in a shaky hand. Tucker had ordered Harvey to see him.

Not good. Had Tucker found out Harvey had outsourced the documentation? Or that he was writing a textbook on company time?

Tucker was talking into his phone and looking out his window. To Harvey's satisfaction, Tucker had developed a slight pouch since his sleek days as a high school quarterback. Although most women still found Tucker attractive, in Harvey's eyes, the man's nose was too long, his eyes too narrow, and his ears too pointy. A giant elf.

Tucker pocketed his phone. "Don't get comfortable, Harvey, because we're going outside for a walk. I have something important to talk about and don't want anyone to hear."

Why go outside?

To fire someone, of course.

Someone caught outsourcing.

Numb, Harvey followed Tucker out the door, down the hallway, and into an elevator. Harvey watched the floor numbers wane—

10, 9, 8—the countdown to unemployment. He guessed he'd never be let back into the building. ('My administrative assistant will arrange for your things to be boxed up and sent to you. The company lawyers are preparing a suit, by the way, so expect to hear from them.')

Tucker wanted him outside to prevent a commotion.

Harvey rarely caused a commotion, but when he did, he threw off months and months of fire and brimstone, all in one volcanic burst, his personal Big Bang. He guessed Tucker was afraid he would toss his office chair through a window, just as he had done that drizzly gray day when the college president had called an all-campus meeting to inform staff and students that Middlebridge College had swirled down the financial flusher. The swivel chair had supported Harvey for many years, as well as the ever-expanding butts of generations of his predecessors. Harvey had launched the chair through a window facing the quadrangle. There was a thunderous crash and a cloud of glass shards. The chair settled onto an overgrown rhododendron bush. Harvey stood at the shattered window, felt the cold but refreshing winter breeze on his face, and greatly enjoyed the moment. Down below, disgruntled students were lugging boxes and suitcases across the quadrangle, but they'd stopped long enough to look up, cheer and clap. Harvey had considered this his finest moment at Middlebridge College.

Harvey and Tucker headed down Boylston Street toward the Boston Public Garden, neither one talking.

Harvey's head buzzed. Without a full-time job, he couldn't pay his mother's mortgage. He was fifty-six and almost broke. He shouldn't be. He'd made decent money all his life and was a saver. But Brenda had opened a yoga studio, a second, a third, all in partnership with the instructor, a dreamy-eyed, bendable guy Harvey detested. The studios sucked up Harvey's savings. Just another month, Brenda kept promising, then they would turn a profit.

They never did. Brenda cleaned out the last of their joint bank account and fled to the West Coast with the yoga freak. She dumped him after a month and took up with the dismal insurance executive whom she was about to wed along with his three-legged dog.

The whole thing gave Harvey heartburn.

And now he was losing his job.

He turned to Tucker and said brightly, "Outsourcing is the future of American corporations."

Tucker grunted.

Stupid, stupid, stupid.

What the hell, why not get it over with. "I know why you brought me out here."

Tucker stopped walking and raised an eyebrow, his curious-elf look. "You do?"

"It's so I won't go ballistic and trash the place after you fire me."

Tucker started walking again. "I'm not firing you, Harvey, even though you're insubordinate, take two-hour lunch breaks, and until recently wrote documentation that read like it came from a roomful of chimpanzees with iPads."

Harvey opened his mouth to protest, then closed it. What Tucker had said was pretty much true. What counted is that he hadn't said, 'You're fired.'

"Then what are we doing out here?" Harvey asked. "Couldn't we have talked behind closed doors?"

"No. Besides, I have a bitch of a headache and need fresh air."

Tucker Aldrich with a bitch of a headache. This should be fun. "So, what do you have to tell me that's so important?"

"Are you looking for a job with another software company?"

"No. Why do you ask?"

"A teaching position instead?"

Harvey hesitated.

"I thought so," Tucker said. He stopped walking and turned

to Harvey, who'd also stopped. "Here's the deal: Stay with the company for one more year, and at the end of that time, I'll give you a bonus equal to your entire year's salary."

It took time for this to sink in. "I don't understand."

Tucker half closed his eyes and stared. "Yes, you do."

"No, I don't."

"We can speak candidly," Tucker said, his voice lowered and conspiratorial. "We both know what's going on, both know about your other job." Tucker laid his hand on Harvey's shoulder. "What you're doing takes a lot of courage."

Courage? Other job? Delivering balloons? Pizzas?

Tucker started walking. "Enough said for now."

Okay, but what exactly had been said?

Well, he hadn't been fired, and Tucker had promised him an unbelievably huge bonus. So what the hell. Who cared why Tucker was acting so mysteriously?

Tucker stopped in front of a clothing store that displayed blank-eyed dummies in men's suits. "This used to be a restaurant, remember?"

Harvey nodded. Back when he and Tucker were best buddies, they'd skipped school, taken the subway into town, bought Red Sox caps, and dined on quesadillas at this spot where now lurked the spicy memory of a second-rate Mexican restaurant. "We skipped out without paying."

Tucker tilted his head back and laughed. "We were indeed troublemakers."

"All eighth-grade boys are troublemakers."

Tucker laughed again.

The friendly Tucker. The easy-to-laugh Tucker. The old Tucker. Harvey liked him this way—or at least didn't despise him so much, and that felt good. Harvey had no idea what had brought on this change and why Tucker had doubled his salary.

Tucker said, "The personnel office got three calls last week from different people wanting to confirm your current address. They weren't told, of course."

"Who called?

"They wouldn't say."

"It was probably just someone doing a credit check."

"Maybe," Tucker said. "But you have to be watchful."

"Watchful for what?"

"Other people asking about you or following you."

"Why would anyone follow me?"

Tucker gave Harvey a hard look. "We can be frank with each other, but I guess you've received instructions not to."

"What instructions?"

Another long look from Tucker. "They trained you well. Let's head back."

"Okay, but—"

"This conversation never took place."

"That sounds like a line from a bad spy movie," Harvey said.

"It should."

Now Harvey was the one with a bitch of a headache and needing fresh air. He slowed his pace. "I'll be along."

Tucker nodded and walked on.

Harvey wondered why anyone would want to follow him. Who would be interested in the doings of a bumbling technical writer or want to know his address? Not a bill collector because he'd finally paid off his charge cards and was up-to-date on his mother's mortgage. Maybe just a case of mistaken identity.

Or was Tucker just making all of this up to scare him into resigning, with his buddy-talk just an act? Could be.

Still, as Harvey retraced his steps back to the office, he found himself studying faces. Why was that woman who was holding the fuzzy white puppy staring at him like that? Why was the panhandler with the Starbucks cup wearing expensive new running shoes?

Three times on the way back to the office, Harvey paused and studied his reflection in a store window to see if anyone was following him, a trick he'd read about in a novel.

But no one was. Or ever would. Harvey felt like a fool. But he told himself he needed to be a careful fool.

Chapter 7

The Egyptian Grain Trade

Harvey stayed late at the office to finish a troublesome chapter ("The Whys and What-Ifs of the Industrial Revolution in Great Britain"), then drove directly to his pizza-delivery job, all the time puzzling over his strange meeting with Tucker.

A taxi veered across lanes and cut Harvey off. He slammed on his brakes and screeched to a stop. The insulated pizza case flew off the passenger seat and hit the floor. Harvey rolled down his window and shouted at the driver, who shouted back and gave Harvey the finger. Harvey responded in kind, adding the f-word.

He rolled up his window and drove on. What had he become? Professor Hudson of the Middlebridge history department would never have given the bird to another driver. Harvey was shocked at his behavior, but also quite pleased with the new Harvey Hudson, foul-mouthed finger-flipper.

Normally, he refused to make deliveries this late at night, but Pete said the client had asked for him by name and promised a huge tip. Harvey asked how they'd known his name and why they'd singled him out. Pete had shrugged and said, "Go find out."

Harvey drove slowly. Streets this close to the harbor were narrow and dim. The GPS took him up one alley and down the other, each narrower and darker than the one before. Brick buildings loomed on each side, with just here or there a lighted window.

He recalled that it was somewhere nearby that his ex-wife had dragged him to self-defense classes. Brenda and the instructor flirted. Harvey finally got even by slamming the guy to the mat and sending him hobbling away, swearing and pressing both hands against the small of his back, which had ended the session for the evening.

Harvey's phone chimed. It was Margo.

"I got your message," she said. "And yes, Tucker has been behaving strangely lately. His girlfriend's giving him grief, which has him pissed, and his Jaguar threw a rod—whatever that means—which has him even more pissed. When he gets like this, he sees boogeymen under the bed."

"Thanks. That's a relief."

"Why?" Margo asked.

"Long story."

"It sounds like you're in your car."

"I'm out cruising."

"Like high school?" Margo asked.

"Exactly."

"Stay out of trouble and wear protection. See you at work tomorrow."

Harvey wasn't quite convinced that Tucker's odd behavior could be attributed to lady troubles or sports-car misfortunes. But in any case, he still had a job.

And so did Amaya. What was she up to right now? It was midmorning in New Delhi, so she might be at her desk, working on the latest round of documentation. Harvey wondered what she was wearing. Was her shiny black hair up, or did it flow down her shoulders?

Harvey felt like a fool and a long-distance stalker.

He steered around a black cat sauntering across the alley.

The GPS lady smugly announced that she'd brought him safely

to his destination, a gloomy, three-story brick building that gave Harvey the chills.

He parked, hesitated, then grabbed the pizza case, climbed out of the car and stood studying the building. A gaudy red-and-yellow sign above the door read, "Jackson Furniture Showroom. Prices You Can Afford!" A small, handwritten note on the door said, "Pizza deliverer, please press the bell and wait to be buzzed in." Pale lights illuminated a row of ground-floor windows, but otherwise the place was dark.

Who had ordered these pizzas, and why had they asked for him by name?

Did he really wanted to go inside?

When he and Tucker were kids, this was the part of the horror movie where they would duck down behind the seats in front of them and shout at the screen, "Don't go inside, you jerk!"

But the jerk always went inside.

So did Harvey. He was no longer a kid or a bookish scholar, after all, but a guy who drove with his elbow out the window and cursed at cabbies. He pressed the button. After all, the minute he stepped inside, someone wasn't going to grab him from behind.

The buzzer sounded. Harvey opened the door and stepped inside, and someone grabbed him from behind.

The pizza case skidded across the floor.

Harvey struggled free, fell to his knees, sprang to his feet, and raised his fists.

The man was tall and thin and had a black, pencil mustache borrowed from an old silent movie, which would have been comical except for the gun.

He waved it in the direction of a couch.

Harvey lowered his arms, backed away, and sat down. His heart thumped. His ears rang. He looked around. There must have been two dozen couches in the showroom: blue ones, white ones, tan ones, striped ones, and some covered in plastic. His mother kept her couch under plastic when no one was visiting. What a blow it would be to her if she lost her other son. And what a blow to him.

His heart thumped harder.

A second man appeared from a side door, settled onto a red velvet sofa ("Only $1,600! No Payments for Three Months!") and, without looking up, started thumbing through a furniture catalog. He was short and soft and had thin brown hair and a piggy red face.

"Who in hell are you?" Harvey asked.

"I'm Luke Smith," the man said, still not looking up, "and my partner is Elliot Smith."

"You're both named Smith?"

"That's our middle names, too."

The two men flashed identity cards too fast for Harvey to read. He said, "What do you want with me?"

"We're part of a secret FBI task force."

Harvey tried to get his head around this. "Which one?"

"You don't get to know. That's the nature of secret task forces," Luke said, continuing to shuffle through the catalog. "A couple of days ago, I was here and got a great deal on a couch like this one, and that's what gave me the idea that this would be a nice, out-of-the-way spot for us to meet."

"This is a meeting? It seems more like a—"

"You should check this place out if you need a second sofa," Luke said, closing the catalog and dropping it onto the end table at his elbow. He looked up. "But I'm guessing a guy who lives in a crappy, one-bedroom apartment above a poultry shop doesn't even have enough extra room for a coat rack."

"How do you know where I live?"

"We know everything about you—where you live and all your old addresses, where you went to college, who you hang out with, and your weakness for Skittles."

Harvey stood up.

Elliot waved his pistol.

Harvey sat down.

Elliot stepped away, returned with the pizza case, opened it and laid its lopsided contents onto the coffee table between Harvey and Luke.

Luke pulled three bottles of beer from a portable cooler, opened them, and handed one to Harvey, along with a $40 tip.

Harvey hesitated, took the bottle, then pocketed the money. This meant they would eventually let him go. Or they'd take the cash back before dumping his body into the harbor.

Elliot said he had to piss, his only words so far.

As soon as Elliot was out of sight, Harvey jumped to his feet.

Luke jerked a pistol from inside his suit jacket. "Uh, uh, big guy."

Harvey settled back onto the couch. Had these two goons lured him here to rob him? But muggers as a rule don't tip or wear tailored suits and shiny black shoes.

Elliot returned, carefully wiping his hands on a paper towel, even getting in between the fingers. A thug with good hygiene.

"What do you want with me?" Harvey asked and immediately realized how ridiculous that sounded.

"First we eat," Luke said. He ripped out a triangle of pizza, the cheese dangling in long strands. He took a bite and said, "Eat."

Numbly, Harvey took a piece and bit off the tip.

Would his last meal be a pizza topped with caramelized onions, apple chunks, and goat cheese? It was Pete's most exotic offer and Harvey's least favorite.

Luke took small bites and kept touching the sides of his mouth with a paper napkin, taking great care not to dribble onto himself or the couch. Elliot folded his slice and shoved in half, with chunks of onion and apple squirting from the sides of his mouth.

Luke swallowed and wiped his mouth. "I'm enjoying your book."

"My book?"

"And the title is a grabber: *Big History: The Birth and Death of Everything.*"

"How do you know about my book?"

"I've been reading it."

"You have access to my computer?"

"I have access to your life. My only real issue is that I don't quite agree with you on the principle causes of the fall of the Roman Empire. In particular, I think that problems with the Egyptian grain trade played a much larger role than you make out."

Harvey shuddered. If these two had access to his personal laptop, then they must know all about Amaya. He hoped he hadn't gotten her into trouble. "I'll take that under advisement. And are you two holding me prisoner because I'm underestimating the importance of trans-Mediterranean wheat shipments?"

Luke laid his half-eaten slice back into the pizza box, took a fresh napkin, wiped his hands, and let his expression turn dark. "We're here," he said, leaning forward, "because you're an accessory to a planned cyberattack by the Russians on the United States."

Chapter 8

The Lovelorn Spy

"Cyberattack?" Harvey said. "Russians? I have no connection with any Russians."

"You write your company's documentation."

Harvey wondered if this had to do with his outsourcing, but it didn't seem like something that would bring in the FBI. "Okay, but—"

"Does the word 'Stuxnet' ring a bell?"

"Uh… I think so. But I don't remember exactly what it is."

"A few years back," Luke said, "the Stuxnet cyberattack caused a number of Iranian centrifuges to speed up and destroy themselves. Their purpose was to create bomb-grade uranium. The Israelis and the U.S. caught flak for the attack, and rightfully so. But the hack delayed Iran's nuclear program by months. It was a slick operation—no missile strikes, no deaths, and not much of an international kerfuffle."

Harvey said, "You're telling me this because?"

"Because you're up to you ears in something similar."

"How? I work for a company that writes software that monitors petroleum pumps. How can—"

"You outsourced your job to Lotus Worldwide Consultants."

Harvey slumped. "Uh… okay, but that's not illegal. I vetted

the company before I signed on, and they checked out as one-hundred-percent legitimate."

"More like ninety percent. It's true they've done above-board business in Europe and parts of Asia, but we've learned that the Russian Intelligence Service secretly owns the company."

Harvey leaned forward. "Russian intelligence?"

"Specifically, the SVR—and don't ask me what the initials stand for. It's the branch of Russian intelligence that's replaced the KGB. The SVR is in many ways comparable to the CIA and Britain's MI6, and—"

"How am I involved?"

"You emailed Amaya on your company computer, right?"

"Uh… okay, but only for the first couple of days, and then I switched over to my personal laptop."

"By then, you'd already given her access to your company's network, and the SVR used that as a portal inside. At first, we thought you were on the take, especially because you had a Russian grandfather who taught you the language, and because you minored in Russian in college. But we checked on your finances, and we talked to people who know you—surreptitiously, of course—and concluded that you're clean. A dumbass about network security, but clean."

Harvey blinked a few times. "How did the outsourcing company know I'd hire them?"

"They didn't. They emailed you and about everyone else in T&M Consultants. Only you bit."

"Does anyone in my company know?"

"Tucker Aldrich since about a week ago."

"Why didn't he fire me?"

"Because we wouldn't let him. We want you to keep on doing just what you've been doing. We told Tucker you were a secret agent working part time for us and as patriotic as the flag. He was impressed."

That explained the strange meeting with him. Harvey said, "He promised me a generous bonus if I stayed on the job."

"Not all that generous because the government will be paying it."

That figured. "Are the Russians trying to pull off another Stuxnet?" Harvey asked.

"Exactly."

"On petroleum pumps?"

"Exactly," Luke said.

"Why?"

Luke picked up a second slice of pizza, hesitated, then laid it back in the box. "Thanks to you, the Russians can now plant a bug on your company's network that will speed up and destroy hundreds of booster pumps throughout the U.S. pipeline grid. If things work out as the Russkies intend, it'll take years to build enough replacement pumps, maybe a decade. Trucks and trains can ship some of the petroleum, but much less than the country needs."

"Which will send the U.S. into a recession."

"Exactly. And it will raise the international price of oil. Petroleum products make up about sixty percent of Russian exports and thirty percent of their gross domestic product, which means their hack will earn Russia tons of money. Putin and his buddies will themselves make billions because they've taken a long position on petroleum futures. They'll win big when the price skyrockets."

Harvey burped up an acidy mixture of pizza and beer, swallowed, then said, "If you knew all this, why didn't you take steps to stop the Russians?"

Luke took the second piece of pizza, after all. "We will, but just not yet. We first want Putin and his gang to take a bath on petroleum futures. But more importantly, we want to use their operation to launch a counter cyberattack."

Harvey let this sink in. Cyberattacks and counter cyberattacks, FBI agents and Russian hackers. Life had taken a strange and frightening turn. "If the Russians had pulled off their operation and destroyed the U.S. petroleum pumps, wouldn't we retaliate?"

"Of course, but not against them. They'll engineer the hack to look like the Iranians are behind it. The Russians would like nothing better than to get the U.S. entangled in another endless war."

"Aren't the Iranians friends of the Russians?"

"Russia has no friends when it comes to self-interest."

Harvey thought about this for a moment. It all made sense. "It's not very sexy."

"What isn't?"

"The Russian hack. I'd think they'd go after our missile systems or the power grids or something like that."

"That's the beauty of their operation. Our military networks are too hard to crack into, and so are the obvious civilian networks such as the electrical grid. But dull targets like petroleum pumps have slipped under the radar."

Again, that made sense. "So, I guess you want me to keep working with Amaya as if nothing had changed?"

"That's right, keep working with *Amaya*," Luke said, putting emphasis on her name. He glanced at Elliot. Both men laughed.

"What?" Harvey said. "What?"

"We'll get to that later."

"I want to hear now," Harvey said.

"Later."

Harvey chugged the rest of his beer and then a second. He was getting a buzz. He needed a buzz. "How does our counter cyberattack on the Russians work?"

"We're letting them mess with what they think is the code, but in fact, the real stuff is off the network and at a place where they can't get at it. When the time comes, we'll insert malware into the code that the Russians have downloaded, and it will infect their systems for months. It should be fun to watch."

"So Tucker is the only person in the company who knows?"

"Him and three programmers sworn to secrecy—just as you are, by the way."

"Margo?"

Luke shook his head.

Disgusting lumps of beer-soaked pizza climbed farther up Harvey's throat. That and fear. He belched quietly and stood up. "I want nothing to do with your goat rodeo. I'm quitting. I'll take my chances on finding another job."

Luke shook his head. "No, you don't."

"You can't stop me."

"Think of your widowed mother," Luke said, his voice trembling with woe. "With you out of circulation and unable to make mortgage payments on her house, the poor dear will be out on the street."

"What in hell do you mean by 'out of circulation'?"

"It would be a terrible blow for a nice lady like that to see her only son go to prison," Luke said, lacing his fingers across his stomach, "but it wouldn't be that much of a tragedy for you because ten or fifteen years in the pokey would give you enough time to finish your book. I'll want to buy a copy, by the way, and I'm sure Elliot will also."

Elliot said, "Yup."

Prison?

"Outsourcing my job isn't illegal," Harvey said.

"No. In fact, that was pretty damn clever. But cooperating with a foreign power is definitely illegal."

"I didn't cooperate with the Russians, at least not knowingly."

"No? Then where did the $250,000 come from?"

"What $250,000?"

"Check your bank balance."

"Why?"

"Just do it."

Harvey took out his phone. "I can tell you right now that there's just a little over $300 in it."

Harvey logged into his account and read the balance. Twice. A third time. A fourth. He had three-hundred and eleven dollars in the bank, as expected, plus a quarter of a million.

Harvey looked up. "You deposited it."

"Yup."

"Not the Russians?"

"Of course not."

"Which means you can't make this stick in court."

Luke picked up his bottle of beer, took a sip, and eyed Harvey. "We're the FBI. We can make anything stick."

Harvey guessed they could. Or at least make his life miserable for years. "You'll take the money back when this is all over?"

"Bet your ass."

"What's Amaya's role in all this? Is she a Russian agent?"

Luke chuckled. Elliot chuckled.

"What's so funny?"

"It means," Luke said, leaning forward and widening his smile, "that you've been sending flirtatious emails to a butt-ugly, bilingual, ex-rugby star, and current Russian intelligence agent named Igor Baranov."

Harvey sagged. "You mean…?"

"That there's no Amaya? That's correct, Igor writes the documentation."

Harvey snatched a handful of napkins off the coffee table and hacked up a mouthful of sour pizza chunks. His head buzzed from beer and disbelief. What an idiot he'd been.

Luke reached into his briefcase, pulled out an eight-by-eleven color print, and handed it to Harvey. "This is Igor. Memorize his face."

Someone had taken the photo through a car window. Igor was

standing on the sidewalk in front of a sporting-goods store with a sign in Russian over the door, a rugby ball tucked under his left arm. He was a huge guy with a huge head and huge hands that could strangle a horse.

Luke reached inside his jacket, pulled out a phone, and tossed it to Harvey. "This is a burner. Carry it at all times. If you need to get in contact with me, use the number I've programmed in. When I want to talk to you, it'll be on that phone."

Harvey slipped the phone into his pants pocket.

Burner phones, Russian agents, late-night meetings with FBI agents, and a secret task force. What a goat rodeo.

And no Amaya.

He was an idiot.

Luke said, "By the way, from our intercepts, we've learned that the Russians have greatly enjoyed your emails. "'If you ever get to the States,'" Luke said in a mocking high voice, "'maybe we can drive to Cape Cod or Vermont.'"

Elliot laughed.

Harvey said, "Fuck you!"

He wanted to melt into the couch. He couldn't remember ever feeling so humiliated, such a fool… and so scared.

"Am I in danger?"

Luke picked up the furniture catalog and fanned through the pages. "Like I said, just keep doing what you've been doing as if nothing had changed."

"That's not an answer."

Luke looked up and chuckled.

"Now what?" Harvey said.

"The Russians have an English-language codename for you."

Elliot snickered.

"Want to know what it is?" Luke asked.

"No."

"Here it is anyway: They call you 'Lovelorn.'"

Chapter 9

Release the Hounds

Harvey sat in his cubicle, his feet braced against the wall, his laptop balanced on his stomach, waiting for the 2:00 p.m. email from India. He no longer pictured a delicate woman in a flowing magenta sari, but a square-jawed and mud-encrusted rugby star working for Russian intelligence.

What a screw up. What a humiliation. What a fool he'd been.

He'd stayed awake fretting much of the night before, then kept nodding off during the morning's team meeting. Only Owen's sharp elbow saved him from snoring. As before, everyone around the table praised Harvey for his documentation. *Amaya will be pleased to hear that*, Harvey had thought, then caught himself. No, the kudos go to Igor.

Fuck!

Harvey wondered if he should quit his job, take off for parts unknown, and find work on some secluded island in the South Pacific as a cabana boy serving mai tais. Tempting, but the FBI would eventually track him down. Also, he'd be broke and unable to pay his mother's mortgage.

But didn't he have $250,000 in his checking account? That would take care of the mortgage and leave enough for a one-way flight to Bora Bora.

He held that thought for a long while, then burped. Harvey's stomach had been churning from too much coffee and too little sleep, from the lingering aftertaste of the gruesome caramelized onion, apple and goat-cheese pizza of the night before, and from fear. Mostly from fear.

Also doubts. Were those two clowns for real?

Just on the off chance, Harvey had Googled 'Luke Smith' and 'Elliot Smith.'

No meaningful matches. No surprise there.

Luke had said he worked for a task force, but refused to say which one, so Harvey was forced to search on 'secret FBI task force.' There were a number of FBI task forces, but none dealing with petroleum pumps as far as Harvey could tell and—understandably—not one referred to itself as secret.

Now what? A dead end.

Amaya's email arrived at one minute past 2:00.

No, Igor's email.

Harvey's heart sank.

Harvey,

I should have the documentation ready by the end of the day.

Amaya

Amaya? Yeah, sure.

Harvey stood up, kicked a dent into the side of his cubicle, then danced around and held his foot.

His big toe hurt. His pride hurt. And he was angry at himself and at Amaya/Igor, at the two FBI agents, at Middlebridge College for mismanaging their finances, and at his ex-wife for losing all their money on her stupid yoga studios, then dumping him for a dull insurance salesman, and he was especially pissed at the two guys in the coffee room bragging about their golf games at the top of their voice.

Harvey punched the wall.

Now his knuckles hurt.

He sat down, rubbed his hand, closed his eyes, took a few deep breaths, talked himself down, and typed a reply:

> I'm looking forward to seeing what you've written. Send it as soon as you can so I can pass it around for review.
> Harvey

Amaya/Igor replied immediately:

> Harvey,
>
> I hope that my current efforts live up to your expectations. I sense you are an educated man with very high standards.
> I have to admit that I often think about you, even though you are oceans away. Nevertheless, I hope that someday we might meet. Do you feel the same way?
> A bit about myself: I won't tell you how old I am—a woman never discloses that—but I live alone in a snug little apartment at the edge of New Delhi and have a younger brother who's forty-seven.
> Please tell me about yourself.
> I feel that I'm being terribly forward, so I'll sign off.
>
> Best,
> Amaya

Harvey read and reread the email. His anger boiled up again.

Rip into Igor? Call him a lying bastard? Tell the oaf that rugby is the brainless sport of thugs? No, of course not.

Have some fun.

> Amaya,
>
> I'm in my early forties, six-feet-four, and many people claim that I'm the spitting image of the young Sean Connery (I blush disclosing this). My many hobbies include race car driving, martial arts, and mountain climbing.
>
> I picture you as an extremely reserved woman, petite, sunny and attractive, a kind individual with a clever wit. Am I wrong?
>
> Yes, I too hope that we may someday meet. I'm dying to get to know you.
>
> Let me end with words from the tragically underappreciated early 20th-century American poet, Thomas P. Philpott, who wrote:
>
> "She is the pink-petalled and fragile first flower of early spring,
> waving in gentle warm breezes,
> lovely beyond words even for the smitten and unworthy versifier laboring at his desk,
> scratching his pen across sad dry paper."

Harvey sent the email, tilted his chair back, laced his hands behind his head, and laughed. When was the last time he'd laughed?

Immediately, he got an email from Amaya/Igor.

No, from Luke.

Was Luke reading emails?

Of course he was. He's the FBI.

Luke wrote:

Six foot four? Sean Connery? A pink-petalled and fragile flower of early spring? Are you trying to sabotage our operation? Write just one more goddamn over-the-top email like that, and I'll release the hounds.

Harvey wrote back,

Gosh, did I overplay my role?
Sincerely,
Lovelorn

Chapter 10

Sliding into Home Plate

Harvey slipped into the company's kitchenette for a cup of coffee and returned to find a fat red balloon bobbing above his cubicle ("Happy Late Birthday!"), its string attached to a wicker basket filled with candy. He sat down and read the note: "From a secret admirer of yesteryear."

Not so secret. Harvey recognized Margo's handwriting.

Harvey was poking through the basket for Skittles when Margo appeared in his cubicle's opening. She thumped the balloon with her knuckles. "Who's the thoughtful individual who sent you this?"

"That twenty-one-year-old Swedish underwear model I've been seeing."

"Uh, huh."

Margo rested her hand on Harvey's shoulder. "Do you miss no longer delivering balloons?"

Her hand felt good. But how did she know he'd quit that job? "Just the Skittles," he said.

"Pizzas are less sugary, but alarmingly high in fat. Still, it is protein."

"Uh… pizzas?" Harvey said. He wondered how she'd also found that out.

Margo unwrapped a Kit Kat and bit into it. "Chester—he's the new guy working with Owen—was watching a Red Sox game at his friend's house when he spotted you at the door, delivering a pizza." She took another bite, leaving a trace of chocolate at the side of her mouth.

Harvey had the urge to kiss the chocolate away, then work his way down. The idea excited him.

He was in fact getting too excited. He was a high-schooler again, back when he produced a woody every half hour. He snatched a three-ring binder off the shelf and laid it across his lap.

Margo said, "You're blushing."

"I am not blushing. I have a fever."

Margo tilted her head sideways and smiled the smile that had made Harvey fall in love with her way back when. She put her hand on his forehead. "You don't feel warm."

Harvey shifted in his seat. At that moment, he wanted more than anything in the world to toss the three-ring binder to the floor, pull Margo down on his bulging lap, and kiss away the chocolate and the decades.

If not that, he would settle for a date. But she was his boss, and that sort of thing was discouraged in the workplace.

But maybe that wasn't a problem because, as half-owner of the company, Margo made the rules. The real problem was that Harvey lacked the courage to ask her out to dinner or to pull her onto his lap and lick chocolate off her chin.

Margo said, "What are you working on now?"

"Writing, as usual."

Which was true, but it was his book, not what the company was paying him for. Harvey felt like a cheat. Margo had hired him, loved him once—or came as close to love as she was capable of—and treated him now as a friend. Harvey was stealing from her company. He should come clean. And he would. Right now and before he changed his mind. He should confess. He really should.

He didn't.

Margo stepped outside the cubicle, looked both ways, then slipped back inside. "Are you free tonight?" she whispered.

"You want me to work late?"

Margo shook her head and poked around in the candy basket, not making eye contact.

Harvey said, "I'll be delivering pizzas."

"Do you want company?"

Was she blushing?

"You're joking, right?" Harvey said.

Margo picked up an Oh Henry!, dropped it, then selected a tiny cellophane bag of Hershey's Kisses, and took one out. "Nope."

"You'd have to like the smell of pizza."

Margo munched on the chocolate. "Everyone likes the smell of pizza. Where should I meet you? And what time?"

Harvey told her.

She touched his shoulder and walked away.

He watched her go. She still had a nice walk.

Back in high school, Margo had been up for anything. She once talked him into helping her shoplift two witchy Halloween masks that they wore around town all day before returning to the same store and un-shoplifting them. Then there was the time they walked through the Harvard campus in their pajamas. Also, the rock-climbing and bungee-jumping. Margo had spirit, drive, wit. And he had loved her. Did he love her now? No. Would he love her again? Maybe.

*   *   *

Harvey was sitting in his car in front of the pizza store and plugging delivery addresses into his GPS when Margo slipped into the passenger seat. She wore a loose blue blouse and tight jeans. She turned toward the back seat and read aloud the label on the stack of insulated carrying cases: "'Pete's Speedy Pizza! Delivered in a Jiffy by Magic Elves!'—I guess that makes you a magic elf."

"You've always known that."

They rode a few blocks before Margo said, "You promised I'd be perfumed with the delicious aroma of freshly baked pizzas, but it's mostly stinky, moist boxes."

"I'm afraid my job isn't quite as glamorous as one would expect."

Margo squeezed his upper arm. "How are you handling it?"

This was her serious voice.

"Handling what?"

"Losing your status as a college professor."

Status meant everything to Margo. In high school, she'd spoken of running for the U.S. Senate or becoming the CEO of a Fortune 500 company. She'd even talked about the U.S. Presidency. Harvey had told her to lower her expectations. She'd called him a loser and slammed the car door behind her.

Harvey said, "Losing my professorship bothered me at first. I was afraid a former student or colleague would come to their front door and find me tugging on a balloon or clutching a pepperoni pizza box, but I've gotten over that."

"Really?"

"Really. What's wrong with delivering pizzas? It's honest work. The only difference between pizza-delivery individuals and U.S. Senators is that we're honest."

Well, not so honest. Again, Harvey wanted to confess to outsourcing his job.

He added, "I like my boss and the others I work with, more in fact than most of the colleagues I had back at Middlebridge College. Pete and the others aren't full of themselves, and they're more friendly, open, and cooperative."

Margo gave him a look that showed she wasn't quite convinced. Neither was he.

Their first deliveries were to apartment buildings near Boston University. At first, Harvey and Margo took turns, but since she got bigger tips, she ended up doing the legwork.

They hurried back to Pete's to pick up a small cheese pizza for a Margaret Thomey.

Margo kicked off her sneakers, shoved her seat back, and put her feet up on the dash. "We had a Margaret Thomey as our sixth-grade teacher. Remember her?"

"She once made me stand in the corner for using a split infinitive."

"Did you learn your lesson?"

Harvey nodded. "I was very careful to never again split an infinitive."

They rode in silence for a few minutes.

Harvey said, "When you eat a pizza, do you ever think about its origin?"

"Not really. I just know it came from Pete's or somewhere like that."

"No, I meant the pizza's real origin, such as who ordered the ingredients, who delivered the ingredients, and who cooked the pizzas. Did the wheat come from Kansas and the cheese from Wisconsin? And who were the farmers who grew the wheat and milked the cows? Did they have families who—"

Harvey felt Margo's lips pressed against his.

He jerked his head away. "Hey, I can't see!"

Margo settled back into her seat.

Harvey drove for another block, enjoying the taste of Margo's minty breath. "You used to do that back in high school to shut me up."

"It still works."

Harvey nodded and drove on.

He rolled up to a narrow brick apartment building in South Boston.

Margo took the pizza inside and in a couple of minutes came back grinning.

"What?" he asked.

"It is indeed our own Miss Thomey. She didn't recognize me. She's gray now and shaped like a bowling pin. I said *ain't* twice and split an infinitive. I thought she'd faint. She didn't send me to stand in a corner, however, but gave me only a two-dollar tip."

Harvey chuckled, then held out his hand and wiggled his fingers.

Margo laid one of the dollar bills in his hand. They were splitting tips.

The next delivery was for three sausage-and-mushroom pizzas at Fenway Park. It wasn't a game night, so Harvey figured some of the staff must be working late.

They went to the side entrance with the number that was written on the delivery slip and banged on the door. A man holding a mop finally opened up, yawned, and signaled for them to follow. He led them down a stairway, through a long, below-ground hallway, and up to a steel door. He tapped the end of his mop handle against it.

A middle-aged man in tan pants and a sleeveless undershirt opened the door a crack.

Harvey said, "You'll have to open farther."

The man reached through the gap and handed Harvey several bills to pay for the pizza but didn't include a tip. "Just leave them outside."

He had an accent, possibly Russian, possibly not. Harvey had Russians on his mind a lot lately.

He set the boxes on the floor.

They started back the way they'd come. Harvey turned to the janitor. "Who is he, and what's that place?"

"He's one of the guards," the janitor said. "That's where they take turns sleeping when they pull night duty." He pointed his mop down the hallway. "Go to the end, up the stairs, and turn right. That's where you came in."

The janitor hurried ahead.

A side door swung open, and a large man stepped out. He wore blue coveralls and carried a pipe wrench. He said, "Who in hell are you?"

Another guy with a Russian accent. Harvey glanced into the mouth of the tunnel off to his left. "And who in hell are you?"

"Wiseass. You're not supposed to be down here. What if I call my boss?"

"Go ahead," Harvey said, then held up the carrying case. "We've just made a pizza delivery."

The man hesitated, grunted, then headed to the room with the steel door.

"Creepy," Margo said, then added, "Hey, we've been left all alone!"

"That's because pizza-delivery specialists are by far the most trusted individuals in the American service industry."

They walked upstairs and toward the entrance off to the right.

Then Margo linked her arm in his and turned him to the left. "This way."

"Why?"

"You'll see." She led him to a ramp leading up to the stands. The lights were off. A pale moon hung over the bleacher seats. She said, "We're going to run the bases."

"You're kidding."

"Come on."

"Uh… okay. Except we can't get onto the field," Harvey said. "There are screens in front of the seats."

"Not in right field."

"How do you know?"

"I know everything."

Harvey watched her thread between the seats in the direction of right field. This was the old Margo from before she'd become the co-owner of a computer company and grown serious and bossy. The Margo he'd loved.

She stopped, turned, and signaled for him to follow.

Harvey did.

They scrambled over the right field fence and jogged to home plate, then took off for first base. They tagged up and rounded the corner. "A double," Margo shouted with a breathless giggle. They both slid into second, lay there for a moment, then got to their feet. Harvey dusted himself off, then Margo, concentrating on her jeans. Especially her jeans. Then Harvey and Margo thumped past third base and slid into home plate, but didn't get up this time. They rolled in the dirt, kissing, snuggling, kissing some more.

It was a strange moment and a wonderful one. Harvey was sixteen again. Time had deliciously folded back on itself. He was reliving his aching longing for Margo, the all-consuming love that only a teenager knows. He remembered their first kiss, and he remembered the time behind the gymnasium when they first got naked, and he relived the nightly sex in the back seat of his father's Mercedes.

He unbuttoned her blouse. She opened his belt buckle.

He said, "This is the dream of every horny Red Sox fan."

She tugged his trousers down.

He pulled her blouse off, then unhooked her bra and tossed it over his shoulder.

"We're making Red Sox history," Margo said. She wiggled out of her jeans and her panties, then kicked them away. "It's right on this spot that Babe Ruth hit his homers, Ted Williams too, and David Ortiz." She lay on her back, her arms stretched out to Harvey.

He lay gently on top of her and kissed her over and over. He said, "This adds new meaning to the expression 'getting to home base.'"

Margo giggled, and the sprinklers whirred.

Cold water splashed off Harvey's head, back, and legs. *"Shit!"* Margo laughed.

Harvey started to rise, but Margo pulled him back down. "Where do you think you're going, buster?"

"Uh, nowhere, I guess."

"That's right. As a historian, you now have a golden chance to make baseball-fan history. So get to it."

Harvey settled back down and got to it.

Chapter 11

A Shoe is Missing

Harvey selected a bench under a willow tree, sat down, and waited for Margo to bring lunch. It was her turn to buy. This had been their routine for the past three days: lunch in the Public Garden, a stroll, a chat, then a carpet quickie behind the locked door of her office. Fun, but also unsettling. They weren't so much a couple as just a pair of consenting adults taking care of their animal needs. *Fuck buddies* was the unpleasant expression his students had used. After sex, Margo would jump up, tug her clothes back on, grab her phone, and start chatting. He would slip away unnoticed.

Margo was incapable of deep affection, so Harvey expected little. Back in high school, it had taken him a while to come to terms with this. Since he'd been so wildly in love with her, he'd believed it was impossible she couldn't love him back with the same blind passion. Certainly, someday she would, he assured himself, but she never did.

His ex-wife had been affectionate, but she'd spread it around.

Harvey's own feelings for Margo weren't progressing, which came as a surprise. Maybe love can't rekindle after forty years. And maybe he didn't want it to.

They were different people now, with different experiences and different hopes. Even their bodies had changed since their sweaty couplings in the back seat of the beefy black Mercedes. Harvey had read that each cell in the human body, except for some in the brain, replaces itself in as short as a few days or as long as ten years, which meant that in some sense he'd replicated himself several times since birth and, in a way, he wasn't the same person he'd been in high school.

That should go somewhere into *Big History: The Birth and Death of Everything*. He made a voice note on his phone.

His stomach growled. Where was Margo? He looked around but didn't see her. He did spot a toddler in a stroller, crying and pointing at his foot. The mother wheeled around, retraced her steps, retrieved the lost shoe, tugged it back in place, ruffled the boy's hair, and rolled on.

Harvey hadn't found his own left shoe that day forty-eight years ago when he'd emerged from the waves as an only child. He'd kicked his shoes off before plunging into the water. He limped home soaking wet, leaving a watery trail, tears running down his face. He didn't want to go back to the cottage. He didn't want to tell his parents what had happened. He didn't want to go on living. He wanted to go back and swim out to the spot where he'd last seen Tommy and just let himself sink to the bottom. Locate his dead brother. Hug him and die.

But he kept walking. What would he tell his parents? How would he word it? Tommy had refused to go to the barbershop before a trip to the beach, and I couldn't stop him? No, he couldn't lie. He must tell the truth. Which is what he had done.

Harvey had wondered for years where his missing shoe had gone. It must have rotted away by now, leaving behind just the metal grommets that held the laces in place, and which actually had a special name that Harvey couldn't remember at the moment. Maybe the shoe had been carried off on that terrible morning in the slobbering mouth of a spaniel that took no interest in a drowning boy. Or the shoe caught the current and floated to Haiti, to be picked up on the beach by another eight-year-old boy, who dumped out the wet sand, laughed, and threw the shoe back into the ocean. Or it had floated all the way to the Moroccan coast.

Harvey looked up and saw Margo approaching. She wore a dark skirt and a white blouse that Harvey pictured himself tugging over her head right after lunch. She plopped down beside him, handed him a tofu salad in a Styrofoam box and said, "This is for my tech writer with benefits."

"Your rug gives me knee burns. I deserve a raise in pay, and I don't like tofu all that much."

Margo punched him on the shoulder. "Suck it up."

A jokey relationship between fuck buddies.

Still, she was kind to him, paid him more than he deserved, treated him as an equal instead of a technical writer perched on the bottom rung of the corporate ladder.

It was a kindness he didn't deserve, the outsourcer, the time-thief.

His throat tightened around a chunk of tofu. He coughed it up and wrapped it in his napkin.

Margo patted his back. "Are you okay?"

No, he wasn't okay. He was a thief, a fake, and a dead weight on the company, and he had to confess. He'd told her the truth about Tommy's death those many years ago, and now he would tell her the truth about outsourcing his job. "There's something I've been wanting to tell you. But first, I want to assure you that I'll find a way to pay my salary back."

Margo paused, a salad-filled fork halfway to her mouth. "What's this all about?"

"I'm stealing from the company."

"Everyone is," Margo said with a shrug. "Our monthly office-supply bill is astronomical."

"No, I mean I'm stealing time."

Margo lowered her fork. "Time? What does that mean?"

"I've outsourced my job. I've hired a woman in India to write the documentation."

Margo's face went blank.

Say something. Tell me what a crook I am, what a loser I am. Throw your salad in my face. Slap me. Fire me. Stomp away.

She giggled and rapped her knuckles against his chest. "You could always make me laugh. That's what attracted me to you. And you were cute, and you had this wild imagination and—"

"No, I really—"

"Hold that," Margo said, raising a forefinger. "If it's who I think it is, I have to take this call."

She reached into her purse, pulled out her phone, lifted it to her ear, and stood up. "What?" she shouted. "They're raising the rent by how much? Tell them we won't pay. Say we'll move the company out of the city if..."

And that was much as Harvey could make out because Margo had wandered off, her phone stuck to her ear, her salad forgotten, him forgotten.

This is how it would be if they became a real couple. She'd pay attention to him only until the next phone call.

He tossed his half-eaten lunch into a trash can, but left her salad on the bench. Maybe she'd come back for it. And for him. But he wouldn't be there.

He crossed the street to Boston Common. He needed to walk. A yellow Frisbee landed at his feet. He whipped it back to the boy, who reached up and snagged it. "Nice throw!"

At least he was good at something.

Harvey was annoyed with Margo, but he was also relieved for having confessed to her. Well, it wasn't quite a confession, was it? Interesting, though. His admission occupied a gray area between truth and untruth, if such a region existed. He had indeed confessed, but she hadn't taken him seriously. So was it a genuine confession? And what is truth? Can there be more than one type?

Hard truth might not even exist in our day when so much of the Web and the political atmosphere is clogged with exaggerations and fabrications.

Is this something that belonged in his book? Is this warp in the fabric of veracity a part of Big History, of our new age? Yes, indeed. He broke into a trot. He had to get back to his desk and write the idea down while it was still fresh.

He paused long enough at a vending cart to buy a wrinkled hotdog. He wondered how many days the thing had been turning on its spindle, and how many tourists had eyed it, noted its shine, shaken their head, and moved on, and then he hurried to his office, up the elevator, to his cubicle, and gnawed on the aged sausage while he typed two pages of notes on truth and untruth just before his phone rang.

It was his mother.

"Did I call at an inconvenient time?"

"No, this is fine, Mom."

"How's work going?"

"Surprising well."

"Is Margo a good boss?"

Harvey's mind shifted to their jolly tumbles. "The best."

"Is it hard working for an old sweetheart?"

Harvey smiled to himself. "When it gets hard, she handles it with great skill."

"You two made a handsome couple back in high school, but you really didn't belong together. In fact, Margo did you a favor when she took up with that dreadful Tucker. You were too easygoing. Margo and Tucker had ambitions and lots of drive, like your father."

That again?

But his mother was right, not about him, but certainly about his father. He'd been ambitious, hard-working, successful, and much admired at the hospital, in particular by the young nurses. He frequently left his family behind and flew the lady of the moment to the Bahamas for a long weekend. Harvey wondered if his mother ever got suspicious about her husband's steady succession of medical conferences in warmer climes. Maybe she just pushed the truth out of her mind and moved on. She was good at that.

Harvey said, "Did you call to talk me into applying to medical schools?"

"No, I just wanted to tell you not to stop by Sunday afternoon because I have plans."

"Okay. What about in the evening?"

"I'm busy then, too. And all of next week. And maybe for a couple of weeks more."

Harvey had visited his Mother almost every Sunday since the death of his father six years earlier. "What's this all about?"

"I'm just making a little change."

"Are you sick?"

"Nope. Healthy as a race horse."

"Getting married again?"

"Goodness, no," she said with a laugh. "I shouldn't have mentioned anything about my plans. You'll find out when you find out. Now I have to run."

Harvey stared at his phone. Plans? He didn't like the sound of that.

*   *   *

Harvey ignored his mother's orders and drove to Brookline the next Sunday afternoon. A dozen cars were parked out front, and three more sat in the driveway. Was it a party she hadn't invited him to? Or was she really getting married?

Just drive on. If his mother didn't want him here, he should respect her wishes. Then he spotted the sign in the middle of the lawn: 'Open House, 1 to 5.'

What the hell!

He swung over to the curb, shut off the engine, and jumped out of the car.

His mother would never sell. She loved the place. She would shrivel up and die if she had to move.

Harvey broke into a run, rushed up the walkway and into the house, elbowed through the crowd, and scurried around looking for his mother. She wasn't in the living room, the dining room, the study, the kitchen.

A woman in a blue pants suit waved her sunglasses in a circle and told her companion that she didn't care for all that dark wood.

Well, fuck you.

He spotted his mother in the backyard, filling the bird feeder. He waved. She hesitated, then waved back. "I'll be right in," she shouted.

She loved birds, loved the sprawling backyard, the gravel walkway that curled through the flowerbeds, and she loved the stone gazebo that he and Tommy had called their fort and played in all summer long.

A woman in jeans and a tight white blouse said to the man beside her, "Should we make an offer?"

"Maybe, but low-ball it," he said. "She's an old lady and probably addled." Then he lifted Tommy's photo off an end table, snickered and said, "That kid on the tricycle has a head like a pumpkin."

Harvey ripped the photo out of the man's hand so hard the frame broke, and the glass hit the floor and shattered. *"Get the hell out of here!"*

The man blinked. "Who are you?"

Harvey took a step forward, pressed his hand against the man's chest, and shoved him backwards. "I'm the guy who's going to kick the crap out of you if you don't get the hell out of here. Now!"

The man and woman hurried out of the room. Everyone followed.

Harvey went from room to room. "Out! The open house is over!"

A middle-aged woman with jangling gold bracelets rushed up, a leather folder in her hand. "What are you doing? I'm in charge of this sale!"

"No, I'm her son, and I'm in charge, and there's no goddamn sale! Why in hell did you talk my mother into putting her house on the market?"

The woman took a step back and clutched her folder to her chest. "I didn't talk her into anything. She contacted me."

"I don't believe that. She loves this place."

"You said you're her son?"

"Yes, but what does—"

"She's selling because of you. She told me her lawyer had slipped up and revealed that you've been paying her bills and mortgage for years."

Harvey fell quiet. A lot to process. His shoulders slumped. "Oh. Sorry."

The woman turned and walked away, waving her folder overhead. "You'll be hearing from me. Or maybe not."

She left just as his mother walked into the kitchen and looked around. "Where is everyone?"

"I chased them away."

"Why?"

"Because you don't want to move, and I don't want you to move."

She set the bag of birdseed on the floor, settled onto a kitchen chair and sighed. "What did the realtor tell you?"

"That you found out I was taking care of the mortgage."

His mother pointed at the chair opposite her. "Sit."

Harvey did.

"I can't let you support me. Your car's a wreck, you live in a hovel, and you're still wearing that dreadful brown sports coat with the elbow patches from your teaching days. I thought you were just going through a bohemian phase, but then I find out your poverty is for real. How would you feel if you were in my position? Would you stay in this huge house while your child lived on ramen noodles?"

"I don't live on ramen noodles, and I'm getting along fine."

She leaned forward and patted the back of Harvey's hand. "In any case, this place is much too large for one person. Geraldine has invited me to move in with her in Fort Lauderdale. She has three bedrooms, so we won't be crowded, and I'll escape these awful Massachusetts winters."

"You hate Florida, and your cousin bullies you, owns too many cats, and smells like dirty socks."

"I'll just have to get used to that, won't I?"

Her voice was strong, but there were tears in her eyes.

Harvey slid his chair next to hers, put his arm around her shoulder, and pulled her in close. Her bones were thin, and she was trembling. He wanted to fix everything, to make everything right. But what could he do? His father had died with almost as many debts as assets. The horse farm and stocks and bonds were gone. Only the house remained, but the mortgage was almost a quarter million dollars.

His mother pulled away and crossed her arms. "I simply will not let you pay the mortgage any longer. I'm sure you're broke."

Broke?

Well, yes and no.

He hesitated. Would he be caught? Maybe not. He'd read that international crooks transferred huge amounts of money using Bitcoins and the like, and where the money went could never be traced. But in his situation, the transfer itself wouldn't remain secret because it came from a bank. Could he claim that someone had hacked into his account and cleaned it out? But Luke and the FBI would trace the transaction in hours. Minutes, maybe.

Not possible, Harvey thought.

His mother stifled a sob.

What the hell, just take the heat. He pulled out his phone and brought up his bank account. "They love me at work."

"That's nice."

"In fact, they're willing to do anything to keep me. That's why they gave me a massive bonus."

Harvey turned the phone so that his mother could see the screen.

She leaned closer and squinted. "You have that much in the bank?"

"Right. My bonus."

"That's a lot of money."

"High tech has a lot of money to throw around," Harvey said. "I had to sign a three-year contract, of course."

His mother nodded and touched her eyes with a tissue.

She'd bought it. She knew nothing about money matters. His father always handled—or mishandled—their finances.

"They must really love what you're doing," she said with pride. "But I can't let you do that, dear. You need the money for yourself."

"No. As I said, I'm getting along fine. And it's not as if I was throwing the money away because... well... uh..." He waved his hands.

"Because you'll eventually inherit this place."

"I hesitated bringing that up."

His mother smiled and squeezed his hand. "What the hell, we're all going to die someday."

"I've never heard you swear before."

"I thought it was about time I started," she said and again wiped her eyes. "Okay, go ahead. Your father always said that real estate was the best investment."

"No," Harvey said, putting his arm around his mother's shoulder. "Families are."

Chapter 12

Can I Get that in Writing?

Harvey headed home feeling more and more apprehensive and driving slower and slower. Cars behind him honked, swung into the left lane, and squealed past. A bearded man in a pickup truck pulled up beside him, gave him the finger, and sped on. Harvey eyed him but didn't respond. He was in too much of a fog.

Now he'd done it, played the good son and promised too much.

Still, he might get away with claiming that someone had hacked into his bank account. Or he could at least find some way to conceal where the money had gone. Every day, terrorists, international drug dealers, and Russian oligarchs transferred millions of dollars undetected across borders. Sure, Luke would know the quarter million dollars was missing from the account, but he wouldn't know where it went.

For the rest of the day and late into the night, Harvey sat with his laptop at the kitchen table, drank cup after cup of black coffee, and studied up on cryptocurrencies, Swiss bank accounts, gold, stock certificates, and plain old cash. Soon it was obvious that monitoring was tight. A money transfer would work only if the source of the funds was unknown, but the $250,000 sat in a closely regulated bank account.

He could back out, but what would he tell his mother? I was

kidding, Mom. I want to keep the money for myself. You'll get used to Florida and how your cousin smells.

Absolutely not.

He might go to prison, or he might get off the hook completely. More likely, it would be something in between. He could argue before the judge that, if he got locked up, he wouldn't be able to pay back what he owed. If that didn't work and he did go to jail, maybe he'd get a sentence of just a year or so. Afterwards, he would tell his mother he'd gone to Katmandu as a visiting professor, and there was no way to phone, email, or send mail.

When he got out, he'd have to pay the quarter million dollars off, of course, but he could do that over a decade or so if he got a decent job and ate ramen noodles for every meal.

Except that felons didn't get decent jobs.

He crawled into bed but didn't fall asleep until three in the morning. He woke at dawn, made eggs and toast, and couldn't get past the first bite. Instead, he drank cup after cup of coffee at the kitchen table and watched the clock. At precisely 9:00 a.m., he called the mortgage company for the balance on the loan. Then he dressed quickly, drove to his bank in downtown Boston, and instructed them to transfer $239,288 to cover the mortgage.

Afterwards, Harvey stepped out into the street and was proud of himself. And worried, really worried.

Since he'd taken the morning off, he still had a couple of free hours. So he drove home, ate a banana and a slice of cold pepperoni pizza, then changed into his running clothes, and headed outside. He paused on the front steps, squinted into the sun, then turned left and jogged down the sidewalk. He was full of energy and more and more ready to take on whatever came his way.

He was halfway down the block when a black car swung up to the curb in front of him and squealed to a halt. Both front doors popped open. Luke stepped from the passenger side and held up both hands for Harvey to stop. Elliot climbed out from behind the wheel.

Harvey jogged in place.

Luke said, "We're here about the money."

That was fast. "Are you referring to that quarter million that had been unprofitably idling in my bank account?" Harvey said, puffing. "I invested almost all of it with a former Nigerian prince who's promised to triple my investment in just six weeks."

"No, you didn't," Luke said. "You paid off your mother's mortgage. Now get the hell into the car!"

Harvey lifted his knees higher and jogged in place faster. "Maybe after I've done my three miles."

Luke nodded to Elliot, who pulled his jacket back to show a pistol in a shoulder holster.

Harvey climbed into the back seat.

Luke sat up front. Elliot got behind the wheel and pulled away from the curb.

Luke threw his arm over the seat back, turned and said, "What in hell made you think you'd get away with this? We know everything you do—when you go to work, when you come home from work, how many pizzas you deliver, and when you take a dump. We've got you by the gonads."

Although Harvey was quaking inside, he forced a laugh. "No, I've got you by the gonads."

"Us? You're the one who's going to the slammer. You're the one who'll end up sharing a cell with a 280-pound biker who calls himself Bubba and has a carnal partiality for ex-academics."

Harvey produced another laugh. "Okay, take me to court. Here's what'll happen: I'll maintain that the $250,000 was my salary from a secret government task force that had hired me to risk my life on a extremely dangerous operation against the Russians."

Luke was quiet for a moment. "The judge wouldn't buy that. To start with, he'll know that the FBI would have withheld taxes before paying you, which means there'd be less than a quarter million in your bank account."

Harvey faked a yawn. "You're missing the point. Yes, the judge might not accept my argument, but in the process of testifying, I'd have revealed the existence of a secret task force dedicated to preventing a Russian cyberattack on U.S. petroleum pipelines. That'll leak out as these things always do. Do you want your little caper to appear on CNN? If I'm taken to court, not only would your mission implode, but the government would have wasted millions of dollars to save a measly $250,000."

Elliot grunted.

Luke was quiet.

Harvey chuckled. "You're not taking me to court," he said with another yawn and wondered if he was overplaying his part.

Elliot circled the block once, twice, three times, cursing at other drivers.

Luke stared straight ahead.

Finally, he said, "Pull over."

Elliot did.

Luke turned in his seat. "For now, I'll let things slide. In fact, I'll even push my boss to let you keep the money once the operation has succeeded."

Yeah, sure. "Can I get that in writing?"

"I'll get the paperwork to you later. This sort of thing takes time. Bureaucracies, you know."

Uh, huh. "Just something hand-written would do for now," Harvey said brightly.

Luke got out of the car and jerked Harvey's door open. "Out!"

"You're not going to drive me back to my place?"

"*Out!*"

*   *   *

Harvey jogged for the next hour, running an assortment of What-If's through his mind. What if he did get to keep the money? Or what if the task force did take him to court after the operation ended? Or what if he did have to share barred lodgings with the randy Bubba?

Once home, Harvey showered, dressed, and hurried to work. He turned on his laptop and found an email from Amaya/Igor:

> Harvey,
>   The latest documentation will be ready by late today. I hope it lives up to your high standards, but I'm afraid it does not, and that makes me sad. To tell the truth, I'm going through a rather low period right now.
>   It seems I've come to realize how dull my life is, how ordinary and regulated. Sometimes, I'm tempted to break free and do something wild. Right now, I'm thinking of how much fun it would be just to hop on a plane and fly to America and visit you. Isn't that crazy?
>   Actually, I may have found a way to make that work. More on that later.
>   Sorry to burden you with my personal problems.
>   Your friend,
>   Amaya

Yes, Harvey thought, it would be crazy to have a hulking, former rugby star show up at his door dressed in a sky-blue sari and attempt to pass himself off as a sweet, middle-aged woman from new Delhi.

Harvey replied:

> Nothing would give me greater pleasure than to meet you in person. I picture you as a petite and fine-featured woman with impeccable taste in dress, but someone who is also athletic. Extremely athletic.
>   Should you come to Boston, you could save hotel

money by staying with me (in separate bedrooms, of course). I'm fortunate enough to own a four-story townhouse in Boston's upscale Back Bay. I live there alone, so there would be plenty of room for a friendly visitor from New Delhi, although I should add that I use the entire fourth floor to display the paintings, sculptures, and Louis XVI armchairs that I've brought back from my countless European voyages.

Please don't delay your trip, however, because I've just learned that I may be moving to a much larger residence that I'll be sharing with many other men.

But that is a story for another day. Right now, I—

"Who's Amaya?"

Harvey slammed his laptop shut.

Margo was standing in his cubicle opening.

He said, "She's that Swedish undergarment model I've been seeing on the side."

"Of course," Margo said. "By the way, I missed finishing lunch with you the other day."

Harvey wondered if he should call her out for forgetting all about him and leaving him alone on the bench in the Public Garden, but he had more important things on his mind: debts, the secretive Luke and Elliot, a Russian agent in a swishy blue sari, and a hairy, horny freak called Bubba.

Chapter 13

Surprise!

After several days of high winds and chilly rain, the weather turned nice, so Harvey walked home from the office instead of taking the subway. Also, he wanted time to think, which he did best on his feet. To the amusement of his former students, he would wander around campus, winter and summer, whispering his thoughts into a handheld recorder. They'd referred to him—presciently—as "Harvey Hudson, International Spy."

The more he thought about Luke and Elliot, the more What-Ifs he generated. Sure, they'd flashed badges at their first meeting, but anyone can order a fake ID card online. They might even be working for the Russians. Or were they themselves somehow trying to influence petroleum futures? They could be as fake as Amaya/Igor.

Harvey stopped halfway across Harvard Bridge, which connected Boston to Cambridge, and leaned over the railing. No, the evidence—scanty as it was—favored Luke and Elliot over Amaya/Igor.

He reached the Cambridge side of the Charles River, walked along with it to his left, then turned right and headed for the snug little abode where he would be safe and secure behind his locked door.

The door wasn't locked. It was open a crack. Had he forgotten to close it on the way out? That wasn't like him.

He pushed it all the way open.

What the hell?

Someone had pulled cans and boxes from the kitchen cabinets onto the floor, knocked books off shelves, sliced open the sofa cushions, and scattered the stuffing.

Harvey didn't budge. Who had done this? The same burglars who'd tried to break into the poultry store downstairs? But even the most addled addict would realize that anyone living in a dump like this had nothing to steal. And it's unlikely a burglar would rip open the couch cushions.

Had Luke and Elliot broken in to look for… for what? Evidence he was secretly working for the Russians? Unlikely.

The Russians themselves could have tossed the place. Maybe there was something in his emails that had aroused suspicion, and Amaya/Igor had sent an agent to the U.S. to check on him.

Or maybe it was just punk kids in a destructive mood.

Numbed, Harvey kneeled, gathered up stuffing, shoved handfuls of it back into the couch cushions, and turned them over, good side up.

He felt violated. He got to his feet, looked around the room, and shivered. He sensed the ghostly person or persons who'd done this, felt them hovering around him. Would they come back? Were they violent?

Were they hiding in the bathroom?

Harvey grabbed the iron frying pan off the top of the stove, tiptoed to the bathroom, raised the pan overhead, turned the knob, kicked the door open, and jumped inside.

No one.

The medicine cabinet door hung by one hinge. Razors, dental floss, and allergy pills lay scattered across the floor. The intruder had sliced the tube of toothpaste open and squeezed its contents into the sink.

Harvey ripped the cabinet door free and set it aside, scrubbed the sink, picked up the items on the floor, and lined them side-by-side in the cabinet. Then he went into the kitchen and filled four trash bags with the cereal boxes and soup cans and cleaning products that the intruder had opened and dumped onto the floor.

Next came the desk. The gold pen-and-pencil set Brenda had given him on their first anniversary was still there. So was the expensive watch for their second anniversary, and which he'd been too embarrassed to wear. That ruled out a burglar.

Then who?

He could call the police, but that wouldn't do any good. And besides, he didn't want them looking into his affairs now that he was tangled up with an FBI task force.

His books lay sprawled on the floor, fanned open, some with pages ripped out.

A knock on the door.

Harvey jumped.

Answer it?

No? Yes?

Another knock.

Harvey grabbed the iron frying pan again, raised it overhead, tiptoed across the room, and jerked the door open.

"Is this your way of asking for a raise?" Margo said.

Harvey lowered his arm. He remembered now that she'd emailed him to say she would drop by after work with important news. Harvey stepped back. "I was… uh… just straightening up."

The kitchen table was still upside down, and the toaster rested on the floor, its crumb flap open.

Margo stepped inside, looked around and whistled. "Have you called the police?"

"Just getting ready to," Harvey said.

He had tried to talk Margo out of visiting because he didn't want her to see how he lived. But Margo did pretty much what she wanted. He stepped aside to let her pass. He said, "This is just a temporary home."

"I should hope so."

"Until my employer gives me that big raise I deserve."

Margo smiled weakly and nudged the toaster with her toe. "Where does all your money go?"

"Did you come all the way across town to advise me on my personal finances?"

"No, but I will now," Margo said and sniffed the air. "By the way, I smell lilac perfume. Have you been entertaining a little someone here?"

"That Swedish underwear model I've told you about."

Margo nodded.

Harvey had forgotten about Margo's acute sense of smell. When they'd been together in high school, he felt he had to shower twice a day.

She picked up the toaster, closed the flap, set it on the counter and plugged it in. Then she went to the bedroom and shuffled through the papers on the desk.

"Just make yourself at home," Harvey said. "And yes, what you're holding are several dozen rejections from colleges and universities. I'm saving them in case I run out of Charmin."

Margo laid the papers back on the desk and turned to him. "It hurts me to say this, Harvey, but you have to face facts. You're a fifty-six-year-old man who's competing with twenty-somethings with fresh PhDs and whose salary would be half as much as yours. In fact, you—"

"Don't you think I know that? But I have some advantages."

"Which are?"

"Two-dozen publications, my past role as president of a respectable international history organization, and my upcoming book."

Margo picked up a lavender paperweight globe, held it up to the overhead light, then set it back on the desk. "How many years have you been working on the thing? Ten? Twelve? Face it, Harvey, you'll never finish."

Harvey wanted to tell her to fuck off, but didn't. From now on, he wouldn't feel a bit guilty about working on his book during office hours.

He glanced at the bed. No, he was too pissed at Margo to suggest that they get naked. "You have to go now. I need to get ready for my night job."

Margo bent down and picked up an astronomy textbook, thumbed through the pages, then set it back on the desk. "I know you're not happy as a technical writer, so I've set up an interview for you."

An interview? A college interview? Margo had contacts with a lot of important people. Harvey's pulse sped up. "Where?"

"Westover Associates."

"Uh… isn't that an insurance company?"

"My cousin's a senior VP," Margo said. "He's expecting you tomorrow at two. The salary's quite a bit more than what you're making now, and there's room for rapid advancement."

"Goddamn it, Margo! You don't set up job interviews for me!"

"I just did."

"I know nothing about insurance, and I sure as hell don't want to."

"You're smart and well-organized. You'll do fine. You don't want to be a technical writer for the rest of your life."

"Maybe I do. I'm good at it."

Or Amaya/Igor was good at it. Harvey knew he would eventually have to go into a different line of work. Just not insurance.

Margo put her hands on her hips. "You *will* go to the interview tomorrow, won't you?"

"Of course not."

"You should," she said.

"Hell, no!"

Margo was quiet for a moment. "I'm leaving."

Again, Harvey glanced at his bed and the sliced mattress. Angry or not, he half wanted her to stay.

She went to the door and paused.

Harvey guessed Margo was waiting for him to call her back, apologize, to hug her, and to undress her.

Instead, she said, "I'll see you at work," and closed the door behind her.

He listened to her footsteps receding down the stairs. He could rush out and call her back, put his arms around her, say he was sorry, scoop her up, carry her back inside, kick the piles of clothing aside, lay her on his bed, and strip off her clothing.

But he didn't.

Instead, he stretched out on the couch and tried to understand what he was feeling. What did he want from her? Love? Marriage? Or just sex? He had no idea.

A knock on the door.

Harvey leaped to his feet.

Margo had come back!

He tucked in his shirt, put his hand in front of his mouth, and sniffed to test his breath. Good enough. He pulled on his sneakers, patted his hair in place, opened the door, and spread his arms.

It wasn't Margo.

It was a stunning woman of about fifty, with long black hair, sparkling dark eyes, and a flowing blue dress.

Harvey dropped his arms.

She said, "Harvey Hudson?"

"Yes."

She smiled a staggeringly beautiful smile.

He said, "Uh… do I know you?"

"Can't you guess who I am?"

Harvey shook his head. "Sorry. Not really."

"I'm Amaya."

Chapter 14

A Poor Jerk Dragged into
a World of Trouble

Harvey stumbled backwards and grabbed a kitchen chair to steady himself.

What the hell?

The woman pointed at the chair with its torn plastic seat. "That must be one of your priceless Louis XVI armchairs."

"What?"

She smiled. "You mentioned them in your email."

"Uh… right."

Her eyes flashed. Novelists talk about flashing eyes, but Harvey had never seen them in real life.

Who was this creature?

She took a step farther inside. "What's happened here?"

"I was burglarized earlier in the day. That's why everything's a mess. My place doesn't usually look like this."

But not much better. Even though Amaya was an imposter, he wished she hadn't seen his sad old brown couch with the leaky stuffing and his sagging brick-and-board bookshelves. His furnishings looked like the things that graduate students rescued from the curb on collection day.

"I flew in a just a few hours ago," Amaya said.

Harvey nodded.

"It took forever."

Again Harvey nodded.

The Russians must have sent this woman.

What would he call her? *Amaya*, at least for now anyway.

He'd never told her where he lived. He guessed that the Russian intelligence service had informed her. "How did you find me?"

Amaya looked around. "May I come in?"

Harvey took a step back to let her pass. "You didn't answer my question."

She slipped inside and gazed around, then unslung her shoulder bag and set it next to her ankle. "I found your address in your application to Lotus Worldwide Consultants."

Slick. She'd delayed replying until she'd come up with a believable answer.

He couldn't decide on his next move. Should he call her a fake and order her to leave? What would he do if he were a real international spy? He'd let her play her role, that's what.

She looked uneasy, which was the natural thing to do. She had the role of a woman who'd just pushed her way into a strange man's home halfway around the world. Harvey wondered if the Russian intelligence service sent their agents through acting school. He guessed she'd rehearsed this scene.

Again, he wondered why they'd sent her here.

Harvey shifted from foot to foot. "Would you like a beer?"

"I don't drink alcohol."

Harvey was wary of this woman. Maybe she was carrying a gun in that bulky leather shoulder bag and was just waiting for him to turn his back.

She reached into the bag.

Harvey stepped back and half raised his hands.

Amaya pulled out a manila folder and held it out to him. "Here's the first half of the next set of documentation. I tried to finish on the plane, but kept falling asleep. I'll work on the rest tonight in my hotel room."

Harvey blinked a few times, listened to his heart pounding, then reached for the folder. His hand trembled. He fanned through pages and pages of stuff he couldn't begin to understand. "Look's great," he said.

"You understand it?"

"Uh… not completely."

Amaya nodded.

"I could if I worked at it, of course," Harvey said, "but I don't have the time to devote all the hours necessary to learn this particular technology."

Yeah, sure. He was hiding his ignorance because he wanted to impress this gorgeous woman, even though she was a phony and a foreign agent out to do damage to his country. And maybe him.

Again, Amaya nodded.

He wondered what Russian intelligence had told her about him, and how they knew what they did know.

"Would you like a beer?"

Amaya shook her head. "You asked that before."

"Right."

Harvey pretended to take an interest in the folder. What in hell was *TWAIN*? Or *thunking*? His new world was filled with mysterious acronyms and goofy vocabulary. His brain thunked. He asked, "Why are you here?"

"You invited me," Amaya said. She looked hurt.

A fine piece of acting.

"Of course."

"Things worked out perfectly," Amaya said with a growing smile. "I'd mentioned in my email that I might get to the States, but I didn't say how. Well, my boss wanted a representative in the U.S., and he gave me the job."

Uh, huh.

"That means I'm here for more than just a visit," she added. "Now we won't have to send emails and documents halfway around the globe."

"Does it really matter if we email from a distance or from just across town?"

Amaya wrinkled her mouth. He'd hurt her feelings again. Or she was acting as if he'd hurt her feelings again. She reached out and tapped his sleeve. "Emails are so impersonal. It'll be much nicer to work with you face-to-face."

This woman had talent. She should have sold herself to Bollywood instead of Russian intelligence.

Amaya touched his sleeve again. "I want you to show me all around town. I want to see the Boston Tea Party Ship, the MIT campus, The Old North Church, and all the other sites I've read about. Will you do that for me?"

Again that smile.

Harvey nodded. He had built up a few vacation days, but he'd planned on hiking in Vermont, not escorting a fetching Russian operative from one tourist spot to the next. He brightened and said, "Sounds like a lot of fun."

He, too, could act.

*   *   *

Amaya smiled and left.

Harvey stared at the closed door and asked himself what in hell had just gone down.

Well, he'd been played, that's what.

Again, he wondered why the Russians had sent her. It was possible they'd somehow learned about the task force and his role in the operation, but unlikely. The FBI ran a tight ship.

Luke had to be told.

Harvey pulled out his phone.

Then hesitated.

Amaya was either an Oscar-winning actor or telling the truth. If the latter, that meant Luke and Elliot were fakes.

Would he really be entertaining any level of doubt about that pair if Amaya weren't drop-dead gorgeous and didn't achingly remind him of Chandra with her big dark eyes, her melting smile, and glossy black hair?

Harvey had to sit down.

Still, it was odd the way Luke and Elliot had lured him to that furniture showroom to deliver pizzas. They could have met him at some Starbucks way out in the suburbs.

But the evidence weighed against Amaya—or whoever she was. Still…

Again, Harvey wondered if he'd be having these doubts if Amaya hadn't brought back memories of Chandra.

Now he really thought of himself as an international spy, a vulnerable pawn sitting alone in the middle of the chess board, a poor jerk dragged into a world of trouble.

He wished he were back teaching, where the only time he'd faced danger had been that icy December morning when he'd slipped on the college library steps and sprained his left wrist.

Harvey toyed with his phone.

Call?

Don't call?

One week. He'd give her one week. By then, he'd know for sure.

He turned off his phone, went to bed, and dreamed of Chandra and this woman who called herself Amaya.

Chapter 15

The Moscow School of Acting for Fetching Lady Spies

Harvey took a long weekend and showed Amaya around Boston, which he told himself wasn't anything like a date, but simply a clever maneuver to find out whether or not she was a spy.

She'd made a list. At top was Harvard Square, which she said was fun but much too noisy and crowded. Then it was off to Quincy Market, where they had coffee and croissants at a stand-up table, and which Amaya also found too noisy and crowded. Later, they walked near the harbor. Amaya pointed at the Boston Tea Party ship. "That's next."

They went aboard and paid to jointly toss a bundle of tea into the harbor, then watched with great disappointment as a bearded man in a Colonial-era sailor suit tugged on a rope and pulled the bundle back over the railing.

Despite this bizarre situation, Harvey enjoyed seeing Boston through a foreigner's eyes. Amaya was bright and observant and said she loved history. He wondered if her Russian handlers had told her to say that because he was a historian. Still, she seemed to be having fun. So was he.

He liked the way men looked at him with envy.

Now and then Amaya brushed up against him, and he smelled

her hair and her perfume.

At each stop, he bought her a tacky souvenir, which made her giggle as she stuffed it into her massive shoulder bag. She made ironic comments about what she saw. She smiled and joked, and there was a bounce in her steps. Harvey got laughs when he made up stories about ghost-sightings at the Paul Revere House. Good company, this *femme fatale.*

Harvey realized how desperately lonely he'd been. Margo was a glorious roll in the hay but spent much more of her time cuddling her phone than she did him. He saw Owen only at work. All of his friends had been on the faculty, some he'd known for decades. They'd scattered to the winds—a few had found faraway teaching jobs, a few went into other fields, two retired, and others stayed home, drew the curtains and drank. One hanged himself.

Harvey and Amaya filed out of the Paul Revere House and sat on a bench across the street. He said, "Now where?"

Amaya stood up and straightened her skirt. "Feed me."

"What kind of food do you like?"

"I usually eat vegetarian."

Harvey led her to a North End restaurant with an outdoor menu listing a half dozen meatless meals. He ordered flounder and a glass of white wine, and Amaya asked for a tofu salad and mineral water.

She said, "I learned a lot about you from your emails, not necessarily from what you said—I knew you were making up stuff to entertain me—but from what you left out."

Harvey wasn't sure what that meant. He said, "I'm a man of mystery," and immediately felt stupid.

Amaya poked at her salad. "I Googled you, of course, and found out you were the president of some historical society whose name I can't remember, and—"

"'The International Society of Big History Educators.'"

"...and I learned that your college folded and left you out of work, but that was about it. So fill me in on the life and times of Harvey Hudson."

As if the Russian intelligence service didn't have a fat dossier on him. But Harvey went through the motions and told her about growing up in Brookline in the big house where his mother still lived, that he'd gone to the University of Michigan and on to Harvard graduate school, then a teaching job at Middlebridge College. "I've led an extraordinarily ordinary life."

Until now.

"Maybe that will change," Amaya said.

Was that a little joke to herself?

"Maybe," Harvey said.

Amaya eyed Harvey's plate. He could see that her heart wasn't into tofu salad. He pushed his plate closer to her.

She took a forkful of flounder, ate it, then asked, "What's Big History?"

"It's the study of everything from the Big Bang, through all of pre-human and human existence, and right up to this moment when you're raiding my seafood."

Amaya made a face and scooped up another forkful. "You must know a lot."

"No, but I know—or knew—a lot of other faculty members who knew a lot. They loaned me books in their field, and I sometimes asked them to guest lecture."

"What made you want to learn everything?"

To get his mind off the death of a brother, to answer all the Whys and What-If's clogging his troubled brain, to look down on the world from far, far above, safe and secure. "I'm just the curious type, I guess."

"Do you miss teaching?"

"Of course."

"Do you like being a technical writer?"

"I'm not one. You are."

Amaya glanced down at her tofu salad and pushed it aside. "You give the impression you've come down in the world."

"I have."

"You shouldn't feel that way. You're doing useful work, and you're not breaking the law, providing one can assume that outsourcing one's job to India isn't illegal." Amaya said that with a quick smile. "Find satisfaction in what life has handed you, Harvey Hudson."

The philosopher spy, the mentoring *femme fatale*.

Margo wanted him to improve himself, but Amaya told him to accept who he was.

Harvey said, "I'll take your wise counseling under consideration and make changes accordingly."

But his outlook on life had already changed. When he was delivering pizzas, and even when he'd worn a spongy red nose for the Rapid Rabbit Balloon Service, he'd experienced a freedom he'd rarely felt when he was teaching. Sure, he hoped to go back to that life, but this time he would do it with a different attitude— less stress, less taking things so seriously, less struggling to make a name for himself, less stomach acid.

Amaya tapped the back of his hand. "I sense you have something deep inside that's troubling you. Do you want to talk about it?"

Does she know about Tommy? Or was this a line she'd learned at The Moscow School of Acting for Fetching Lady Spies?

Harvey shook his head. "Where did you grow up, and what were your parents like?"

"I grew up in New Delhi. My father was a businessman. He died when I was in my teens. My mom was a homemaker. She passed away just three years ago."

Was she telling the truth? Or had Russian intelligence scripted her story? Harvey said, "I'm very sorry," because he figured that was his next line in their little play. "Siblings?"

Amaya looked away. "A brother."

The question had bothered her. Or had she pretended it bothered her? Harvey didn't press her. "Have you always worked for Lotus Worldwide Consultants?"

"No. I taught computer science at a small women's college in New Delhi. Then I went through a really awful period and..."

And Amaya stopped talking and stared into the distance.

A painful memory or another terrific performance.

"It was a truly awful period," Amaya said. "I quit my job, went home, and closed the shutters. Once every week or two, I would leave the house to shop for groceries and essentials, then race right back home. Eventually, I ran out of money and took a job at Lotus Worldwide Consulting."

Harvey didn't know how much to believe. But the uneasiness over her brother—if there really was a brother—and the part about the really awful period sounded genuine and made him curious. She seemed to have gone off script. Right now, the frustrated director of their little play stood in the wings and wildly waved her arms. Harvey said, "Do you want to talk about what happened that made you leave teaching?"

Amaya shook her head, dabbed her eyes with her napkin, and forced a smile. "I'm so excited to be in Boston. I'd hoped to study at MIT, but after my father died, my mother couldn't afford it, even with a scholarship." Amaya lifted her arms, palms up, and forced another smile. "But here I am, anyway."

"You've never told me why."

She had, but Harvey wanted to see if her story was the same as before.

"I have already. Don't you remember?"

"Tell me again."

"My boss wanted a representative in the U.S. and gave me the job."

Same story.

Amaya glanced around the restaurant.

Harvey recognized that look. He pointed at the restrooms in

the far corner. He and Brenda had eaten here several times.

Amaya stood up and handed Harvey her purse. "Hold this, please."

He watched her work her way through the crowd.

Okay, how much of her story was true? Probably some. The more closely the tale fit with a spy's real past, the less likely they would slip up. Harvey had read that somewhere.

He clutched Amaya's big leather purse on his lap. A real secret agent would search through it, he guessed.

So he did.

He found the collection of cheesy Boston souvenirs he'd bought her, a driver's license with her photo, her passport, a Visa card, a note card with his address on it, and about fifteen pounds of lotions and cosmetics. Everything checked out. Harvey snapped the purse closed and felt better.

But only for a moment. Of course, everything checked out. She'd set him up. No woman had ever handed him her purse when she went to the bathroom. That's where they reapplied lipstick, checked their eyeliner for smudges, or ran a brush through their hair. She'd given him her purse because she wanted him to search through it.

Amaya pushed through the crowd and smiled at Harvey. Men checked her out, then turned to him. Lucky guy, they were thinking.

What if this was a real date, that Amaya was who she claimed to be, and that she liked him as much as she was pretending to?

So many What-If's. Harvey's head buzzed. So many What-If's.

Chapter 16

A Chipped Black Mug

Whenever Harvey had free time over the next few days of vacation, he and Amaya continued touring Boston and the surroundings. She wanted to see everything: the Battlefield in Lexington, the two Colonial museums in Concord, even Fenway Park.

On the day it rained, they visited the Museum of Fine Arts. They were standing in front of a Degas when Harvey's phone vibrated. It was his mother. Could he drop by? Kathy was coming over. You've been neglecting us lately.

He hesitated. Would it be wise to let a Russian spook into his mother's house? Amaya didn't seem dangerous, however, and by introducing her to his mother, he would give Amaya the impression that he trusted her. In any case, Harvey figured the Russians knew all about his family, since they knew almost everything else about him.

Could he bring a friend? Of course, his mother replied.

Harvey and Amaya drove to Brookline. His mother hugged him at the front door, then hugged Amaya, which from her expression both surprised and pleased her, and led them into the living room. More hugs from Kathy.

She had big eyes like Harvey, but had missed out on his red curls and instead inherited dark hair from her mother. Kathy was tall, lithe, and athletic, and she went everywhere in baggy blouses, and from time to time still wore jeans with the knees blown out, which had always driven Brenda crazy.

Harvey and Amaya sat side by side on the big white couch. Kathy and Harvey's mother took chairs across from them. Harvey's mother poured tea from a delicate pink pot into three matching cups for the ladies and a chipped black mug for Harvey. "You get the cheap cup," she said to him, "because you and Tommy broke three of these that day you were tossing a ball around in the dining room, which I'd told you a hundred times not to do." She sat in her rocker and turned to Amaya. "Is he any better behaved now?"

"Worse."

Harvey's mother took a sip of tea. "I've failed as a parent."

"You didn't have much to work with," Amaya said. "I hope Tommy is better behaved."

"Much better. He's the good son."

Harvey glanced at Kathy. She rolled her eyes.

Apparently, the Russians didn't know that Tommy had drowned a half century earlier, or they did know and had failed to tell Amaya. Harvey himself hadn't told her about Tommy. He'd been putting off the pain.

She looked around and said, "You have a lovely home, Mrs. Hudson."

"Thank you. And please call me *Hazel*."

A first. She'd never granted previous girlfriends that privilege, and years passed before she'd let Brenda use her first name.

Harvey's mother reached over and patted Harvey's hand. "I've almost forgiven him for breaking those cups." She took another sip of tea and added, "My boy takes just wonderful care of me and visits every Sunday."

Harvey glanced at Amaya. Were her eyes wet? It certainly looked like it. Thespian tears.

Harvey's mother asked Amaya where she was from, where she'd

gone to school, where she'd met Harvey, and where she'd bought those darling sandals. Amaya glanced at her feet. Harvey's mother made appreciative sounds. Kathy made appreciative sounds. Harvey abstained.

Surreal. His mother and his daughter were sitting here and admiring the footwear of a woman who could very well be a secret Russian agent.

He recalled a play from when he was four or so, way back at the edge of memory's dark curtain, when he'd been given the role of a frog and instructed to say "Ribbit" at the appropriate moment. He'd never acted before, had never seen a play before, and for him the scene blurred the real and the unreal. He knew he was a boy in an itchy, hooded, bright-green frog costume, but everyone treated him like a frog, which in a way made him one. A dizzying experience. He felt a bit like that now.

Harvey had tired of sandal talk. "Yesterday, we went to the new astronomy exhibit at the Museum of Science."

His mother turned to Amaya. "Did he lecture?"

Amaya laughed. "A little."

"He does that."

"Of course I do," Harvey said. "I'm a professionally trained lecturer, and I know everything about everything."

"Actually, he was cute," Amaya said, then pointed at the photo on the mantel of Harvey and Tommy, each holding a bunny. "I'm guessing Harvey's the taller one?"

"That's right. He and Tommy look so much alike that it's sometimes hard to tell them apart."

Again, Harvey and Kathy exchanged glances.

"I love those blue curtains," Amaya said. "What's the material?"

Harvey slipped into the kitchen before he heard the answer, dumped his tea into the sink, and made a strong cup of coffee.

Would he ever tell his mother that her drape-admiring visitor was a Russian agent? Probably not. If, in fact, Amaya was a Russian agent. He hoped not, but he had to admit she probably was. Still, the two phone conversations he'd had with Luke over the past few days hadn't given Harvey much confidence in him, either. Luke had been irritable and unwilling to give Harvey straight answers to his questions.

What if both Amaya and the clown team of Luke Smith and Elliot Smith were Russian operatives?

A new and unsettling What-If.

Harvey dropped onto a kitchen chair, overwhelmed.

Life as an international spy was exhausting.

Kathy pushed the door open, stood over him, and rested her hand on his shoulder. "I can take just so much window-treatment-and-footwear talk. Besides, I wanted to get you alone." She squeezed Harvey's shoulder. "I like this one. She's gorgeous and smart and seems really nice."

"Yup."

"And way too good for you."

"That, too."

"I hope you don't spend all your time burdening her with your famous What-Ifs. What if the sun was twice as far away? What if humans had two heads? What if the world really was flat and people fell off the edge, and what if—"

"I get it."

Kathy tugged at the sleeve of Harvey's jacket. "You need to stuff this horrible brown thing into a trash can and get yourself an entirely new wardrobe. Also, get rid of that wreck you drive and buy a new one, or at least take it to a car wash, and you should—"

"Stop listening to advice from people half my age."

Kathy rolled her eyes.

Harvey had seen her interacting with her professors and fellow medical students, and she'd always been cool and witty and adult, and she had certainly never rolled her eyes. But she often did with him. She would slip back to her teenage years, and he liked that.

He didn't quite want to see her grow up. He remembered changing her diaper, helping her up after she'd tumbled off her tricycle, and bandaging her skinned knee that time she'd fallen out of a maple tree.

He couldn't imagine his baby girl slashing someone open and tugging out a troublesome appendix.

Kathy said, "One of these days, you'll have to tell Amaya that Tommy's not alive."

"I know, and it'll be hard."

Kathy leaned down and hugged him.

She smelled of strong soap, surgeon soap.

"But not just yet," Harvey said.

Kathy released him and straightened up. "I should go back."

Harvey watched her leave, then got up, went to the counter and dug a chocolate-chip cookie out of the Mickey Mouse jar, which had been a Mother's Day gift that he and Tommy had bought with the money their mother had paid them for pulling weeds from the rose bed. Harvey took a big bite and let the cookie dissolve on his tongue. A delicious memory.

He pulled the kitchen door open and hesitated. His mother was holding up her knitting for Kathy and Amaya, apparently the start of deep blue scarf. Kathy fingered the edge and said something he couldn't make out. Amaya made little knitting movements with her hands. His mother nodded and smiled.

A warm family scene.

If only.

Chapter 17

Slamming Doors

Harvey woke at dawn, stared at the ceiling, and wondered for the hundredth time if Luke and Elliot were who they claimed to be. Without the pair's real names or that of the task force, his Google searches had failed.

Something else was bothering him, but he couldn't remember what. Maybe he needed to renew his car's inspection sticker. Or a bill was due. Or was it someone's birthday?

He pushed these concerns out of his mind. They weren't life and death. Luke, Elliot, and the Russians were.

Harvey slipped out of bed, made a pot of coffee, sat at the kitchen table and brainstormed. He could show up at the FBI building outside Boston and pretend he had a package to deliver to an agent whose first name was Luke but whose last name was illegible. Yeah, sure. Deliver a suspicious package to the FBI? They'd escort him into a windowless room and grill him for days. If not that, his face would at least be on their security cameras.

What if he called in and asked to speak to an agent named Luke whose last name he'd forgotten but needed to be reached because he'd left his jacket at a birthday party at Harvey's sister's house? Fat chance they'd buy that either.

Besides, Luke was probably a made-up name. Smith certainly was.

Harvey asked himself what a real spy would do. Well, they'd spy, that's what they'd do.

He grabbed a slice of pepperoni pizza from the refrigerator, snatched yesterday's *Boston Globe* off the counter, picked up his cup of coffee, ran downstairs, and jumped into his car.

Driving fast, it still took a half hour to reach the Chelsea FBI office, a glassy, nine-story building four miles northeast of Boston. He parked in the employee lot, just one of six cars this early in the day.

He called Margo and told her he'd be late to work, then opened his newspaper, chewed on the slice of pizza, and sipped his coffee. He wanted to look like some guy who wasn't yet ready to face another dreary day at his desk. Harvey wore a Red Sox hat with the bill pulled low. Between that and the newspaper, he figured he was safe from security cameras and from Luke or Elliot—if they should actually show up.

Three cars arrived and their drivers got out. Strangers.

Harvey settled in for a long wait. This could take hours, days even.

But then he spotted Luke pulling into a spot just two rows over.

Harvey slumped, raised his newspaper, and peered over the top.

Luke stepped out of a black Ford sedan, a car like the one Harvey had seen parked in front of the furniture showroom that fateful night when he'd delivered a pizza and got dragged into the dark world of espionage.

Luke waved at a man who waved back, then stopped to chat with a tiny woman holding a large brown briefcase with both hands.

So Luke was for real, and so was Elliot.

Which meant Amaya was not.

Harvey scrunched down farther into his seat. Not good. Not good at all.

But maybe things weren't as bad as they seemed. Because Luke, Elliot, and the task force were genuine didn't prove that Amaya was a Russian agent. Luke and Elliot could have made a mistake. No one's perfect, after all. And the two devious FBI agents might, for some reason, be hiding the truth about Amaya from Harvey.

So he had to give her every chance to prove she was who she claimed to be. It was only fair, after all.

*   *   *

Harvey drove home. His seven-day deadline had ended. He'd been sure he could find out in that time who Amaya really was, but he'd failed. So he extended the deadline to ten days. Another three days certainly wouldn't matter. Or even an extra week. Maybe two.

That weekend, he and Amaya hiked in New Hampshire, visited the Museum of Fine Arts (Amaya lingering before the Monet collection, with Harvey promising to sneak back that night and steal for her a painting from the Rouen Cathedral collection, maybe two), and they skipped stones on the Charles River. Amaya said her father had taught her how, much to the disapproval of her mother, who said that wasn't a proper activity for a young lady. Amaya teased Harvey because she got more skips. Harvey insisted she'd found better stones.

They held hands a couple of times and kissed twice, just friendly pecks on the cheek, but real kisses.

Harvey liked the way Amaya's hair smelled, and he liked how easily she laughed, and how deep-down nice she seemed to be. He teased her and got teased in turn. He had to keep tugging himself back to reality, however, and often wondered what was going inside that beautiful head. How long could this last? And how long could he keep postponing his deadline?

Some days, he told himself, he should spill everything to Luke and Elliot. Other days, he thought he should call her out. Most days he didn't care. Live for the present. The new Harvey Hudson.

They were strolling through Cambridge and eating chocolate

ice cream cones—Amaya's weakness—when it started to rain. Harvey suggested his apartment. Just until the storm ended, he added in haste. Just to get out of the rain and nothing else.

He said that twice.

Amaya made coffee. Harvey produced the remains of a three-cheese pizza left over from his last delivery. Amaya said she normally didn't indulge in pizza, but she ate two slices.

Harvey bent the box in two and stuffed it into the trash container under the sink.

Amaya said, "Don't you recycle cardboard?"

"Pizza boxes can't be. They're too messy."

"Then they'll end up in a dump along with old shoes, broken canary cages, and all the rest of what we throw away," Amaya said. "I hate the way modern civilization is so reckless with resources. I think about how someday—maybe in a hundred years, maybe in a thousand—mankind will simply run out of raw materials. What if future generations are forced to mine our dumps for usable materials like copper and aluminum and precious metals?"

Amaya's What-If pleased Harvey, but he didn't let himself be drawn into the discussion. He was too distracted by the strand of wet black hair hanging down her forehead and the curves behind her damp blue blouse. He suggested they sit on the couch and listen to music.

They did. She liked jazz and classical, just like him. Or said she did—Harvey didn't mind one way or the other. He played an old Dave Brubeck, a favorite of his, even though a purist might not call it real jazz. She said she hadn't heard it before. He put his arm around her shoulder, kissed the top of her head, behind her ear, her lips.

He heard her breath catch. He heard her murmur. He felt her right breast pressed against him. He carried her to bed.

They lay facing each other. She made a nervous joke about what skipping stones can lead to. He wanted to tell her about an exciting collection of fascinating stone tools recently discovered in a Nigerian cave, but caught himself. They stared at each other for a long time, then he touched the side of her face, pushed the hair out of her eyes, kissed her again, and told himself he shouldn't be doing this.

"Do you have a boyfriend back in New Delhi?"

Amaya shook her head.

"Were you ever married?" Harvey asked.

Again, Amaya shook her head, but only after a hesitation.

Apparently she had been. Or still was married. At the moment, neither mattered. Harvey cupped her left breast.

She didn't take his hand away. "Are you seeing anyone?" she asked.

Harvey shook his head and said, "No," and he felt guilty for lying to her.

Then again, wasn't Amaya probably lying to him about everything?

He kissed her again and again—her mouth, her chin, her forehead. He unbuttoned her blouse. She pressed her body against his and said, "Yes," and someone knocked on the door.

Harvey sat up.

Amaya rebuttoned her blouse.

Harvey whispered. "They'll go away."

"Did you lock the door?"

"Uh... I don't think so."

They waited. Another knock.

Was it Luke and Elliot? Kathy? Russian agents?

The doorknob turned.

Harvey and Amaya hopped out of bed and stepped into the living room.

"Harvey, are you home?" Margo called.

Harvey mumbled, *"Uh, oh."*

The door swung open, and Margo stepped inside. She wore a

full-length black dress with a white shawl around her shoulders.

Now Harvey remembered what had been bothering him all day: Margo had bought opera tickets for them weeks earlier, back before Amaya had shown up. Margo had stopped having sex with him after he'd refused to go to that dismal interview she'd arranged for him at the insurance company, but apparently she wasn't going to waste expensive tickets to the opera. Margo hated waste.

Her eyes shifted to Amaya, then Harvey, back at Amaya.

No one spoke.

Then Harvey introduced Margo to Amaya as his boss, and Amaya to Margo as a friend.

Margo put her hands on her hips. "A friend?"

Harvey nodded.

Margo pointed at Amaya. "A friend with a misbuttoned blouse?"

Amaya turned her back, redid the buttons, and said over her shoulder, "Harvey, is it normal in America for a person's boss to show up at their home in party clothes?"

Blood rose to Harvey's face. "Uh…"

"Who is this woman?" Margo said, shaking a finger in Amaya's direction.

Harvey said nothing.

Amaya turned back around and sniffled.

Harvey put his arm around her shoulder.

She pulled away.

Harvey wished the floor would open up beneath him, that he would tumble through to the store below and land on a soft, welcoming pile of decapitated chickens. Which he deserved.

Margo tightened her hold on her shoulder bag, pointed at Harvey, and turned to Amaya. "He's yours. Maybe you can make something out of him. I failed years ago and again recently. I only hired him because he was broke and pathetic."

Amaya sobbed.

Again, Harvey tried to hug her. Again, she pushed him away.

Margo hurried to the door, turned back, and glared at Harvey. "You're insubordinate, overpaid, and… and… *fuck!*"

She slammed the door behind her.

Amaya said, "You knew her before she was your boss?"

"From high school," Harvey said.

Amaya snatched a napkin off the kitchen table and blew her nose. "Were you lovers?"

Harvey nodded.

"And still are?"

"That's ended," Harvey said.

"Then why is she so angry?"

"Residual jealousy," Harvey said. "Also, she was obviously put out because you're so much prettier than she is, and—"

"Spare me your flattery," Amaya said and blew her nose again. "When I asked you if you were seeing anyone, you lied to me."

"Not really. As I said, it's all over between us, and I'm very sorry about what just happened, and I'll make up for it by—"

"A lie is a lie. Period."

"I didn't lie, and if you'll just let me…"

Amaya, too, slammed the door on her way out.

Harvey stood staring at it for a long time. He'd hurt Margo, and he'd hurt Amaya, and he'd lied to her, the woman who was probably lying to him about everything. The woman he loved.

Chapter 18

Flattery, Flowers, Hail

After three days of flattery, flowers, charm, explanations, and apologies, plus the promise that he'd never again see Margo outside of work or even go into her office and not leave the door open, Harvey won Amaya back. He found her anger believable and concluded that, if she was a spy for Russian intelligence, she would have played her role and forgiven him right away just to keep him close by. Harvey told himself that Amaya was who she said she was, and that was that.

He hadn't gotten her back to his apartment and into bed, however, but he was happier than he'd been for a long time.

They spent all their free hours together. They went for walks along the Charles river, dined out, went on pizza deliveries—which Amaya thought was all the fun in the world—and she asked Harvey to drive her to Marblehead and walk along the shore. She said she'd read about the place in a guidebook.

Harvey refused to take her there and refused to say why. His parents had sold the cottage two months after Tommy drowned, and they never returned to Marblehead. Neither had Harvey.

As a substitute, he drove Amaya to the North Shore and Plover Beach, a tiny, horseshoe inlet with high rocky sides. Although the area was called a beach, no one swam there because of the gigantic waves and powerful undertow. Harvey took Amaya by the hand and walked her to the edge of the water. It was a chill, gray day. The sea was rough, the waves high, the wind strong, not unlike the day Tommy had drowned.

Harvey could still hear his mother's instructions: "Walk Tommy directly to the barbershop and come right back afterwards."

If only.

Too many If-Onlys, Whys, and What-Ifs clogged Harvey's brain. One that pressed down hardest was a fantasy about what it would be like if everyone got one big do-over in their life. Harvey knew exactly how he would use his. He pictured himself clutching Tommy's hand and steering him up the three steps into the barbershop with its shelf of green-and-tan lotions, the dark clippings that circled the floor beneath the chair, the barber who wore a hairpiece some days and went bald on others, and for a short time Harvey would feel good. But then his fantasy would burst, and his heart would sink, and he…

Amaya shook his arm. "You're off somewhere."

Harvey pulled free.

"And a bit jumpy," Amaya said, stepping away.

"Sorry. I have a headache."

"That's what men say when something's going on that they don't want to talk about."

Harvey stepped away, then stopped and studied Amaya. She looked both curious and put out.

Now? Yes, the time had come.

He took Amaya by the shoulders and gently turned her toward the water. "See those rocks at the edge of the cove?"

Amaya nodded.

"Tommy was climbing on rocks just like those," Harvey said, pointing out to sea, "when a rogue wave knocked him down and dragged him away." Harvey swallowed. "Forever."

Amaya turned back to him, her eyes wide, her jaw slack.

"Forever? You mean he's—"

"Dead. Yes."

"But your mother talks as if he were alive?"

"In her mind, he still is. Or somewhere between alive and dead."

Amaya put her arm around Harvey's waist. "The poor woman. And poor Tommy. And poor you."

"I jumped in and swam out to where I'd last seen him. I dove, over and over, but couldn't find him. I wanted to drown with him, but didn't have the courage."

"How awful, how awful. I'm so sorry, Harvey."

"Mom was institutionalized for a while. After she got back, she went around the house talking to Tommy and sometimes talking to me as if I were Tommy. I had been told to take him to get a haircut, but instead we went to the ocean and climbed on the rocks. My parents never punished me for disobeying and never said a word about Tommy's drowning. I wish they had. They left me to punish myself, which is the worst kind because it never ends."

Amaya was silent for a while, then said, "How old were you?"

"Eight."

"You were just eight years old, and your parents sent you off all alone to walk your brother to the barber? Is that normal?"

"The shop was only a dozen blocks away," Harvey said.

"You have a daughter. If she were eight and had a younger sister, would you have sent them off alone to the hairdresser?"

Harvey shrugged. "Probably not."

"Your parents didn't discipline you because they knew they were at fault."

"Maybe."

"I understand exactly how you feel, Harvey, and—"

"How could you?" Harvey said and pulled Amaya's arm from around his waist. "How could anyone?"

"I know exactly how you feel," Amaya whispered, dragging out her words, "because I've been through the same thing."

"You've lost a sibling?"

Amaya turned toward the ocean. "No. I lost my daughter and my husband in a car accident. And it was my fault."

Harvey fell silent, then said. "I'm sorry, really sorry. Then you do understand."

Amaya nodded and sobbed.

"You were driving?"

Amaya shook her head. "I'd taught my last class for the day and wanted to go shopping for something—probably another pair of shoes I didn't really need. My husband was home with our daughter, who'd just turned three. I didn't have a car at school because I always got a ride with a colleague. When I called my husband, he told me my daughter was napping and that I should take a taxi to the store, but I said taxis were dirty and smelly, and why couldn't he do this one little favor for his wife? I'm afraid I was a bit spoiled back then. Finally, he agreed. That's how our last conversation ended, an argument followed by his giving in."

Harvey hugged Amaya's shoulders and guided her to a stone bench. They sat down. "There was an accident?"

"A truck swerved into their lane. They died instantly. Two police officers came to the school and told me, and I…"

Amaya bowed her head, then looked up. "My daughter and my husband died on account of me."

"No," Harvey said, "they died because a careless truck driver swerved over the center line."

"That doesn't help, just as it apparently didn't help you when I pointed out that your parents shouldn't have put you in charge of a six-year-old boy." Amaya took Harvey's hand in both of hers. "You're a good person. You make me happy, and you make me laugh, and I love you."

Tears rolled down her cheeks.

Harvey had wanted to hear her say that for what seemed like forever, just not in circumstances like this. He kissed her forehead.

"And I love you."

They sat holding each other's hands, not talking. A mixture of emotions swirled through Harvey: telling his painful story to Amaya, listening to hers, hearing her say she loved him, and telling her he loved her.

A tumble of regrets, guilt, joy.

Harvey saw his future: He would never let go of this woman, whoever she was. They were good for each other. No, perfect for each other. Soulmates.

They stood up, walked to the edge of the water and stood on wide, flat rocks covered in shiny green seaweed. The sun came out and flickered off the waves. Amaya skipped a stone—three skips. Harvey skipped his four times. She said he'd found a better stone. They laughed.

Bliss, Harvey thought: A beautiful beach, a salty breeze, and a woman who understood his guilt. Despite the FBI task force and the Russians, a good life lay ahead. Somehow, he would make everything work out. He had to. He took a deep breath and let it out slowly. Bliss.

Amaya picked up a seashell and examined it. "This is how I'd imagined New England to be: foggy and cool sometimes, sunny sometimes, but always beautiful. I hated it the first day I got here because it was so gray and chilly, and there was even a hailstorm. I wanted to get right back on the plane. But now I love it here, and this is where I want to spend the rest of my life."

"So do I."

Should he add 'together'? He didn't know. She'd said she loved him, and he'd said he loved her. Wasn't the next step a bigger commitment? Living together? Marriage?

Yes, just do it, he told himself. Make the move.

Amaya said she was getting cold, so she walked back to shore and sat on the stone bench, smiled at Harvey, dangled her legs, and kicked her heels together.

He started toward her, trying to find just the right words. Should it be a long preamble about how wonderful it is when people find love again later in life and never want to be alone? Or just come out and ask her to marry him.

How lucky he was. What if she'd gotten back on the plane that day it hailed? What if he'd never met her, never fallen in love, never seen her sitting on that stone bench, pushing her hair out of her eyes, and looking so beautiful and happy, and what if…

Harvey stopped walking.

He'd been in his car the day it had hailed. Stones pinged off the roof, bounced off the hood, and danced on the blacktop ahead of him.

It had been a Monday. No, it couldn't be. Yes, it had been a Monday because he'd had his teeth cleaned that afternoon.

Amaya had shown up at his door the following Thursday. He remembered her words: "I just flew in a few hours ago."

He remembered now how Margo had arrived at his apartment right after the break-in and said she smelled lilac perfume.

Amaya wore lilac perfume.

Chapter 19

Not Again!

Harvey eyed Amaya, the actor, the deceiver, the heartbreaker.

She waved and patted the bench. "Come and sit beside me."

She sounded happy.

He bent down and picked up a flat stone, perfect for skipping.

Maybe he'd gotten this all wrong. After all, anyone can mess up the days of the week. He was always doing that when he taught, showing up for a class a day ahead, or a day late, or missing one altogether. And lilac perfume? Other women besides Amaya must wear it.

But not burglars.

"You look worried about something," Amaya said.

Harvey dropped the stone. He could just slip back into his bubble as if nothing had happened. Or he could set up a meeting with Luke and Elliot and tell them about Amaya. Or confront her right now and get the truth out in the open.

Amaya scooted aside to make more room for Harvey.

He didn't sit down. He took her by the shoulders and pulled her to her feet.

"Hey!" she shouted. "Not so tight!"

He turned her to face the ocean. "Do you know how much it hurt my mother and father and me when Tommy drowned?"

"Yes, of course I do. I told you how I lost my—"

"Do you know how much pain I felt talking about his death?"

"I do, and I'm sorry, but now let go! You're hurting me!"

Harvey released her. "Did you make the story up on the spot?"

Amaya took a step back. "What story?"

"That crap about a husband and a daughter dying in a car accident. Or did your handlers back in Moscow concoct that tale so you could play on my feelings about Tommy?"

"Moscow? What are you talking about?"

Amaya stepped farther away, fear in her eyes.

Harvey moved closer. "You know what I'm talking about."

"No, I don't, Harvey. Why are you behaving like this? You're frightening me."

Harvey turned his back to Amaya and looked toward the ocean. Big waves had started coming in, the wind blew hard, a gull cried. He swung around. "How long have you been working with Igor Baranov?"

Amaya took a step back. "Who? I don't know anyone with that name."

Her lower lip twitched, and her eyes were wide with panic. Now he knew for sure.

His heart sank, and the energy drained out of him. What a fool he'd been to let this woman play on his lonely guy needs. "No more lies."

Amaya sagged, looked down, then up. "I didn't make up the story about the car accident." Her voice was small.

"Maybe, maybe not," Harvey said. "But what I do know is that you're working for the Russians. They sent you to charm me, break into my apartment, and lie to me."

Amaya said nothing.

"You're a spy," Harvey said. "My country's enemy and my enemy."

She burst into tears and pressed her hands against her face.

"Crying won't help. Even if it's for real, which I doubt it is."

"You don't know the truth," she said. Her voice trembled.

"Yes, I do."

"Not the real truth," Amaya said, lowering her hands.

"You mean there's real truth and unreal truth? That's nonsense!"

"Don't shout at me!" Amaya said and walked toward the water.

Harvey watched her go. Just minutes earlier, he'd loved her. Now? He didn't know.

She climbed onto the rocks.

Go over and tell her he loved her no matter who she was? Or drive home and try to forget about her?

He sat on the sand, bowed his head, and closed his eyes. If it hadn't hailed that day, he might never have found out the truth about Amaya. If he hadn't outsourced his job, there would be no Amaya. If Middlebridge College had handled their expenses better, then...

A roar.

Harvey looked up. A rogue wave was thundering toward shore.

"Amaya, watch out!"

Harvey leaped up and raced toward her.

The wave lifted Amaya off the rocks, swept her away, and rumbled up the beach.

Harvey tumbled backwards and went under.

He struggled, gasped, grabbed a rock, and clung to it.

The wave flowed out.

Harvey jumped to his feet, tore off his jacket, kicked off his shoes, and dove into the water.

"Amaya!" he shouted. "Amaya!"

He spotted her bobbing on the surface, arms flailing, legs kicking. A weak swimmer.

He opened his mouth to shout again. His throat filled with cold salt water. He rolled onto his side, spit, and turned back onto his stomach.

Where was she?

Another huge wave lifted Harvey and dropped him.

He spotted Amaya and swam toward her.

His trousers were soaked and heavy. His arms ached. His lungs hurt.

"Amaya!" He shouted. She disappeared under the water.

He stopped swimming, rose and fell with the waves, panted and peered around.

No Amaya.

Not again! Not again!

There! There she was, off to the left! Paddling. Struggling.

Harvey splashed toward her.

She saw him and shouted something.

Harvey swam as hard as he could.

Finally he reached her.

He put his arm around her shoulders, turned her on her back, and started towing her toward shore.

She coughed and spit and tried to talk.

"Later," Harvey said. "We'll talk later."

The waves pushed them to shore.

They lay gasping on the wet sand.

"Thank you, thank you," Amaya said between breaths. She rolled onto her side and pressed herself against him. "I love you."

Harvey felt her shivering. "And despite everything, I love you, too," he said. "That's all that matters."

"I want to tell you everything."

"You don't have to," Harvey said.

"Yes, I do."

Chapter 20

A Much Better Idea

Harvey pulled Amaya closer to him. She was wet, shivering, and gritty with sand. So was he. Neither of them had the energy to stand.

Harvey said, "You broke into my apartment."

"Igor's orders. I was to look for evidence that you were working for the CIA or the FBI."

"Why was the Russian intelligence service suspicious of me?"

"They're suspicious of everyone."

Harvey brushed wet sand off Amaya's forehead. "Have you made up everything about yourself? Is your name even Amaya?"

"Yes, it is. And what I told you about my past—teaching, quitting after my husband and daughter died—all of that is true."

"I'm sorry it is," Harvey said. "When did you start working for the Russians?"

"I didn't start out working for them, not exactly. After I'd gotten back on my feet, I applied for teaching jobs but couldn't find any, so I went to work for Lotus Worldwide Consultants, writing English-language documentation for Toyota. But after just a few weeks, the company made Igor my boss. He was a shadowy figure. I'd seen him around, and I knew he was Russian but nothing else about him. No one did. His first week, he took me off the Toyota job and gave me your project but wouldn't tell me why."

"Igor wrote the emails and the documentation?"

"No, I wrote them. His English is good, but he's not fluent. Also, he's not all that technical. He, of course, read everything I wrote."

"Including our emails?"

Amaya nodded. "Not long after I started working with you, I cleaned out a jam in a photocopier and found a memo describing a hacking operation intended to destroy petroleum pumps. The memo mentioned my name but gave no indication why. Shocked, I confronted Igor. He said the United States was attempting to sabotage the Indian petroleum industry, and the project's goal was to prevent this."

"So you stayed on the job?"

"Of course. I believed him, and I was angry with your country."

"You didn't yet know you were working for Russian intelligence?"

"No."

"Why was I singled out?" Harvey asked.

"You weren't. Lotus Worldwide Consultants solicited a number of people in your company. But you were the only one who responded."

"The only one stupid enough."

"Not stupid. You had no idea what you'd gotten into," Amaya said. "Just as I didn't know at first I was working for the Russians."

"When did you find out?"

"One day, Igor called me into his office and said they were sending me to Boston. Then he told me the truth about the project."

"Why would he do that? Wasn't he afraid you'd contact the Indian intelligence service?"

"He showed me photographs of my brother walking hand-in-hand with his young daughter in a park, one of him standing in line with his wife at a movie box office, and even one through their kitchen window while my sister-in-law was doing dishes."

"So, you cooperated to save your brother and his family?"

Amaya bit her lower lip.

Harvey pictured Kathy taking notes in class and his mother trimming rose bushes. "I'd have done the same."

And he'd have fears just like hers. After the Russians were through with her, they would never let go of her, and they might not even let her live. "After you got here, what did you tell Igor about me?"

"I said you were just a technical writer and suspected nothing."

Should he tell her? Yes? No? Yes, it was time for all of the truth. "I'm working with an FBI task force. They know all about what the Russians are planning."

Harvey expected Amaya to look shocked. But she wasn't. She said, "I suspected something like that."

"Oh?"

"That time we were visiting your mother, and you slipped into the kitchen to get away from our shoe talk, she told me you'd gotten a $250,000 bonus at work and how proud she was of you for using it to pay off her mortgage. But I knew that beginning technical writers don't get bonuses like that, if any at all. That's when I started to wonder about you."

"You didn't tell Igor?"

"Of course not."

"So you suspected me just as I suspected you, and you protected me just as I protected you."

"Exactly. But eventually Igor will find out I'm no longer cooperating, and then—"

"We'll work something out," Harvey said with a confidence he didn't feel.

"How?"

"I'll approach the two government agents I work with, tell them everything you told me, and ask for their help."

"What can they do?"

"If you cooperate, they'll protect you and smuggle your brother and his family out of India."

"I doubt they'd agree to leave."

"Okay, then what if the task force tips off the Indian intelligence service? They could roll up Igor and all the others and close the company."

Amaya shook her head. "Moscow would suspect me."

"What if we ran away?"

"The Russians would track us down. They're good at that."

Harvey was exhausted and shivering and had run out of What-Ifs. "I'm sure the task force has a better solution."

"I doubt it," Amaya said, "but I have no other choice."

Harvey got up, pulled Amaya to her feet, and kissed her on her chilly, damp forehead. "Before we visit the task force, let's dress up in our best clothes, go to the fanciest restaurant in Boston, and order their most expensive meal and wine."

Amaya put her arms around him, pressed her body tightly against his and said, "I have a much better idea."

Chapter 21

A Little White Cottage

Harvey and Amaya lay in his bed, fully clothed and facing each other.

"I believe this works best without garments," Harvey said.

"I've heard."

Neither made a move to undress.

Harvey patted his stomach. "Too many Skittles, too much pizza."

"You look fine."

Harvey hesitated, then reached over and unbuttoned Amaya's blouse, still damp from the ocean.

"Pull the shades, please," Amaya said.

Harvey got up and pulled them. By the time he got back, Amaya had undressed and pulled a sheet up to her neck.

He stripped quickly and slipped beneath the sheets. They lay side by side for a minute, then rolled to face each other.

"This is awkward," Harvey said.

"Just a bit."

Then he pulled Amaya in closer and kissed her lips, her forehead, her lips again.

She said, "This is much better than a meal in a fancy restaurant."

"Way better."

And it was.

Afterwards, they clung to each other, breathing hard.

About now, Harvey thought, Margo would go for her phone.

He said, "Are you hungry?"

"Starving, but I'm exhausted and don't want to get out of bed." Amaya pulled the sheet up over them. She was quiet for a couple of minutes.

Harvey said, "You're lost in thought."

"I was thinking about you, of course."

"You had to say that."

Amaya made a face. "And I was marveling how as a girl I'd always wanted to come to America, and finally I'm here. It's not exactly the sunny situation I'd fantasized, but at least I made it."

"Did a love interest figure in your fantasies?"

"Yes, but you're much better."

"You had to say that, too."

Amaya tilted her head back. "What did you dream about becoming when you were young?"

Harvey didn't want to admit that, from a young age, he'd wanted to be a history professor just like the kindly, bearded, and distracted man who lived next door. "I wanted to be a cowboy, a train robber actually, with a hideout in the dusty, tan hills of Montana, with a black hat and a black horse. Or maybe a black horse with a black hat."

Amaya laughed. "Did people still rob trains from horseback when you were a boy?"

"I planned on resurrecting the practice. What did you want to be?"

"A ballerina."

"You could dance?"

"For years, my mom took me for lessons because she loved to dance. I did too, but I never got very good, so the teacher kept me in the beginners' group year after year, and finally I quit out of embarrassment. When we're young, we dream of what we want to become. When we're older, we dream of going back in time and correcting our mistakes."

"But we can't."

"No, we can't change the past, but we can change the future by changing the present. We shouldn't dwell on our mistakes but must remember those things that we've done that were right—our sacrifices, our kindness to others, that sort of thing."

"Have you always been this wise?" Harvey said.

"Since birth. All women are. Men not so much."

"Not even me?"

"Maybe we should order takeout."

Harvey laughed. Not something he'd done much of lately.

They lay quietly for a couple more minutes, then Harvey said, "You still want to turn yourself in?"

"It's best."

"I can't guarantee anything."

Amaya lifted her head from Harvey's chest. "Of course you can't. I might get deported or sent to prison."

"Or neither," Harvey said, attempting to sound upbeat. "Whatever happens, we won't be apart forever."

"When I was little, I had an American book, and on the cover it had a tiny, white cottage with a white picket fence and red roses climbing all over it. Someday, we'll get a small house with a picket fence. I'll plant the roses. "

"I was thinking of a cabin in Oregon, on top of a hill with a breathtaking view and a winding, gravel driveway, far from civilization, and where it'll be dirt cheap to live."

"That would be okay, too, I suppose," Amaya said, "but you'll have to build me a white picket fence."

"And we'll plant a massive garden and rows of fruit trees. To economize, we won't buy a car, but go everywhere on bicycles, winter and summer, rain or shine."

"Even if we live on a hill?"

"Maybe we'll need a car. But something cheap and reliable."

"We'll find part-time work as teachers," Amaya said.

"Or open a pizza parlor."

Amaya laughed. "Even better."

She pointed at the two heaps of clothing on the floor. "Changing the subject somewhat, you have a closet full of dry things to wear, but everything I have is damp."

"You'd look irresistible in my favorite Red Sox T-shirt and shower clogs."

"In your dreams."

Harvey threw back the sheet and grabbed shorts and jeans from a dresser drawer. "I'll take our things to the laundromat down the street and pick up some takeout."

Amaya rolled onto her back and pulled the sheet up to her chin. "And I" she said, "shall take a nap."

Harvey finished dressing, stuffed their clothing into a trash bag, and walked to the laundromat. He tossed everything into a washing machine, sat on a bench, and called Luke. "It's me," Harvey said. "We have to meet."

"Why meet? We've got burner phones."

"Nope. Face-to-face."

"How come?" Luke asked.

"Because I said so."

Silence. "Okay. Come to the furniture store, 9:00 p.m. tonight, only make it two pepperonis this time."

"That place again? Why?"

"Elliot's dip-shit brother-in-law owns it."

As soon as the washer stopped, Harvey transferred their clothes to a dryer, walked home, and found Amaya curled up and asleep. He opened his laptop and typed up everything she had told him about the Russian project and everything he knew about the task force, then printed the document and sealed it into double envelopes. He went down to the street and slipped the letter into a mailbox. He then picked up their clothes at the laundromat and bought two large orders of pad thai noodles with basil fried rice.

Amaya was still asleep when he returned. She looked young and innocent and like that girl with a bubbly dream about a little white house in America, not the grown woman who was up to her pretty neck in trouble. At best, she'd be sent back to India. Would the Russians leave her alone after that? Harvey guessed not. And if she stayed here, she might be tossed into a federal prison. She was in her early fifties. If she got fifteen years and served eight or ten, she would come out in her sixties. How would she look after so many years locked away? Harvey didn't care. He'd wait. He pictured her standing at the prison gate, glancing back and forth for him to show up, clutching a brown paper bundle wrapped in string. He would run up to her, hug her, lift her off her feet, swing her around, and tell her how much he loved her.

Amaya.

Chapter 22

Bora Bora

Harvey and Amaya drove to Pete's and picked up the two pepperoni pizzas Luke had ordered, then headed toward the waterfront. Harvey dropped Amaya off at an all-night diner. If Luke refused to deal, Harvey would hurry back, pick her up, and rent a hotel room for both. First thing in the morning, they would empty their bank accounts and go off the grid.

Harvey continued on to the furniture store. He went inside and found Luke and Elliot sitting side-by-side on a low-slung, puke-hued sofa. They looked like a couple of out-of-shape, middle-age guys waiting for a Patriot's game to start. He set the two pepperoni pizzas on the coffee table and dragged a hard chair over. He wanted to sit higher than Luke and Elliot and force them to look up at him. This was a negotiation, after all, and not a Superbowl party. For the same reason, Harvey refused the bottle of beer that Luke held out to him, and he didn't touch the pizza.

Luke and Elliot peeled off slices.

"Why face-to-face?" Luke said, biting down hard.

"What's the FBI's protocol for a foreign agent who has turned?"

Luke chewed, swallowed, eyed Harvey. "Why do you ask?"

"I might know someone who wants to surrender to you."

Luke spread a napkin across his lap. "Talk."

"You were wrong when you told me that Amaya wasn't for real and that I'd been communicating with Igor Baranov."

Luke and Elliot kept on chewing.

Not what Harvey had expected. "She's here in the U.S.," he said. "She's an Indian national the Russians forced to work for them."

Luke looked up. "Forced?"

"Her brother and his family were threatened. Amaya did what she had to in order to protect them. I'd do the same, and so would you."

Luke shrugged and sipped his beer.

Again, not the expected reaction.

"Amaya wants to turn herself in," Harvey said, "but first you have to promise that, in exchange for her full cooperation, she won't be prosecuted. Second, you must promise that you will protect her older brother and—"

"Younger brother," Luke said. "Younger brother."

Right, younger brother.

How does Luke know that?

Luke lifted a napkin off the coffee table, wiped his fingers with great care, reached into the briefcase near his foot, and pulled out a manila folder. He flipped it open and read: "Amaya Patel, maiden name Ahuja, a fifty-one-year-old widow, five-feet-four, slim build, brunette, attractive, dark eyes, no visible scars or tattoos, lifelong resident of New Delhi. She got a master's degree with honors in computer science from the University of New Delhi, taught in a girl's college for twenty-four years, and was unemployed for twenty months before taking a job at Lotus Worldwide Consultants." Luke looked up. "Does that sound about right?"

Harvey nodded. "If you've known about her all along, why in hell did you tell me she didn't exist?"

"We didn't find that out until after we'd talked to you the first time."

"Why not tell me afterwards?"

"Good question," Luke said.

"And?"

"And we have our reasons."

Harvey let this sink in. "You wanted to test me."

"Good thinking," Luke said and turned to Elliot. "Our boy is learning the trade."

Elliot said, "Yup."

Harvey said, "You've been watching us?"

"Sometimes."

"Why didn't you grab her?" Harvey said.

"And compromise the operation?"

Of course. Now Harvey felt even more of an idiot. "Regardless, Amaya is innocent and deserves immunity for turning herself in."

Luke shook his head. "We decide who gets immunity and who doesn't." He grabbed a napkin and wiped up the big glob of tomato sauce he'd dropped on the couch. "Did Amaya tell you why the Russians sent her?"

"To check me out. She wasn't sure why they thought they had to."

"It's because your pal Tucker screwed up, that's why. He goes to a lot of cocktail parties in Washington, DC so he can schmooze and try to pick up government contracts. A while back, he went to one and spent most of the evening peering down the gown of a Swedish model who, in fact, was a Russian agent sent to mingle at parties to learn whatever she could from drunken dickheads like Tucker. To impress her, he intimated he was part of an intelligence operation to protect the U.S. from a foreign cyberattack. The babe forwarded the information to Moscow. We tapped into the message. Since Tucker is half owner of a company that writes code for petroleum pumps, a red flag went up."

"Was the operation compromised?"

"No, because we send disinformation back and forth over a European network we know the Russians have broken into. We convinced them that Tucker was making up the story just to talk the babe into bed. Still, there was enough lingering suspicion for the Russkies to send Amaya to find out what she could about the company and about you."

Harvey said, "She ransacked my place."

"Not surprising."

"Did the Russians send someone to check out Tucker, too?"

"They didn't need to because they still have their Swedish babe rubbing up against him. Through her, he passes on the disinformation we give him. He's actually doing a pretty good job because I ripped a strip of flesh off him."

Harvey winced.

"Not literally," Luke said, "but by the time I got through shouting at him, he probably wished I had taken a slab of skin instead." Luke dabbed again at the tomato stain on the couch and frowned. It wasn't coming up. "Bring Amaya here. I want to talk to her."

"Not until I get a deal: Amaya goes free, and her family gets protected."

"That won't be easy."

"No? Well, make it happen," Harvey said. "If you don't, she'll go off the grid, the Russians will get suspicious, and your whole damn operation will spiral down the flusher."

"We would find her. We're the FBI, remember? But okay, I'll bring this to my supervisor, and I'm sure she'll agree to your terms."

Too easy. "That's a promise?"

"Of course."

"And I can trust you?"

"I said you could."

"Would you if you were in my position?" Harvey said.

A slight hesitation then, "Of course."

"Well, I sure as hell don't trust you," Harvey said. "Do you think

I'd waltz in here without a backup plan? Of course not. I typed up and printed everything I know about your operation, about Amaya, and about the Russians, double-enveloped the letter, and mailed it to my lawyer. If Amaya disappears or winds up in prison, or if I disappear or wind up in prison, my lawyer will open the inner envelope and release the letter to the press."

Luke exchanged glances with Elliot, then turned back to Harvey. "Am I to believe that?"

"What would you do if you were in my place?"

Luke picked up his bottle of beer, paused, then set it down. "Just what you did."

"So we have a deal?"

Luke nodded. "Bring Amaya here."

*   *   *

Harvey picked up Amaya at the diner and drove her to the furniture showroom. He assured her that everything would work out just fine.

He could tell she didn't buy this, but she didn't say a word. He reached over and took her hand. It felt cold.

They parked outside the furniture showroom. Harvey helped Amaya out of the car, put his arm around her shoulder, steered her inside, and introduced her to Luke and Elliot.

Luke sprang to his feet, hurried to get a chair for her, offered her pizza and beer—which she refused with a shake of her head—and called her "Mrs. Patel."

The power of a beautiful woman. Or maybe this was how FBI agents dealt with foreign agents who turn.

Luke waited for her to sit, then lowered himself back onto the couch, careful to avoid the tomato stain. He opened the manila folder and read to her the same information he'd read to Harvey. "Is that correct?"

"Yes."

Her voice shook.

"Don't worry," Luke said. "You've made the right decision by coming to us."

Amaya said nothing.

Luke closed the folder and stood up. "Please come with me, Mrs. Patel. I have a few questions."

They walked out of earshot and sat on facing sofas.

Harvey said, "How long will he interrogate her?"

Elliot shrugged.

"She'll get to go free, right?"

Another shrug.

"I'm guessing Luke will interrogate me next. He'll want to see if our stories match up."

No response.

"Do you ever talk?" Harvey asked.

"Yesterday. Twice."

The two men sat in silence until Luke returned with Amaya, left her with Elliot, and led Harvey to the far side of the room, where they plopped down on facing sofas. Luke read questions from a notepad. Harvey guessed they were the same ones he'd just asked Amaya. Then Luke added some extras.

"Did you trust Amaya at the beginning?"

"No," Harvey said.

"Then exactly when did you start trusting her?"

"It wasn't a single moment."

Luke scribbled on his pad. "Did you trust us?"

"At first, but later not so much."

"Why did you later stop trusting Amaya?"

"I caught her lying."

"That's when you started trusting us again?" Luke said.

"Mostly trusting you."

"Was it her idea to turn herself in or yours?"

"It was a joint decision," Harvey said. "And you asked me that once before."

"Has it occurred to you that Amaya might be playing all of us?"

"No."

Luke was quiet for a moment. "Are you two sleeping together?"

"None of your business."

"That means yes," Luke said and wrote that down. Then he asked all the same questions again but with different wording.

After several more minutes of interrogation, Luke closed his notebook and stood up.

Harvey and Luke rejoined Amaya and Elliot, who was waving his hands in the air and describing the safety features of his new car, talking a streak. The power of a beautiful woman.

Luke pulled a photo from his briefcase and held it up. It showed a beefy man stepping from a dry cleaners, a suit covered in plastic and folded over his arm. Luke handed the photo to Amaya. "Do you recognize him, Mrs. Patel?"

She shook her head, then handed the photograph back.

"That's Boris Semenov," Luke said. "I want you to know what he looks like. He's Igor's boss back in Moscow. Boris was behind at least one poisoning in London, and he ordered a couple of killings in Sweden. And that's just what we know. He's traveled to Boston twice and stayed in safe houses."

"You knew about the visits?" Harvey said.

"Of course. We're the FBI."

"Then why in hell didn't you grab the guy when he was here?"

"It's more useful to monitor where he goes and who he sees," Luke said. "Besides, snatching him would compromise our operation."

"Is he a danger to Amaya?" Harvey asked.

"Of course not," Luke said, a little too loudly. Then he grinned. "I can't say that he's not a danger to Igor, though."

"Because?"

"Because Igor's been porking Boris's wife, which is about the most dumb-assed move I can think of. We picked it up on telephone intercepts. If Boris ever finds that out, well..." Luke made a throat-cutting gesture.

Elliot chuckled.

What a world I now live in, Harvey thought. "What happens to us?"

"You two will keep on doing exactly what you've been doing, but with guidance from us," Luke said. "You, Harvey, will merrily continue on as an ersatz technical writer and keep delivering pizzas, both to make it look like everything is normal and because Elliot and I enjoy them so much. Mrs. Patel, we want you to continue to work at T&M Consultants and report to Moscow, but we'll tell you exactly what to say to them. We'll be monitoring your emails, of course. And Harvey's."

"You already are," Harvey said.

"Just a reminder. And don't worry. We'll be watching you."

"To keep us safe," Harvey said.

"Of course.

"And to prevent us from taking off for Bora Bora."

Luke flipped open the second pizza box and pulled out a slice. "That too."

Chapter 23

Sweet Dreams

Harvey stepped into the conference room and joined Owen at the window. They were the first to arrive. Below them lay the rows of brick buildings of Back Bay, with the Charles River beyond. A pair of eight-person sculls raced side-by-side. The rowers bent their backs, stroked, straightened up, leaned down, stroked again—over and over. A small motorboat followed, with the coach sitting at the bow and shouting into a megaphone. Harvey wanted to trade places with the guy. He wanted to trade places with just about anybody.

"You're jumpy today," Owen said.

"Too much coffee."

Harvey knew he was jumpy. He'd spent the night with Amaya, hugging her until she fell asleep, after which he dreamed of Russian agents and poisonings and of a car chase with Tommy in the back seat, calling for help.

On the walk from the subway to the office that morning, Harvey had glanced behind him every minute or two. He saw a pair of women in dark business suits, walking together and gripping briefcases by the handle, two men wearing blue work clothes and peering into an open manhole, a girl skateboarding, a bicycle messenger riding on the sidewalk, and two vaping teenagers slouched against the front of a coffee shop. Anyone of them could be a danger. So much to fear.

As soon as other team members started wandering in, Harvey and Owen grabbed their usual spots that faced the window. Margo settled down at the foot of the table to Harvey's right and didn't look in his direction. They'd hardly spoken since the night she'd found Amaya at his place.

Everyone praised the latest round of documentation. The ex-basketball player with the tiny ears lobbed a question that Harvey sidestepped. The red-bearded guy who always brought a sticky bun asked something that Harvey could actually answer. The girl who yawned through meetings said nothing, which was a relief because her questions were always tough and ill-tempered.

Tucker stood at the head of table—he never sat during meetings—and thumbed through pages of the document, commenting on this and that and heaping praise on Harvey even though he knew Harvey hadn't written the stuff. Liars make the best actors, Harvey told himself.

Which he was too, a fake technical writer and a fake human being. What did he know about anything? What had he ever done to change the world, to leave his mark? Semester after semester, he'd stood before a podium and pontificated to his classes about the Big Bang, the emergence of *Homo sapiens*, the building of the Great Wall of China, and the explosive changes brought about during the electronic age, but those were just word balloons he'd sent floating out over the heads of drowsy students and not events he'd taken part in or even witnessed. He'd been a fake contributor to society, a fake technical writer, a fake husband, a fake son, and a fake caretaker of Tommy.

Did others beat themselves up like that? Owen certainly did. Amaya to some extent. Tucker never, nor Margo.

Even physical objects could be fakes. There were phony Picassos, phony medications, and phony breasts. And although this conference table was trying to pass itself off as solid maple, it was in fact just molecules that were 99.99 percent empty space, as was he. Harvey thought of himself as an empty shell like the table, like his chair, and like this building. He was hovering fourteen stories aboveground on a swirling mass of subatomic particles ruled chaotically by quantum mechanics, balanced atop a planet that was itself preponderantly space, in a universe of emptiness. A staggering thought. And what if…

"Give Harvey a hand," Tucker said brightly.

Harvey blinked and looked around.

Applause ensued.

Harvey nodded in embarrassment at the praise he didn't deserve.

Once in a while, a class would clap after his final lecture of the semester in the earlier life that now seemed so far in the golden past. They'd clapped either for his brilliant insights or because they'd never again have to listen to him lecture.

He'd received an email invitation this morning to return to campus for a job fair for ex-faculty. He'd debated whether to go, but finally accepted. He knew Luke wouldn't let him take another job, but this would give him the opportunity to chat with the few former colleagues who were still in town. Plus, he'd have the chance to walk Amaya around campus. He liked that, returning to the college and showing her off. He would introduce her as a former professor, but—as much as he'd like to—he thought it wise not to mention that his comely companion was an international spy.

*   *   *

Harvey did his pizza deliveries, then drove home and crawled into an empty bed. Amaya was staying at her hotel for the night because she wanted to pull an all-nighter and not disturb him while she worked on the next batch of documentation.

In his dream, a red-bearded and shirtless Russian agent stood over him, a silvery, two-headed axe raised high overhead.

Harvey woke with a jolt and jumped out of bed. Sweat ran down his back. He pulled on his clothes and shoes and went outside for a walk, his usual cure for sleeplessness.

In any case, he needed cash, so he headed for an ATM a few blocks away, glancing around in the night for muggers, mobsters, and Russian agents wielding double-bladed axes.

Why are humans so afraid of the dark? They shouldn't be, since they descended from nocturnal, tree-dwelling primates. He guessed that the first humans had terrific night vision, but it had atrophied after they climbed down from the trees. If people today could still see in the dark like cats and owls, there would be fewer nighttime driving accidents, fewer plane crashes, and fewer drunks stumbling into manholes. But would daylight be blinding? Harvey guessed not. Human eyes would have evolved to accommodate large changes in brightness. Would sleep be harder or would eyelids be thicker? Probably thicker. The concept of day and night might even disappear. Restaurants would serve diners around the clock, movie theaters would be open twenty-four hours a day, and...

And Harvey walked right past the ATM. He swung around and bumped into a wide-shouldered man with a gray crew cut and a ratty black jacket.

Harvey recalled the Russian who'd axed his way into his nightmare.

Harvey crossed the street.

Would he be looking for Russian assassins for the rest of his life? Probably.

The smart move would be to skip the ATM and head home. But the tough-looking guy was probably homeless, someone not to fear but to pity. Just stick to well-lighted areas, get the cash, then hurry home, pop a pill, and climb into bed.

Sleeping problems had started right after Tommy's death. Harvey remembered waking up thrashing and shouting. His mother could never calm him, but his physician father could. Using his best bedside manner, he would talk Harvey back to sleep with stories about the Iowa farm where he'd grown up. He created vivid images of cows, corn fields, hay barns, and a sprightly pet lamb that would bound into Harvey's dreams. Over the years, the nightmares became fewer and fewer, and the lamb grew up and moved on, but the insomnia endured.

Harvey had often prepared classes in the middle of the night, or he wrote articles, ate popcorn, and watched *Seinfeld* reruns. Sometimes he went for walks. He liked the quiet, liked to let his imagination run free. Was that prowling gray van on its way to a burglary? Is that car filled with men in black-brimmed hats heading to a gangster sit-down? Is that pretty lady driving alone at this hour of the night a hooker? A fellow insomniac? Sometimes he'd run into his night-owl neighbor, and they'd walk together. He was an amiable and taciturn elderly man who later turned out to be wanted in Arkansas for bank robbery.

Harvey withdrew $200 and headed home.

And spotted the crew-cut man peering from an alley.

Harvey picked up his pace.

The man stepped from the alley.

Harvey broke into a trot, leaped a low fence, fell, jumped up, and ran on.

He glanced back to see his follower clear the fence by two feet.

An agile guy for someone who looked homeless.

Stand and slug it out? He knew how to box, and that would be the manly thing to do.

Yes? No?

No. The guy might have a knife or gun.

Harvey ran in the direction of his apartment, breathing hard, his heart pounding.

He looked back and saw no one. He slowed to a walk and took big gulps of air.

No more sleep tonight.

He had the key in his hand and hadn't yet unlocked the door when he heard footsteps. He spun around.

The man had caught up.

He waved a knife and muttered something under his breath.

It sounded like Russian.

Harvey froze. This wasn't a mugger, but an assassin. Moscow had found out he was cooperating with the FBI.

Don't they use poison? Why a knife?

To make it look like a mugging.

Harvey backed away from the door. He remembered the self-defense classes he'd taken with his ex-wife.

If your opponent has a knife, wrap your jacket around your left forearm to ward off the blow. Keep your right free for striking back. And stay calm.

Harvey wrapped his jacket around his left forearm.

But he didn't stay calm.

His heart banged.

Kill or be killed.

The knife looked about eight inches long. One side serrated.

Is this how he would die?

They circled. Once, twice.

The man looked wild and angry. His eyes flicked back and forth.

More circling. Around and around.

Then the man lunged.

Harvey blocked the blade with his jacket and punched his attacker in the jaw.

He stumbled backwards, then came at Harvey.

Time slowed. Harvey waited… waited… waited. At the last second, he grabbed the arm with the knife, jerked the man forward and off balance, spun him around, and slammed his head against the brick wall.

The attacker said, "*Oof!*" and fell face down. His knife flew into the bushes.

Harvey kicked him in the side. He didn't move.

Blood flowed from his ear.

Was he dead?

Harvey jerked his phone out and called Amaya. "Something's happened. Don't leave your hotel room. Lock your door, brace a chair under the handle, and don't let anyone inside."

"What's going on?"

"I'll explain later."

Harvey shoved the phone back in his pocket.

The pool of blood expanded.

Harvey unlocked his door, stepped into the hallway, and called Luke.

"Goddamn it, Harvey! It's the middle of the night!"

"A Russian agent tried to stab me. I think I killed him. The guy's lying out front of my place."

"No, shit? You're sure he's Russian?"

"I'm pretty sure, and why aren't you asking if I'm okay?"

"Because you sound okay. I'll call the cops and get back."

Harvey climbed the stairs to his apartment and turned off the lights so the police wouldn't come upstairs and question him. He dropped onto a kitchen chair, lay his arm on the table, and unwrapped the jacket. He saw a slice through the cloth, then a slice through his flesh. Now he felt the pain.

He took a first-aid kit from the bathroom cabinet and bandaged his arm in the glow of the streetlight. Then he returned to the kitchen table, drank a beer, and waited for Luke to call.

An ambulance wailed up, a police car right behind. Harvey stood up, pulled the curtain back a couple of inches, and looked down. The EMTs loaded the victim into the ambulance. One cop glanced up at the building and said, "Should we go inside and ask questions?"

The other cop said, "Let them sleep. He's just some addict who fell down and banged his head."

The ambulance and the police car pulled away, sirens howling.

The phone rang a half hour later. Harvey snatched it off the table. It was Luke.

Harvey said, "Is the Russian assassin dead?"

"Nope. Did you want to kill him?"

"Of course not."

"You were right that he is a Russian, but he's not an assassin," Luke said. "You beat the crap out of a garden-variety mugger. He's got a long record and a history of violence."

Harvey let out his breath. He hadn't killed the man. An assassin hadn't attacked him. That was a relief and, oddly, somewhat of a disappointment. He said, "You'd have made the same mistake."

"I never make mistakes. But at least you did society a service by getting that piece of garbage off the streets for a while. Now go to bed, Mr. Bond. Sweet dreams."

Chapter 24

A Tiny Boot

Harvey picked Amaya up at her hotel and assured her for the tenth time that his panicky call of the night before was a false alarm. He told her he'd feared someone was breaking into the building and coming after him, but it turned out to be just another burglar trying to get into the poultry store downstairs. Harvey told her the place attracted break-ins because it was a reputed money-laundering operation, with a lot of cash lying around. He wasn't sure she believed him, but she didn't push it.

It was Kathy's twenty-fourth birthday. Harvey hated to see her grow older, and he feared she would someday take a job in a faraway state. He wanted her near him. He wanted her to be six again. He wanted to take her for ice cream and balance her on a bike without training wheels, and he wanted to bandage her scraped knees.

What if time could be frozen? Or if, as we grow older, we could go back to our best moments and relive them? What if…

"You should have worn something lighter," Amaya said, tugging Harvey's sleeve. "It's going to be hot."

"You sound like my mother."

"Good."

Harvey's long-sleeved shirt concealed the bandage. If Amaya

or his mother saw it, they'd make a fuss, and if Kathy saw it, she would make him let her treat the wound. The cut wasn't deep, but it was painful enough to have kept him awake the night before, that and the realization that the fight could have gone the other way. He silently thanked Brenda for dragging him to those self-defense sessions. What if she hadn't? He'd have been the guy the EMTs had shoved into the ambulance.

*   *   *

Harvey's mother opened the door. She wore her diamond earrings and an expensive-looking black cashmere sweater. Harvey figured she'd dressed up for Amaya. Twice the day before, she'd called Harvey and ordered him to bring her. The two women liked each other. His mother had referred to Brenda as "that woman," and that woman had referred to her mother-in-law as "that bitch."

Harvey and Amaya gave Kathy long hugs and said, "Happy Birthday."

Harvey's mother headed for the kitchen and invited Amaya along.

Kathy led Harvey into the living room and sat beside him on the couch. "You look stressed and exhausted. Does it have something to do with Amaya?"

"Nope."

"How are things going with you two?"

"Fine."

Harvey remembered sitting Kathy down just like this and quizzing her about boyfriends.

"Are you having trouble forming full sentences?" Kathy asked.

"Yup."

"I like her a lot. She's much too good for you, by the way, but I believe I told you that before. Grandma adores her, and I'm surprised she didn't have a justice of the peace waiting here for you."

"Next visit."

Amaya returned with Harvey's mother, laughing about something.

After champagne, chatting, more champagne, and more chatting, the presents appeared. Harvey's mother gave Kathy an expensive gold necklace, Harvey gave her a sports watch, and Amaya handed Kathy a blue silk scarf that the three women enthused over.

Kathy tried it on, then Harvey's mother tried it on, then Amaya tried it on. Harvey asked for a turn but was ignored.

He'd given his daughter a fancy sports watch because the old one had stopped working. Kathy jogged, swam, and did yoga, and she nagged Harvey to exercise more. People needed to stay in shape, she said, in order to ward off aches and pains as they got older.

And to ward off muggers.

Harvey's book contained a short section about the role of physical fitness in the evolution of humans. The strong and fast survived, and the weak and slow perished. It was as simple as that. What if everyone today followed a routine that mimicked as closely as possible that of our distant ancestors, specifically the survivors? It would involve long runs, climbing trees to escape danger, digging caves, and whacking meaty, small game over the head with wooden clubs. He imagined opening a fitness center devoted to those activities. He would name it "Origins" and put everyone into scanty, leopard-skin, cave-person outfits, and then…"

"I said," Harvey's mother said, "are you ready for cake? I asked twice before, Harvey, but you didn't hear me. You're just like your father. He would wander off into his own world and have to be dragged back."

This was about as close as she ever came to criticizing her late husband. That always puzzled Harvey. She would talk about what a good man he was and about how he left her so well-off—at least until she finally found out the truth—and how he spent so much time with his family. Did she know about the girlfriends? Probably, and she'd simply fit them into her cheerfully tilted worldview.

She brought in a chocolate cake with pink frosting. Harvey watched Kathy blow out the candles in one explosive burst from her well-exercised lungs. Everyone ate cake, drank coffee, nipped at a second bottle of champagne, talked louder and louder.

Harvey's mother set her empty plate on the coffee table and turned to Amaya. "Have you ever been married."

"Mom!"

"It's a perfectly reasonable question," she said and turned back to Amaya. "I didn't offend you, did I dear?"

"Of course not. And I was married for sixteen years," Amaya said in an even voice.

"Any children?"

Amaya hesitated. "A daughter."

"Wonderful. How old is she?"

A longer hesitation.

"Twenty-four," Amaya said in a small voice. "Just like Kathy."

"What does she do?"

"She's… in medical school."

"Again, just like Kathy," Harvey's mother said. "How lovely. Harvey has probably told you that my late husband was a prominent surgeon. Do you see your daughter often now that you're in the States?"

"Not often enough," Amaya said and looked around the room but not in Harvey's direction. "She's very busy, but when we get together, we have a wonderful time. We shop and go to cafés and laugh all the time, and…."

Amaya stopped talking and stopped smiling. She stared at the carpet, her eyes unfocused.

Harvey wanted to say something but didn't know what it would be. Go along with the story? Make up something of his own? Tell his mother that he'd met the daughter, and she was a wonderful person?

No, stay out of this. Amaya had gone to her happy place, her crazy place, her necessary place. The story had rolled off her tongue. She'd no doubt been perfecting it over the years, adding stuff and subtracting stuff, a pale rendering of the daughter who never had the chance to grow up. Amaya had just now revisited the parallel universe where there were no accidents, no dead daughters, no guilt.

If his mother knew the truth, she would understand.

So did he. Sometimes he imagined Tommy as still alive, an engineer because he'd loved to build stuff with Legos. He was living nearby, happily married, with a son and a daughter. Harvey and Tommy hiked together, swam in the ocean, went to Red Sox games, talked politics and climate change, competed over every little thing, shared a garden tiller, a snow blower, a life.

Kathy tried the scarf on again and thanked Amaya again, who sat in silence, her lower lip quivering.

Harvey got up and sat beside her on the couch, put his arm around her, and kissed her on the top of her head.

Amaya leaned on his shoulder.

Harvey's mother beamed.

Kathy broke the silence. "Thanks everyone for the wonderful presents."

Harvey's mother refilled their coffee cups. "Tommy's favorite birthday present was the cowboy boots I bought him. He was so cute in them and wore them everywhere."

And he died in them. Two days after the rogue wave had pulled Tommy out to sea, a tiny boot washed ashore. A policewoman had shown up at the front door and asked the grieving family to identify it.

Harvey's mother hadn't said a word. She'd hugged the soggy boot to her chest, carried it upstairs, and stood it on Tommy's bureau in the room that he and Harvey shared. Over the years, she left everything unchanged on Tommy's half of the room: a poster of a spaceship, its plastic version on the bureau, and a baseball cap autographed by a Red Sox pitcher.

Harvey would lie awake staring at the boot glowing in the nightlight, hating it, wanting to pitch it out the window, but fearing he would somehow make Tommy unhappy.

In the weeks after the drowning, people spoke softly to Harvey, patted his head, squeezed his shoulder, told him he was a brave little fellow, and they assured him his mother would soon be back from her little trip, and everything would return to normal. Harvey would slip out of their grasp. He knew everything would not return to normal.

No one blamed him. He always thought it would be better if they had. He wanted to be punished, but never was. So he punished himself.

He was angry with himself and angry with his parents for sending him off alone that day with Tommy. He was angry with the power of waves and water and with the fragility of the human body.

And he was angry with Tommy for leaving him with a lifetime of guilt.

Chapter 25

The Center of the World

Harvey pulled into Middlebridge College and parked in front of the student union. Plywood boards covered the windows. Someone had spray-painted "Fuck!" in red across the front door.

Amaya stepped out of the car and glanced around. "What a pretty campus."

Harvey agreed. Ivy climbed the sides of the red-brick buildings, ancient oaks shaded the curving sidewalks, and pink rhododendron bushes fronted the buildings.

Would the place become a high-tech center? Or would some college take the school over as a satellite campus? More likely, a developer would level the buildings and erect condos.

Harvey took Amaya on a melancholy tour of the grounds, pointing out various buildings where he'd lectured, as well as the library, the science hall, and the chubby statue of the felonious railroad baron who'd founded the school a century earlier. Then he led her to the pond behind the gymnasium. They sat on a stone bench with 'Class of 2005' carved into the back of the seat. "After lecturing, I'd often sit here to decompress," Harvey said. "The last time was the day I found out the school was closing, and I threw my office chair through the window."

Amaya's eyes widened. "You really did that?"

"I sure as hell did."

Harvey stood up, took her hand, led her to a brick building facing the quadrangle, and from there up three floors to his old office. Plywood covered one window. Harvey pushed the other one open and pointed at the overgrown rhododendron bush below. The chair was missing, but one castered leg remained.

"That's not like you," Amaya said.

"Actually, it is. I hold things back until I explode. My personal Big Bang."

"I hope I never see that."

Harvey hoped so, too.

They walked arm-in-arm to the job fair in the gymnasium. Red-and-gold banners boasted of basketball triumphs. The Middlebridge College team had been champions for three years in a row in the nineties, but had not had a winning season since. Harvey had never gone to a game, but wished now that he'd involved himself more in campus activities. Still, that might have made his departure even more painful.

Former members of the faculty shuffled from one card table to the next. Harvey spotted no close friends—a disappointment. He knew that a few had found summer-school jobs here and there, that a half dozen others had retired, some had drifted into industry, a biologist had attempted suicide, and a sociology professor had succeeded.

Harvey looked around for Russian agents, but didn't see any. Or didn't think he saw any. There were a few people Harvey couldn't recognize. Russians? Or agents Luke had sent to follow him?

A former professor of Asian history sidled up to Harvey, a freckled and unpleasant man with garlic breath, an ego the size of his area of specialty, and a weakness for alliteration. He'd always dismissed the teaching of Big History. After the collapse of the college, he'd warned Harvey that he would never find another teaching job, that his field wasn't so much an intellectual discipline as a disillusioned dilettante's meadow of miscellany. Harvey moved away without introducing Amaya.

They shuffled dutifully from table to table where sat scrubbed young people behind discouraging signs reading, "Atlas Chemical Industries—We Need Reps!" "How to Earn your Real Estate License!" "Your Future in Surgical Supply Sales!"

Harvey knew of no one who'd taken up as a hobby the selling of chemicals, bungalows, or scalpels. That's how he separated occupations: those with amateur participants and those without. There were professional photographers and professional astronomers and enthusiastic amateurs in both fields, but there were no amateur technical writers. Each semester, he'd explain this to his students, who would look on dully. Don't pursue a profession without participating amateurs, he would advise. He knew that most of his listeners would come to understand this only later in life, when they were off marketing chemicals, bungalows, scalpels.

A group of acquaintances had gathered at a free-throw line. Harvey took Amaya by the arm and joined them. There was a botanist who now sold life insurance ("Here, Doctor Hudson"—a business card tucked into his shirt pocket—"Everyone should provide for their loved ones."), a bird-like chemist who now worked in private industry and, after prodding, admitted she'd doubled her salary. Then there was a tanned and independently wealthy engineering instructor—name forgotten—who lived on his yacht in Boston Harbor and said he'd decided never to work again, followed by a young and frequently stoned assistant math professor who now worked for the Yum-Yum Custard Company as their traveling magician.

Harvey said he and Amaya were deep into international affairs, really deep. Then he took her arm and hurried away. He'd seen enough.

The dean, the event's organizer, blocked them at the exit. He was a thin, dark, humorless, and rather spooky man whose trousers always hung an inch above his ankles. Harvey remembered how hard he'd made life for him, assigning him extra classes, holding back raises, delaying his sabbaticals.

Unprompted, Harvey reported that he now had an extremely important job in an up-and-coming high-tech company at an embarrassingly high salary and with wads of bonuses. "Even though my current job pays me an embarrassing high salary and gives me wads of bonuses," Harvey said, "I've wearied of the fast-paced corporate life and am hoping to go into another field such as pizza delivery. I'm extremely disappointed to discover that you've neglected to bring in a representative from that particular profession."

The dean looked puzzled. "Pizza delivery?"

"Or international spy."

"International spy?"

Amaya dragged Harvey out the door.

She laughed all the way to the car.

A pretty sound, Harvey thought. Something he hadn't heard lately.

She settled into the front seat. "You must really miss this place."

Harvey started the engine, then leaned back and turned to Amaya. "Less and less. For years, this was the center of the world for me, but I now realize how isolated I was. I can't imagine growing old here, lecturing to sleepy students about the origin of the universe and the evolution of man until my notes curled up and turned brittle, and I curled up and turned brittle. I've stepped away. I'm a player in the world now, not an outside observer."

Amaya squeezed his shoulder and smiled. "It sounds as if you've moved on."

"I just wish I hadn't moved on to international espionage."

Chapter 26:

Waxed Dental Floss

Harvey sat typing in his cubicle, absorbed in finishing Chapter 28 ("The Treaty of Versailles and Its Tragic Aftermath") but was becoming more and more irritated by the strand of dental floss lodged between upper-left molars 14 and 15. Every few paragraphs, Harvey caught himself tonguing the minty thread, which by midmorning had expanded to the diameter of clothesline rope.

Enough, he decided. He closed his laptop, grabbed his umbrella, and headed to the drugstore.

Amaya had called him earlier and apologized for not telling his mother that her daughter had died in a car accident. She said she'd made up the story on the spur of the moment only to save the poor woman from thinking about Tommy. Harvey knew that Amaya hadn't invented the tale on the spot, but he didn't call her out. He told her that he, better than anyone, understood what she was feeling, and that his mother would have understood only too well.

He bought a pack of waxed floss at the drugstore, scooped his change off the counter, and headed outside. As he walked, he thought about what his spunky cave-dwelling ancestors did when a strand of stringy gazelle got hung up between a couple of cuspids. Did they search for a thin twig? A rose thorn? A fish bone? Or did they just go around grumpy all day long, whacking each other over the head with fat, cartoonish clubs?

Harvey got a half block from the drugstore before he noticed that rain was flowing down his collar. He hurried back to the store and found his umbrella still leaning against the counter, and at the same time he remembered he was almost out of antiperspirant. He located the appropriate aisle and its many choices. What would society be like if no one had invented deodorants? If everyone smelled bad, would anyone even notice? Probably not. Then again, in past centuries, some of the European nobility had splashed themselves with perfume, both women and men, and…

And out of the corner of his eyes, Harvey spotted a tall, husky man looming over shelves of medications, picking up an item, putting it back, picking up another, putting it back. He gave the impression that he, too, was overwhelmed by too many choices.

Except he wasn't. Except he was Igor.

Harvey recognized him from the photo Luke had shown at their first meeting.

Igor the rugby player, the Russian agent, the giant with hemorrhoidal issues.

Harvey's pulse quickened.

If Igor had trailed him to the drugstore, then why hadn't he followed him out the door? Was Igor working with a team, and it had been his turn to drop out of rotation? Or was he on his own, and itching had trumped duty?

Run? Stick around?

Stick around.

Harvey was careful not to look directly at Igor. That's how a trained agent would operate. Instead, he pretended to concentrate on his search for just the right underarm product.

Harvey lifted one antiperspirant after the other off the shelf and made a show of perusing the labels. "Spring Fresh!" one declared brightly. Another shouted that it was "Like a Summer Breeze!"

A third bragged puzzlingly that it was "One-hundred percent organic and non-GMO!"

Harvey selected a bright green box, pulled his phone from his jacket, and swiped through screens to make it look as if he were checking product reviews. He tilted the phone just enough to take a quick photo of the fearsome rugby star standing only a dozen feet away. Harvey slipped his phone back in his pocket, chose an antiperspirant in a purple box solely because it came without an exclamation mark ("Keeps You Fresh All Day"), paid at the counter, and left the store.

He tilted his umbrella into the wind and felt proud of himself. He'd outed a Russian spy.

He glanced back. No Igor behind him. Were others lingering in doorways?

Just a few weeks earlier, he'd never have imagined himself in a position where he'd be scanning for murderous foreign agents. It was a creepy feeling. And scary. And exciting.

Once inside the building, Harvey hurried to his cubicle and sent Igor's image to Amaya, then Luke.

Seconds later, Harvey's burner phone vibrated.

Luke said, "Where did you take this?"

"At the drugstore a couple of blocks from where I work."

"When?"

"Just now," Harvey said. "What do I do?"

"You do nothing. Just act normal. Or as normal as someone like you is capable of acting. I'll get right back to you."

Harvey slid the phone into his jacket pocket. His hands shook. Some international spy, he thought.

He unspooled a foot of floss and removed the offending string on the first try. At least something was going well.

Amaya called. "What's Igor doing here?"

She sounded scared.

"I have no idea. Maybe Luke knows. You're in your hotel room?"

"Yes."

"Don't let anyone in until you hear from me or Luke."

"I'm frightened."

Harvey hesitated. "Don't be. There's really nothing to worry about."

But he knew that wasn't true. And Amaya must be thinking the same thing.

"I love you," Harvey said. He leaned back in his chair and closed his eyes. Poor Amaya. What could he do to keep her safe?

Nothing. He could do nothing. Things had spun out of control.

Meanwhile, an argument broke out in the kitchenette next door between the ex-basketball star and the thin woman who yawned throughout team meetings.

He said he was allergic to her cat.

She said she loved her cat.

Well, he hated cats and loved dogs.

She hated dogs because they were so needy, and they have to be walked a hundred times a day, and they spend half their waking hours sniffing butts.

He said he hated her cat, and he hated her.

She said he could go to hell.

She stomped past Harvey's cubicle. The former point guard thumped off in the other direction.

The burner phone buzzed. Harvey jerked it out of his pocket. "Yes?"

"I'm going to send a Zoom invitation to you and Amaya."

"Will that be secure?"

"I'll make it secure. I'm with the FBI, remember? Now get out of the building so no one will walk in on you."

Harvey went down the elevator and jogged three blocks to the Public Garden. The rain had stopped. Water dripped off the statue of George Washington on horseback, off red-and-yellow tulips, and off the bench that Harvey sat down on. He had more important things to worry about than a damp butt. He made a show of thumbing through his phone, casually looking up now and then for Russian operatives crouched in the bushes.

The Zoom invitation popped up, and Harvey clicked on it. Luke and Elliot were sitting on hard chairs side-by-side in front of a blank white wall, and Amaya was at her desk in the hotel room. She wore a blue blouse and a worried look.

Harvey waved. Amaya waved back. So did Luke.

Harvey said, "I wasn't waving at you, dickhead. Why in hell didn't you tell us Igor was in town?"

"We didn't know."

"You keep bragging that the FBI knows everything."

"We have long borders," Luke said, "plus tens of thousands of foreigners arrive every day. It's not that hard for someone to slip through."

"It's too bad we don't have people watching for that sort of thing, like, I don't know, maybe uniformed guards at airports and border crossings?"

"Wiseass. The Russians are masters at faking documentation, so Igor probably didn't come directly from Moscow but stopped in Brussels or somewhere else and bought tickets using false papers."

Amaya bit her lower lip. Harvey wanted to reach out and hug her, calm her, run away with her to some place where she'd be safe, maybe to a mountain-top cabin in Vermont and go into town only twice a year to stock up on food.

He said, "Igor didn't follow me out of the drugstore, so I'm guessing he wasn't working alone."

"Right. One guy trails you for a while, then drops out and another picks you up. Igor thought he could safely follow you because he believes you don't know about him, but he wouldn't trail Amaya, since she can ID him."

Harvey said, "Others are watching her?"

A hesitation, then Luke said, "Probably."

"Why are they here?"

"Because Amaya's not a regular agent but was forced into her role. It's standard Russian practice to watch someone in her situation."

"Will you grab Igor?" Harvey asked.

"And ruin the operation? Of course not. All we can do is contain him and the rest of his team."

What a clusterfuck. Harvey had just about enough.

He waited for the policeman on horseback to get past, then said, "Listen, damn it, I'm quitting unless you give Amaya around-the-clock protection, put teams in her hotel, and post a guard outside her door."

"That's all you want?" Luke said.

"That's a start. And do it now!"

"We're dealing with professionals. It would take them about two minutes to spot our agents lingering inside the hotel, and then what would the Russians conclude? That Amaya's been turned, that's what. Her best protection is for the Russkies to keep thinking she's working for them. She's their asset, and they won't harm her."

"For now," Harvey said, "but what happens after they discover you've spoiled their cyberattack, and later on when they find your software bugs chewing their way through their computer networks?"

"We'll deal with that when the time comes," Luke said. "Anyway, you have nothing to worry about."

"'Nothing to worry about?' Bullshit! You have to…"

Luke ended the session.

Harvey phoned Amaya. "Can we talk?

"Sure, but stay where you are. I need some air."

Harvey stared at his phone, now silent. The Russians will be following her, and they probably had eyes on him right now. Not a good feeling. He yawned, leaned back, stretched, and looked around, the picture of serenity.

Fifteen minutes later, a taxi pulled up at the far side of the park. Amaya climbed out, paid the driver, and hurried toward Harvey. She wore jeans and the pretty blue blouse from before.

My one job in life is to protect this woman, Harvey told himself. Her and his mom and Kathy. And Amaya's brother and his family. A big order.

"A nice day," Amaya said. She kissed Harvey and sat beside him. From her tone, he knew she wasn't thinking it was a nice day.

She reached into her purse, pulled out her phone, and held it up so Harvey could see the screen. "I just got this. That's my brother. The woman is his wife, and that's their daughter blowing out the candles. She's the cutest thing. It's her fourth birthday. I wish I could have been there for the party. She's like a substitute daughter," Amaya said, her voice strained. She looked up. "I worry about them."

Of course she did. The Russians had them under observation.

Amaya got to her feet. "Let's walk. I need to move."

Harvey stood up. "Do you still hate your hotel?"

Amaya nodded.

"My place isn't a whole lot larger," Harvey said, "but there are two rooms, and it has more windows than where you're staying, and lots more privacy. The downstairs poultry store can get noisy during the day, and there's no yard, of course, and I have to lug my wash to the laundromat down the street, and whenever it rains—"

"Yes."

"Uh… yes what?"

Amaya stopped walking, took both of Harvey's hands, squeezed them and said, "Yes, I will move in with you. Isn't that what you were leading up to?"

Harvey nodded. "You'll be safer there."

"How romantic."

"And because I love you," Harvey added in haste.

"You'd better say that." Amaya looped her arm into his and

started them moving again. "One condition: I have to replace that ugly brown couch."

"Sure."

"And get rid of the kitchen table with the shaky leg."

"Okay."

"Plus the lumpy mattress, those horrible gray drapes, that leather footstool that leaks stuffing, and the rug that smells like a dead possum."

"That's all?"

"And a few other things."

"Will you leave anything of mine?" Harvey asked.

Amaya was quiet for a minute. "I like the Degas print over the couch, but it needs a better frame."

Harvey said, "I'll pick up the cost, of course."

Amaya shook her head. "I have loads of money. My company pays well, and the Russians give me bonuses."

"Sounds like you're doing okay financially. Still, have you ever thought of a third source of income?"

"No. And like what?"

"Like a job at my company, supposedly as my editor. I've already spoken with Tucker, and he's agreed because he knows all about your work with the Russians and my connection to the FBI. You and I could share an office, which means I could protect you around the clock, and—"

"And I could protect you," Amaya said.

"Uh… right. Anyway, what do you think?"

"Moscow will love it, and I'll save all my salary for our little white house with the white picket fence."

Amaya smiled.

Harvey hadn't seen her do that in days.

They walked on.

Amaya said, "All your stained dishtowels will have to be tossed, too."

"Are you keeping anything?"

Amaya leaned her head against his shoulder. "Just you."

Chapter 27

Take Me Hiking

Harvey woke at dawn, rolled over, and hugged Amaya. This stopped her from shouting in her sleep. It was another nightmare, like the night before and the night before that. He said, "It's Saturday. Let's get out of town."

"Take me hiking."

Harvey climbed out of bed, stepped into the living room/kitchenette, slipped sideways between the new couch and matching easy chair, and pulled his stomach in so he could ease past the shiny new kitchen table. He turned on the coffeemaker, also brand new.

Amaya had moved in two days earlier. Harvey had come home from a pizza delivery to find all his furniture piled up at the curb. The apartment was unrecognizable now—bright and cheerful and filled with color. And crowded.

While Amaya showered, Harvey called Luke and told him that Amaya had moved in with him and had taken a job at T&M Consultants.

Harvey waited for an explosion.

Instead, Luke said, "Smart move on both counts. But why in hell didn't you talk to me ahead of time?"

"It just slipped my mind."

"Yeah, sure."

Harvey and Amaya had a quick breakfast, hopped into his car, and headed north to New Hampshire and Mount Monadnock.

Amaya loosened up more and more as they got farther from the city. She spoke of her childhood, of birthday parties with other girls, her disastrous dance lessons, her teaching, and her family and friends back in New Delhi.

Harvey picked up on her good mood. He told her about how he and Tucker used to set off fireworks at night in their teacher's front yard, sneak into movie theaters, and spy on Tucker's neighbor while she showered.

Boys, Amaya said, shaking her head.

Harvey pretended to get lost three times so he could switch back and look for anyone tailing them. He guessed Amaya knew what he was up to, but she said nothing.

Finally, they ran out of talk. Amaya looked out her window, hummed quietly, and fell asleep.

An hour later, Harvey pulled into the lot at the foot of the mountain and touched Amaya's forearm to wake her. He opened his door and stepped outside. The air smelled clean. Birds chirped. Squirrels scampered past.

Amaya got out, yawned and stretched. "Lovely."

"Someday," Harvey said, "I'll build a tiny hideaway for us on the far slope where no one will ever find us."

"It better have indoor plumbing."

They headed toward the trailhead and started to climb.

The day was cool and sunny and filled with insects. Harvey and Amaya took turns slapping them off each other's back and neck.

Most of the offenders were the persistent little black gnats that hover around a person's nose. He'd once read that carbon dioxide attracted the critters. They were almost microscopic, which meant their brains were microscopic, which amazed Harvey.

An elephant's brain weighed about eleven pounds, he'd read somewhere, over three times that of a human's. Yet, elephant brains and human brains functioned the same, each one doing a fine job for the body they occupy. One would think that the animals with the biggest brains would be the smartest, and that elephants and sperm whales would concoct life-saving vaccines, solve global warming, and compose glorious symphonies. And if brain size did control intelligence, then gnats would be too dumb to fly. They would just lounge around all day saying, "Huh? I don't understand. What's going on here?"

But that wasn't how things worked. Harvey made a mental note to fit brain size somewhere into his book.

He took out his phone and made his daily call to his mother. She was doing fine, she said, a little breathless, heading out the door to accompany her new neighbor to the mall where they would shop for shoes. Then Harvey spoke with Kathy until he lost his signal.

And his good mood. He worried about his mother, his daughter, and Amaya, and he fretted over Igor and especially Boris the Poisoner. Evil incarnate.

Amaya said, "You've fallen quiet."

"Lately, I've been pondering the nature of evil and people's conflicting ethical beliefs. For example, what I take as the truth can be the total opposite of what others believe. I often wonder how I can be so sure of what I take for the truth, and how another person can be equally sure of what they believe. I once had a student who insisted that for decades a government satellite had been beaming down mind-altering rays and ruling the planet. I couldn't talk him out of it, nor could his classmates. Aside from this one bizarre belief, the kid seemed normal enough. That got me to thinking. What if he was right and every other person in the world was wrong? That's highly unlikely, but not mathematically impossible. The kid's classmates argued they had the facts on their side, but he had his own take on the same facts. That sort of thinking is more and more common these days. I'm afraid we live in an age where the distinction between fact and opinion is disappearing. If things keep going in this direction, the time might come when—"

"Look at that beautiful red bird," Amaya said.

They walked on.

A few minutes later, they spotted a deer ahead on the path. They froze. The deer froze. It watched them for a minute, then bounded into the thicket.

Amaya was captivated.

And happy. She told more stories about when she was a little girl, of the Minnie Mouse watch an aunt had hidden in Amaya's slice of birthday cake, ruining the watch, but Amaya wore it anyway. And she spoke of taking hikes outside New Delhi, and how the birds and vegetation back home were so different from those she saw here. *Look at that blue bird. Isn't that a strange bush with the funny little red berries? I've never seen a pine cone shaped like that.*

Harvey began seeing the world through her eyes. The tall pines looked different, exotic even. So did the hawks, the squirrels, and the moss on the tree trunks.

Amaya told him to listen to the songbirds, the wind in the treetops, the leaves crunching underfoot. "Isn't that glorious?" she said.

Harvey wished she was this happy all the time.

And he wished that man wasn't following them.

Harvey had spotted him ten minutes earlier. When they stopped, he stopped. When they sped up, he sped up. He was a tiny fellow and an awkward hiker. Who sets out to climb a mountain in street shoes and no hat? Someone who doesn't expect to hike, that's who.

Tell Amaya and spoil her good mood?

Maybe later.

They walked on.

Amaya fell silent, stopped walking, and sat on a large, flat rock. She scooted sideways to make room for Harvey. "When did you spot him?"

He sat down. "A few minutes ago. You?"

"Just now. Is he trouble?"

"Not as long as he stays far away," Harvey said.

"What do we do?"

"Just keep climbing. If he gets any closer, then we'll have to deal with the situation."

"What does that mean?" Amaya said.

Harvey shrugged.

They continued their climb.

After a quarter hour, they no longer saw the man.

"He's probably gone back to the parking lot to wait for us," Harvey said.

"Why did he bother to follow us in the first place? He knew we'd eventually have to return to our car."

"Maybe he suspected we were meeting someone up here, but he got winded and gave up."

They reached the top of the mountain, peered around at the lesser hills, and sat silently for a few minutes, their good mood spoiled. Then they started down.

They were halfway to the bottom when they heard moaning.

"An injured animal?" Amaya said.

"Sounds more like a person."

"There," Amaya said, pointing at the gully to their right.

It was the man who'd been trailing them. He lay on his back, his right leg twisted underneath.

Harvey pulled out his phone. No signal. Same for Amaya's.

"We can call when we get closer to the parking lot," Amaya said. "But it'll take hours for rescuers to get to him."

The guy had been up to no good, that was for sure. Leave him here to suffer? To die even? Of course not. "He's small," Harvey said. "I can carry him."

Harvey worked his way down the gully, slippery from the damp leaves.

He kneeled, rolled the man onto his side, and helped him straighten his leg.

He moaned in pain.

"You'll be okay," Harvey said and stood up. "Climb onto my back."

The man sat up, reached into his jacket, and jerked out a pistol.

Harvey kicked the man's hand. The gun flew into the bushes.

The man clutched his hand and screamed.

"You bastard!" Harvey shouted. He grabbed the man by the collar, lifted him up, and shook him until his head bounced back and forth. "Who in hell are you?"

He said nothing.

Harvey saw terror in his eyes. What had the man been told that made him so afraid of me that he had to pull a gun?

"I could drag you farther into the woods and leave you there to die. You know that, don't you?"

Again, that terrified look.

What now? Punch his lights out and leave him here to be eaten by wild animals?

Of course not. Harvey turned his back. "Get on."

The man hesitated.

"Get on!"

He climbed up and clung to Harvey's shoulders.

Harvey held the man's uninjured leg with his left hand, and with his right, he grabbed roots and brush and pulled himself up the muddy slope.

When he reached Amaya, she said, "You did the right thing."

"I hope so."

"Can you carry him all the way?"

"If not, I'll at least make it easier for the rescue team," Harvey said. "Walk behind me and keep an eye him. Shout if he makes a move, and I'll drop the bastard."

It was slow going. Harvey tripped over roots twice, dumping

the man both times, who yelped in pain. The second time, Harvey thought about just leaving him there for the rescuers, but he didn't.

Amaya finally got bars on her phone. She called 911.

Harvey said, "We'll wait in the parking lot with him until the ambulance arrives, then take off. We don't want to stick around to answer questions."

They reached the entrance to the lot in fifteen minutes. They were halfway across, when a beefy man in a brown leather jacket stepped out of his car, opened the rear door, and signaled with his pistol for Harvey to put the injured man in the backseat.

Harvey tensed. He whispered to Amaya, "Stay back. Get ready to run into the woods if things turn ugly."

He walked to the car, turned around, and let the man slide onto the back seat.

Harvey raised his hands and positioned himself between the shooter and Amaya.

Without lowering his gun or taking his eyes off Harvey, the man in the leather jacket kicked the rear door closed and climbed behind the wheel.

The car screeched away just as an ambulance wailed into the parking lot.

Harvey and Amaya hurried to their car and sped off.

Harvey's back throbbed and threatened to seize up. "Nothing like a nice long hike to calm one down," he said.

He took out his burner, called Luke, put it on speaker, and told him what had happened. "I don't know how they could have followed us," Harvey said. "On the drive here, I switched back three times to watch for them."

"Which is a maneuver that trained agents look for. Did you get the license plate?"

Harvey glanced at Amaya. She shook her head.

"No," Harvey said.

"You screwed up big time," Luke said.

"I was somewhat distracted," Harvey said, dragging out his words. "That seems to happen whenever someone points a gun at my face."

"Yeah, well, for what it's worth, you and Amaya can give us descriptions of the two goons. You said you think the injured guy's a Russian?"

"No, I know he's a Russian."

"How can you be so sure?" Luke said.

"Because I stole his wallet."

Chapter 28

A $2.99 Air Freshener

Harvey stood at the entrance to a squat, brick apartment building in Boston's Back Bay, a pizza box in hand, and in the dim streetlight he studied the list of residents until he came to *Percy Daniels.* Harvey pressed the button.

He hoped it wasn't the Percy Daniels he'd had in class his last semester at Middlebridge College, a brilliant and thoroughly disagreeable boy with long feet.

The door opened.

It was the same kid.

"Professor Hudson?"

"Uh, nice to see you again," Harvey mumbled, then opened the box. "Caramelized onion, apple, and goat-cheese."

Percy reached into his back pocket.

"On the house," Harvey said, closing the box. "I'm the new owner and CEO of a huge, nationwide pizza business, and from time to time I get down into the trenches and make runs just to keep in touch with all aspects of operational matters."

Percy blinked.

Harvey handed him the box. "I'm going international next year."

Percy blinked again.

"Business is booming."

"Uh… goodbye, Professor Hudson," Percy said and eased the door closed.

Harvey shuffled back to his car.

What the hell, did it really matter that the little prick didn't believe his story? He had cranky FBI agents and Russian spies to worry about.

Harvey settled behind the wheel and yawned. This was his last delivery for the night. He was still taking painkillers for the back spasms resulting from carrying the Russian down the mountain, and twice that morning, the pills had made him drift off during a company meeting.

He sniffed the air, then eyed the bouquet-shaped air purifier hanging from his rearview mirror. The perfumy smell stank up the car and seeped into his soul. He'd bought the thing just that morning because Amaya kept complaining that his car reeked of soggy pizza boxes. It was rare for her to grumble, but she'd been on edge lately and waking up from nightmares.

Harvey pulled away from the curb and wondered if Amaya would be awake when he got home. Probably not. He would pop the question right after breakfast, maybe after second cups of coffee. Yes, that would be the perfect time, when both of them were wide awake. He should have bought flowers for the big occasion, but it was too late now because all the florists had closed up hours ago.

Brenda had proposed in the shower while Harvey was soaping her back. He hesitated, soap bar in hand, then agreed. As she shampooed her hair, she went into precise detail about the wedding, the honeymoon, and the house they would own. All planned out.

Brenda had said they were meant for each other. Harvey hadn't been so sure, but he hadn't backed out, either. It had felt like an arranged marriage.

Arranged marriages were still common in some parts of the

world. Harvey had discussed them in one of his lectures, kicking it off with, "How would you feel if your parents arranged your marriage?" Percy Daniels of the caramelized onion, apple, and goat-cheese pizza had pointed out loudly from the front row, his arm waving importantly overhead, that mothers still tried to arrange marriages.

After his divorce, Harvey's own mother had invited candidates to their Sunday get-togethers. There were nice ones and quiet ones, and not-so-nice ones and not-so-quiet ones, with the last being a sweet, petite brunette with an inherited Toyota dealership and a leaky left eye.

Harvey watched the brunette grow taller and taller while her bad eye expanded to the size of a pie plate and squirted sticky, yellow fluid in his face, and she came lurching toward him with her fangs dripping, and she make a terrible screeching sound like metal scraping and…

And Harvey woke up, he swung the car away from the tree trunk, thumped over the curb, and steered back onto the street.

The right side mirror dangled from its viscera.

Harvey pulled over and parked.

Just a short nap, he told himself. He was a danger to himself and to others.

He tilted the seat back, closed his eyes and dreamed he was sharing a pizza with the auto heiress and Percy Daniels, who was smearing tomato sauce on her face and licking it off.

Harvey awoke to a stiff back, his watch said 2:57 a.m., and the car stank. Something perfumy. He'd once accidentally knocked one of Brenda's perfume bottles off her chest of drawers and onto the floor. It broke and filled the air with a scent that lingered for days. Brenda shouted that it was a Jean Patou! He shouted back at her, then her at him again, then he shouted back, late into the night.

Harvey's head cleared. No, the smell wasn't a $600 bottle of

French perfume, but a $2.99 air freshener. He rolled the window down and tossed the thing into the night.

*   *   *

When Harvey arrived home, he was too exhausted to undress, so he kicked off his shoes, lifted the edge of the blanket, and started to climb into bed.

Amaya sat bolt upright. "Just where have you been?"

Harvey paused, his right foot raised. He set it down. "Working. I told you I was making deliveries."

Amaya snatched the clock off the nightstand and held it up for him to see. "It's three-thirty in the morning!"

"Right. I took a nap in my car."

Harvey made a move to slip into bed.

Amaya jerked the blanket out of his hand. "A nap?"

"At the side of the road."

"I doubt that."

"What's this all about?" Harvey asked.

"You smell of perfume."

"It's my car's air freshener."

"You don't have one."

"I bought it today."

Amaya said. "Show it to me in the morning."

"I threw it away."

"Sure, you did."

Amaya got up, grabbed her robe, and wrapped it tightly around her, keeping the bed between them. "Yesterday afternoon you spend half an hour in Margo's office. You'd promised never to go in there with the door closed."

"She made me shut it because she wanted to discuss my bonus."

"Is that what people call it now? A bonus?" Amaya folded her arms across her chest. "In the bathroom a couple of days ago, I overheard two administrative assistants gossiping about how you and Margo used to have sex on her office rug. Is that true?"

Harvey hesitated. "It was before I met you."

"And she's always talking to you. Yesterday in the hallway, I saw her stop you and put her hand on your arm."

"She's a toucher."

Amaya grabbed Harvey's pillow and threw it at him. "You're sleeping on the couch."

"Goddamn it, Amaya, I was not with Margo tonight!"

"Don't you *dare* swear at me!" Amaya said, shaking her finger. "I deserve better. I can put up with this dingy place that smells like raw chicken from the store downstairs, and your snoring, and your hideous brown sport coat, but I will *not* tolerate being sworn at, and I certainly will *not* let you get away with cheating on me! My husband used to come home smelling of sex, but I put up with his affairs for our daughter's sake. But no more!"

"You're punishing me for what your husband did."

"No, I'm punishing you for what you did. What would you think if I came home at three-thirty in the morning smelling of aftershave? How would you feel if I saw other men?"

"You've got this all wrong," Harvey said. "I'm not like your husband. I would never cheat on you, and I never had on Brenda, even after I suspected she was cheating on me. Your nerves are shot, and I understand. This business with the task force and Igor and Boris has me climbing the walls, too. So, let's make some tea and sit at the kitchen table and talk this over like a couple of adults."

Amaya climbed into bed, rolled toward the wall, and said nothing.

"Well?" Harvey said.

Silence.

Harvey muttered "Fuck," then grabbed a blanket from the closet, snatched the vase of red roses he'd bought Amaya the day she'd moved in, and smashed it to the floor.

"You're behaving like a child," Amaya said.

Harvey shuffled into the other room, stretched out on the couch, and pulled the blanket over him. His feet hung over the end, and the box holding the engagement ring pressed against his thigh. Harvey rolled onto his back, took out the box, removed the ring, and held it up to the light. What now? Toss it into the trashcan? Drop it into the cup of some homeless person? Try to return it?

He wondered what he could do to convince Amaya that he was telling the truth. Ask Margo to talk to her? But Amaya would insist she's lying.

He thought back to episodes like this with Brenda. Years and years of ups and downs. Most times she started the fights, sometimes he did.

Maybe he should just split with Amaya and live alone. Life would be simple and steady. He'd have to quit his job, of course—he couldn't do the work without her. He would tell Luke and Elliot to go to hell, and then he'd work full time for Pete, an existence of no stress and free pizzas.

Who was he kidding? He couldn't imagine life without Amaya.

Chapter 29:

Punching the Wall

Harvey stepped into the meeting room ahead of everyone and set a cup of cappuccino at the place to his left where Amaya always sat. He took a chocolate croissant from a paper bag—one of her few dietary weaknesses—and laid in on a plate.

Would she even show up? Harvey didn't know. She'd slipped out of the apartment while he was still asleep on the couch.

His back ached from lying on it, and his heart ached from losing the woman he loved. He shouldn't have sworn at Amaya and smashed the vase. He'd texted three apologies and emailed twice, but she hadn't responded.

His burner phone vibrated. Harvey stepped to the window and looked down. Clouds hung low, and a drizzle streaked the glass, but a half dozen tilted sailboats were out on the Charles, all in a clump, all going the same direction. A race, he supposed.

"Yes?" Harvey said.

"We went through the wallet you lifted from the injured hiker," Luke said. "You were right. He is a Russian agent."

"Why was he following Amaya and me?"

"Like you said, he probably thought you were meeting someone on the mountain."

"Amaya needs better protection," Harvey said, "as well as my mother and daughter, and…"

Several team members walked in, followed by Amaya.

Harvey said, "We'll talk later," and he pocketed the phone.

Amaya carried a cup of coffee. She didn't look at him.

He pulled the chair out for her, a gallantry that went unacknowledged.

He shouldn't be doing this. His clumsy efforts were making him look guilty. He remembered the furs and jewelry his father would buy after his trips to mythical medical conventions.

Amaya pushed the cappuccino aside and shoved the chocolate croissant across the table to the bearded, sticky-bun programmer. He'd been eyeing the plate like a hungry hound.

Harvey leaned close to Amaya and whispered into her ear, "We need to talk."

"I have nothing to say."

Harvey straightened up. "Well, I do, dammit!"

The techie paused, the croissant halfway to his mouth, then lowered his eyes and took a bite.

Others went silent. Then the last members of the team arrived, followed by Tucker.

The project manager lobbed a question at Harvey, who, out of the corner of his eye, read the answer Amaya had typed into her laptop.

He leaned close to her and whispered, "Thanks."

"I'm not doing this for you," she whispered back, "but because it's my job."

Then a dense, testy, and highly technical argument broke out between the lanky basketballer and the woman who always yawned. The pair were still split up. Harvey felt for them.

His thoughts drifted to earlier that morning, when he'd received an email from a prestigious journal enthusing over the article he'd sent them ten months earlier. Harvey had worried back then that they wouldn't print his paper on how civilization might have escaped the rise of Hitler if the Depression hadn't occurred, a What-If that existed in a parallel universe and, Harvey admitted, a trite and much-tread thesis.

So what if the damn paper got published or not? His life had taken a sharp turn into its own parallel universe. He had stepped from the narrow professor's lane to the... the what? The dark path of bogus technical writers, unpaid employees of the FBI, and his role as a lovelorn fool dumped by a fetching Russian spy. A world of hurt.

Still, Harvey thought himself a little special as he sat at this meeting surrounded by fresh-faced techies whose lives were open books—high school to college and right into well-paying, nine-to-five jobs. Wouldn't it be fun to blurt out that he, Harvey Hudson, was an international spy living at the raw edge of danger, sharing digs with a Russian agent, and he wasn't at all the mild and reflective fellow they took him to be?

The whimsy of fortune could well have led him down a different path. Some wealthy, white-haired, and addled alumnus could have stepped forward and written a check that saved Middlebridge College. Had that happened, Harvey imagined himself right this moment standing before a summer-school class and expounding on how Napoleon could have defeated the Russians had he properly planned for the harsh winter, and how that would have changed for decades the balance of power in Europe as well as just possibly blocking the later formation of the Soviet Union, and two boys in polo shirts would doze in the back row and, right in front of the lectern, a conscientious and sweetly moon-faced scholarship girl in jeans and sandals would scribble notes, and he'd be in bliss.

Or at least content. And unafraid.

There would be no Amaya, however. Also, no $250,000 to pay off his mother's mortgage. Plus, he was now leading a life of greater stimulation. Never had he pondered things so deeply, asked himself so many questions, thought harder, and found so many answers.

Life had become more exciting and infinitely more precious. Until now, his existence had progressed logically from one day to the next, one week to the next, one semester to the next. He'd been living in his comfort zone, in a bubble of contemplation and What-Ifs and Whys, an existence devoid of technical documentation, Igor and the toxic Boris, Luke and Elliott, and late-night pizza deliveries.

Everyone should be forced for one week of the year to slip out of their comfort zone and randomly switch occupations with someone else. Barbers should become bankers, bankers should become ballerinas, and ballerinas should become butchers as a way to keep their minds nimble and to better understand the lives that others lead.

Or maybe not. Harvey wasn't certain that these alliterative career swaps would always be advantageous. Would he want to step into an airliner piloted by a lobster trapper, and would he be all that comfortable having his appendix detached by a taxidermist? In fact...

In fact, everybody was staring at him.

Owen nudged him with his elbow.

Harvey glanced at Amaya's screen, then said, "Give Appendix B another read. If it's still not clear, then check back with me."

The project manager nodded.

The ex-couple renewed their noisy argument. Margo broke in and said, "Take it offline."

After the meeting, Harvey ran into Margo in the coffee room. Standing close to her—too close to her—was a tall, chiseled-chinned hunk in an expensive suit that Harvey couldn't afford, with a gold watch he couldn't afford, and a haircut he couldn't afford. Margo clutched the man's upper arm. She introduced him as Chad-Someone-Or-Other. A handshake ensued.

Harvey watched the attractive pair leave together, chatting and smiling. The hurt was much less intense than back in high school when he'd spotted Margo kissing Tucker in his shiny red convertible, or when Chandra had written from India and bubbled over with joy that she was soon to marry an orthodontist, or when Harvey had learned of Brenda's serial infidelities. Still, the sight pained him.

He and Margo weren't a match. He should actually be happy for her. So what was it that bothered him?

Well, he knew. She was a part of a couple, and he was alone.

Harvey felt like punching the coffee-room wall.

So he did.

Hard.

He broke through the wallboard and halfway up to his elbow.

Harvey twisted and turned to pull free.

Owen stepped into the room, stopped, and raised an eyebrow.

Harvey jerked his arm out. "Don't ask."

Chapter 30

Besties

Harvey pulled up in front of his mother's house, grabbed a bouquet of pink tulips off the front seat, and climbed out. He waved at the elderly woman raking the front yard of the ugly yellow colonial across the street. The rental sign was finally missing.

He was halfway up the walkway when his burner phone buzzed. Harvey stopped and answered. "I'm busy right now, Luke."

"Not that busy. I won't let you accept that offer."

"I guess you're listening in on my calls," Harvey said.

"Bet your ass I am. So?"

"So, Tufts University offered me a full professorship," Harvey said, "and my choice of courses. A dream job, starting in the fall."

"You can't quit, goddamn it!"

"What can you do about it?" Harvey asked.

"Make your life miserable."

"You've already made my life miserable," Harvey said. "Try to stop me, and I'll go to the press."

"You wouldn't do that."

"Just watch."

A long silence, then Luke said, "You're letting your country down."

"The head of the department said to take a week to think about her offer. But I don't need a week. I'm calling back this afternoon."

"Fuck!"

"And turning her down."

Silence, then Luke said, "I guess you've got a patriotic streak after all."

Harvey did, but wouldn't admit it to Luke. Besides, he didn't know if he was even ready to go back to all the stress that comes with academia. His life had changed. He had changed. "No, I'd just miss you and Elliot so darn much. You're a couple of really swell guys to hang out with."

"Everyone says so."

Harvey pocketed his phone.

His mother and Kathy greeted him at the door.

Harvey stepped inside and handed the tulips to his mother.

They hugged in a threesome.

His mother looked at his bandaged right wrist. "What happened?"

"I was trying to punch my way into a parallel universe."

"I have no idea what you're talking about, but I never have, even when you were a boy."

Kathy said, "Let me look at it."

She unwound the bandage and manipulated the bones.

Her hands felt warm and professional, and he felt loved and cared for. A reversal of roles. Here was the little girl who was always tipping over her tricycle and coming home with skinned knees for him to clean up and bandage. A lump filled his throat.

"Nothing broken," she said.

"Is this covered by my insurance?"

"The first consultation is free. Did you hit someone, Dad?"

"A wall."

"You're in the habit of hitting walls?"

"Only when they have it coming."

Harvey's mother stepped into the doorway, shaded her eyes

with her hand, looked toward the car, then turned back to Harvey. "So, where is she?"

"Amaya's not coming."

"That's a disappointment. Well, make sure to bring her next Sunday."

"She won't be able make it then, either."

His mother closed the door and gave Harvey a hard look. "Did you break up with her?"

"She broke up with me."

"Men always say that. What happened?"

"She accused me of cheating."

"Did you?"

"Of course not."

"Men always say that, too."

They shifted to the living room. Harvey and Kathy sat side-by-side on the couch. His mother snatched the plate of chocolate-chip cookies off the coffee table and walked to the kitchen. No cookies for him. Punishment for the breakup. That time he and Tommy had cut their mother's roses and sold them on the street, she'd deprived them of cookies for a week.

Kathy squeezed Harvey's good hand. "So, it's all over?"

"I hope not, but it looks like it."

"I'm sorry."

"Me too."

They sat in silence.

Harvey tried to tell himself this might be for the best. After all, things would get messy after the project ended. If the task force succeeded, the Russians would suspect Amaya and him as well. The FBI would put them into separate witness protection programs with fake names and fake pasts and possibly even arrange for plastic surgery. He would never see Amaya again. A lonely existence lay ahead.

Still, he loved her, and maybe there was a way to get her back.

"Did you read about that little boy?" his mother called from the kitchen.

Harvey looked up. "Uh… what little boy?"

"The one who'd wandered off from home and everyone thought was dead but turned up twenty-eight years later, safe and sound. Oklahoma, I think. Or maybe Arkansas."

Harvey had read the article, plus the follow-up disclosing that the man was an imposter after an inheritance.

"I did," Harvey said.

"One must never give up hope."

Harvey exchanged looks with Kathy, who shook her head and whispered, "Poor woman, she's never given up."

Harvey hadn't quite either. Two days earlier, he'd seen a man on the street who was the age Tommy would be if he had lived, and the man looked how Harvey thought Tommy would look, walking with a woman and two lanky teenage boys, all laughing over something.

Moments of magical thinking. Hard to shake.

His mother returned with a tray of tea and the plate of cookies.

Forgiveness.

The bell rang.

Harvey's mother hurried to the door. "That's Mary. She's just moved in across the street. I absolutely insisted she meet you, Harvey. She gave me all sorts of silly excuses not to, but I finally forced her into it."

A gray-haired woman with a cane stepped into the living room, air-kissed Harvey's mother on each cheek, hugged Kathy, shook hands with Harvey, dropped into the easy chair across from him, and spoke at length about her two grown sons living on the west coast, her twin granddaughters who both played the violin like angels, her arthritic hip, what a nice neighborhood this was, and back to her ailing hip, adding, "It's no fun growing old."

Not so old. She hadn't leaned on her cane when she came

through the door, her skin lacked age-appropriate wrinkles, and faint, brown roots were showing.

Why would a woman dye her hair gray?

Harvey leaned forward, took on a solicitous expression, and asked Mary about the ages of her grandchildren, where she'd lived before moving to Brookline, how long she'd lived in her previous home, and what schools she'd attended. All the stuff a spy master would ask and watch for a stumble. Then Harvey started over with the same questions, but coming at the subject from different directions to see if the woman would slip up.

"That's enough, Harvey." His mother turned to Mary. "My son is full of questions. He was just like that as a boy, trailing me all day long, asking strange things I could never answer."

The three women turned the conversation to politics, brands of herbal tea, and politics again. Then hugs all around, and Mary left. She seemed in a hurry to get away.

Harvey said, "How well do you know her?"

His mother held out the plate of cookies. "We're already best friends—well, almost, anyway. She's about my age, but much more fit and puts me to shame, and she has me walking for hours. We do yoga twice a week and go shopping together and to museums."

Harvey took a cookie. "You don't like museums, and you hate shopping."

"I sacrifice for Mary's sake. She lives alone in that big house. Her two sons have moved all the way across the country, and she's a widow like me. I feel sorry for her, so alone."

A nudge. Visit more often.

Kathy said she had to get back and study for an exam. Harvey offered to drive her home.

His mother poured the cookies from the plate into two plastic bags and handed one to Kathy and one to Harvey, then gave both of them long hugs at the door.

Kathy walked with Harvey to his car. "I'm sorry about Amaya."

"So am I."

"You'll find someone else."

Harvey shook his head. No one could ever replace Amaya.

*   *   *

By the time Harvey dropped Kathy off at her apartment, they'd eaten most of their cookies.

He hugged her goodbye and called Luke.

"Yeah?"

"Thanks," Harvey said. "I appreciate it."

"Appreciate what?"

"For planting that agent with the careless dye job in the house across the street from my mother."

Long pause. "You owe us."

"No, I don't. My mother wouldn't need protecting if you hadn't dragged me into your sleazy goddamn world of espionage."

"I wouldn't have had to drag you into my sleazy goddamn world of espionage if you hadn't outsourced your job."

True, Harvey thought. "In any case, you're taking care of my mother, so I guess you're not the unfeeling bastard I thought you were."

"You need to work on your compliments."

"What about my daughter?"

"We still have teams on her campus and others watching her apartment."

"Thanks."

"That's the spirit," Luke said.

"What about Amaya?"

"She's also under observation."

Harvey guessed that was for her protection but also to prevent her from taking off for Bora Bora. But it made sense they'd keep tabs on a turned Russian agent.

Luke said, "Amaya's alone a lot lately. Troubles?"

"Troubles."

"Figures." Luke said. "You must be a hard guy to live with."

"Speaking of which, you've been married, what, three times? Or is it four?"

"Keep in touch."

Chapter 31

That's a Problem?

Harvey wished that museum benches had backs because his own still throbbed from carrying the Russian off the hill and from sleeping on the couch. He'd been sitting on the same bench for almost an hour.

He'd called Amaya earlier in the day and invited her to join him at the Museum of Fine Arts for the new Monet exhibit. She hadn't committed to coming but had sounded interested. Or at least Harvey convinced himself she'd sounded interested. But no Amaya. He'd chosen this place to meet her because she liked the Impressionists.

So did Harvey, not just for their art but for the way they evoked Paris in the 19th century. He pictured himself back there, his favorite time in history, where he took on the role of Impressionist painter, a bearded and carefree frequenter of sidewalk cafes.

Sometimes when his students had looked especially inattentive, he would wake them up by asking them when and where in the past they would like to have lived. This got them sitting up. He discovered he had a classroom of queens, explorers, feted scientists, and fellow Impressionists. "What if you were a barefoot serf?" Harvey would ask. "Or a doomed soldier on Napoleon's frozen trek into Russia? Or a single mother of four, living in the

Middle Ages in a shack with a dirt floor and two abscessed teeth?"

Harvey Hudson, spoiler of time-travel reveries.

He himself would be a cavity-free Impressionist painter.

The guard had been giving Harvey suspicious glances after the first half hour, and so had the man at the far corner of the gallery—a burly fellow with meaty hands who was feigning an interest in a row of Monet's cathedrals.

It was no surprise that Igor had followed him, and it was no surprise that he himself had no trouble recognizing the giant with a fake black beard and tinted horn-rimmed glasses. It's hard to disguise oneself when one looks like a refrigerator in size sixteen loafers. Harvey had identified Igor that day in the drugstore without Igor's having caught on. That gave Harvey great satisfaction. He was learning the trade.

He waited another half hour for Amaya, then gave up and stepped outside.

A blast of wind and rain knocked him sideways. He opened his umbrella and watched it snap inside out and break. Lightning flashed, thunder boomed. Harvey dashed toward his car and lobbed his ruined umbrella into a trash can as he ran.

A hard, horizontal gust shivered across the puddles in the parking lot. Water ran down Harvey's face and the back of his neck. His socks were squishy. He jumped into his car, grabbed a handful of Pete's napkins ("Rated Best Pizza in Boston Two Years in a Row!"), wiped his face, neck and hair and spotted Igor splashing through the puddles.

And a man trotting a couple dozen paces behind.

Harvey started his engine and turned on the wipers. He recognized the second man as the leathery goon who'd whisked the injured hiker away at gunpoint after Harvey had carried him down Mount Monadnock. Small world.

He guessed Igor and the man behind him were operating as a surveillance team.

Then Igor looked over his shoulder and broke into a run. So did the second man.

Not a team.

Harvey jerked out his phone to call Luke.

Igor ran out of the parking lot and turned left, the other man close behind.

Harvey lowered his phone.

Just sit back and let things play out? Without Igor around, Amaya would be safer.

No, he couldn't let anyone get hurt, even Igor.

No time to call. Harvey put the car in gear, squealed out of the lot, and turned left.

Igor and the other man crossed the trolley tracks at Huntington Avenue and turned right.

Harvey swung onto the street.

He watched the pair turn left into Ruggles Street.

Harvey laid on his horn and cut left across approaching traffic. Brakes squealed, and horns blared. A hulking, black delivery van banged into the right rear fender of Harvey's car, sending it sliding sideways. Harvey spun the wheel to the left, straightened out, and floored the accelerator.

Then braked. Hard.

Traffic had stopped ahead of him.

Damn! Damn! Damn!

The pursuer was getting closer and closer to Igor.

Harvey beeped the horn.

Cars didn't move.

The wipers thumped back and forth, beating out lost time.

He honked again. And again. Nothing.

Harvey cranked the steering wheel to the right, thumped up over the curb, and drove down the sidewalk.

Igor crossed Parker Street and disappeared down the next street to the right. The other man followed.

Harvey swung back onto the street, sped through a red light, and turned the wrong way down the one-way street where he'd last seen Igor and his pursuer.

Both had disappeared.

Harvey slowed to a crawl and glanced to the right. A tall fence. Too high to climb. He squinted straight ahead. No one there. Harvey looked left.

There!

He slammed on his brakes, backed up, and swung into a tiny parking lot just in time to see the killer stab Igor.

Igor clutched his shoulder and staggered backwards.

The attacker stepped closer.

Harvey gunned the engine. The tires squealed.

Igor's attacker spun around to look.

Thump!

Harvey slammed on his brakes.

The man slid halfway up the hood on his stomach, arms outstretched, eyes wide open, face-to-face with Harvey, then he slowly slipped off.

Harvey jumped out of his car.

The man lay motionless.

Harvey kicked the knife away, then bent closer. Had he killed him?

He shook the man's shoulder. No movement.

Dead.

Oh my God!

Igor lay on the ground and moaned. Harvey rushed over to him.

Now what? He had two Russian agents on his hands, one maybe dead and one maybe dying.

Call Luke.

Harvey reached for his phone and staggered sideways. The left side of his face exploded in pain.

Igor's attacker swung his fist again.

Harvey ducked, planted his feet, stiffened, and threw a hard uppercut to the jaw.

Teeth clanked.

The man fell.

Harvey bent down and shook him, then slapped him across the face. Hard. No reaction. Another slap. Blood flowed from both sides of the man's mouth. This time he was down for the count.

"Want me to call an ambulance?"

Harvey straightened up and turned around. An elderly man stood at the cross street, both hands holding a dripping newspaper over his head.

"I've already called," Harvey said. He pulled out his wallet and flashed his defunct Middlebridge faculty card. "I'm with the FBI—you don't want to get mixed up in this."

The man scurried off.

Harvey dragged the would-be killer to his car, tied the man's belt around his wrists, dumped him into the trunk, and grabbed a first aid kit tucked into the spare tire well. He slammed the trunk closed, hurried over to Igor, kneeled beside him, ripped his shirt open, and taped a wide bandage onto his shoulder.

Harvey said, "Who are you?"

That's how a professional spy would handle things. Pretend he didn't know who Igor was.

Igor said nothing. His eyes were glassy.

Harvey put his arm around Igor's waist, helped him to his feet, walked him to the backseat of the car, eased him inside, and slammed the door.

Igor slumped in the seat and closed his eyes.

Harvey stepped away and called Luke.

"What do you want?" Luke asked.

"We have to meet."

"In this weather?

"Igor's been stabbed. I rammed his assailant with my car, then knocked him out."

Long pause. "You've gotta be kidding."

"Meet me at Benson Hospital—it's the closest one."

"No, that'll bring in the police. I know someone who'll patch those two up. Where are you?"

Harvey told him.

"I'll be there in five."

"Hurry," Harvey said, "I've got one Russian agent bleeding all over my backseat, and a second one tied up in the trunk."

"That's a problem?"

Chapter 32

Your Merry Career as Assassin

Harvey spotted a police car approaching. He crouched behind the dumpster at the end of the parking lot, heard the cruiser back up, idle, then drive on. Harvey's pulse thumped.

Just minutes later, Luke swung into the lot and slammed to a stop. He jumped out of his car, opened the trunk, and grabbed a jack handle.

Harvey stepped out from behind the dumpster.

Luke walked over and stood beside him. "Open your trunk."

Harvey eyed the jack handle. "The hell I will."

"It's not what you think. I'll use this only if the guy tries to escape."

Harvey hesitated, then hurried to his car and opened the trunk.

The passenger moaned.

"Still alive," Luke said and slammed the trunk closed. "I'll ride with you."

They jumped into Harvey's car and pulled away.

Luke turned to Igor, slouched in the back seat, his eyes half closed. "Why did that guy stab you?"

No reply.

"Don't want to talk? We'll see about that," Luke said and turned to face forward.

Harvey handed him a billfold and whispered, "This belongs to the goon in the trunk. His driver's license and charge card say he's Vladimir Volkov. He's the guy who drove off with that injured hiker."

"I'll get him run through the database." Luke whispered back. "Turn right at the next light. I've already warned the doc we're on our way."

"Why not a hospital?"

"I told you: We don't want these two goobers on the books. Turn right at the next street."

Harvey did. "Is he a real doctor?"

"Yup. He regularly does stuff for us and for mobsters with gunshot wounds that they don't want reported."

Harvey looked over at Luke. "You have a dicey circle of acquaintances."

"You among them."

At Luke's signal, Harvey turned west on Huntington Avenue.

Luke threw his arm over the seat back and said to Igor, "One more time: Why did the thug in the trunk try to stab you?"

No answer.

Luke asked the same question again, only louder.

Still no answer.

"We know exactly who you are," Luke said. "You're Igor Baranov."

Harvey glanced in the rearview mirror. Igor was shaking his head.

"My name is Leonid Novikoff," Igor said in heavily accented English. "I am tourist. I am injured. Take me now to doctor."

"A tourist, huh?"

"Yes. And I am hurting bad."

"So am I," Luke said. "It hurts me when someone lies to me."

"I am visitor to your country. A very bad thief attacked me."

"Bullshit."

"No, is true."

Luke turned and faced forward. "Swing around, Harvey. We'll take this peckerhead to the usual spot north of town where the outgoing tides are the strongest."

"Uh... right."

Harvey did a U-turn.

Igor said, "You cannot do that to me!"

"Wait and see," Luke said. "Your pal in the trunk is also going for a late-night swim. The world will be a better place without you two shitbirds."

Harvey glanced over at Luke. A bluff? For real?

Then Luke gave him two more turns that led away from the ocean.

Harvey relaxed. But only a little. He was still driving around town with two Russian agents in his car, one bleeding in his backseat and the other unconscious in his trunk.

Igor groaned.

Luke said, "You can let us drown you in the ocean—providing you haven't bled out in the meantime—or you can cooperate, and we'll get you fixed up. I don't know why the jerk in the trunk tried to kill you, but I assume you've been targeted for some reason, and the next guy who comes after you will take you out. If not him, then the one after that. We could protect you, but it sounds like you'd rather go for a swim."

Igor was quiet for a minute.

"Well?" Luke said.

"I will cooperate. Take me to doctor."

"A smart move," Luke said.

"Where to?" Harvey asked.

"Just keep going straight."

So, they'd been driving toward the doctor's office all along.

Luke said, "Is the guy in the trunk a fellow agent?"

A hesitation, then "Yes."

"Why would he try to kill you?" Luke asked.

"He got sent by my boss. I sleep with his wife."

"Boris's wife?"

"Yes."

"Not smart," Luke said. "Why in hell did you do that?"

"I was drunk. She seduced me. Several times that happens. I could not stop her."

"I'm sure you couldn't," Luke said. "Why did Boris make the hit in a public place? Why didn't he just send someone to poison you?"

"To look like a mugging here in the U.S. so Russian police do not get involved."

"He sent you all the way to the States just to get killed?"

"No," Igor said. "He did not know yet I sleep with wife. Later he find out."

"What was your mission here?"

"They sent me to study the situation."

"'The situation?'" Luke said. "You'll have to be more specific if you don't want to end up sucking salt water."

"They said, 'Go find out if everything is okay over here.'"

Luke said, "What does 'everything' mean?"

"I do not know. They do not give details."

"That's bullshit," Luke said. "If you didn't know what they'd sent you here to look for, then how in hell could you assess the situation?" Luke tapped Harvey's shoulder. "Turn around and head back to the ocean."

"Wait! Wait!" Igor shouted. "We broke into the T&M Consultants' network. We will destroy your pipeline pumps and economy and raise gas prices for good of Russia."

"You've got to be kidding," Luke said. "I don't believe it."

"It is true. Now take me to a doctor."

"Only if you keep talking."

Igor did. He told everything he knew, which confirmed

everything that Harvey, Luke, and the task force already knew.

The world of spies and counterspies is a complicated place, Harvey told himself. Lies on top of lies on top of more lies. His new world.

Igor said, "We have also agent here named Amaya Patel."

Luke said, "No kidding?"

Harvey took a deep breath. A big relief. The Russians didn't know that Amaya had turned. He lifted his foot off the accelerator because he thought that was what a good spy would do after hearing such startling information. "Amaya?"

"Yes."

"She can't be!" Harvey said.

"She is."

"She's... uh...," Harvey said, filling his voice with hurt.

"She's your lady friend," Igor said with a weak laugh. "But she is not. She has you twisted around her... her... uh..."

"'Little finger,'" Luke offered.

"Yes, that. And you have even a codename. I will tell you what it is."

Harvey knew already. "Don't."

"*Lovelorn*," Igor said.

He chuckled. So did Luke.

Harvey leaned over the steering wheel, looked straight into the night, and said nothing.

*   *   *

The doctor's office was above a hardware store on a side street of a broken section of Boston. Lightning flashed, thunder rumbled, and rain fell in buckets. Harvey parked in an alley. He and Luke took Igor by the arms and together walked him up the back stairs to the doctor's office. They stretched him out on the examination table, then carried Vladimir up and laid him on the floor.

The doctor was a fragile and elderly man, with a shaggy gray mustache and nervous eyes.

Luke introduced Harvey as 'Marvin Miller,' but didn't tell Harvey the doctor's name or identify the wounded Russians for the doctor, who didn't seem to expect to be told.

He made a quick examination of both men. "I'll start with the one that got hit by the car."

"Nope," Luke said. "The one on the examination table."

The doctor shrugged and lifted a corner of Igor's bandage, no questions asked. A guy accustomed to dealing with mob bosses. Did the doctor know that Luke was with the FBI? Would he have cared?

Harvey looked around. The room had a sink, a plaid easy chair, several glass-front cabinets of bandages and bottles, and a shelf supporting a couple dozen medical books and a dozing black cat.

Also, a framed diploma on the wall from Harvard Medical School.

"Is that for real?" Harvey asked.

The doctor was scrubbing up in a stained sink. He looked up. "It certainly is. I was second in my class and for twenty-two years was on the staff at Mass General, but I took a liking to painkillers, and I ingested a few too many one day and collapsed in the operating room. I lost my license, of course.

Harvey stepped closer to the diploma. The date was the year before his father had graduated from Harvard Medical School.

Harvey opened his mouth to ask if the doctor had known his father, then remembered that Luke had introduced him as Marvin Miller. "My late father was a well-regarded surgeon."

The doctor snapped on a pair of blue latex gloves. "Which means he probably never collapsed in the operating room."

"Actually, he did. He died of a heart attack and speared his patient on the way down."

The doctor laughed, then looked up and said, "I'm sorry."

"So am I."

If his father had lived, he would be retired by now and probably beyond the age of Caribbean excursions with curvy nurses, and he would stay home and be a companion to his wife.

Across the room, Vladimir groaned and rolled onto his side.

The doctor paused, needle and thread in hand, and said to Harvey. "Go check his pulse. Tell me if it's low, or if he falls back unconscious or turns pale."

Harvey kneeled beside Vladimir and took his pulse. Fifty-eight, which was low, but the guy had been unconscious. His coloring looked okay, however, and now and then he moved his head.

It felt good to be taking care of someone, even a Russian assassin. Harvey wondered if he should have become a doctor.

Vladimir opened his eyes and raised himself on his elbows. "Why did you hit me with your car?"

His English was stiff but correct, with a slight British accent.

"To save you from a murder charge."

"Who are you?"

"I'm an international agent," Harvey said.

He liked the sound of that, then realized that the man he'd bashed into with his car really was an international agent.

Vladimir lay back. "Are you going to turn me over to the police?"

Harvey had no idea, but he said, "Not if you cooperate."

"Cooperate? If my people found that out, I'd be as good as dead."

"They won't find out. You just have to give us a bit of innocuous information, and I promise we'll patch you up. Soon you'll be free to continue your merry career as an assassin. Now tell me, when did you—"

"I'll take over," Luke said, shoving Harvey out of the way.

"But I was doing so well."

"Yeah, sure. Okay, Vladimir, how long have you been in the country?"

"Two days."

"So, you're not a permanent resident agent?

"No."

"Why should I believe you?" Luke asked.

"I've got a plane ticket," Vladimir said and patted his jacket pocket. "Now get the doctor over here to fix me up."

Luke ignored the order and went through Vladimir's pockets. He pulled out the plane ticket and handed it to Harvey.

The ticket was in Russian. Harvey read it. "This checks out."

Just a garden-variety hitman. Several levels below international spy.

The doctor walked over and kneeled beside Vladimir. "The man with the stab wound will pull through. Give me room so I can see about this one."

Harvey got to his feet, went to the surgical table, and rested his hand on Igor's bandaged shoulder. "What's the post-mission plan for Amaya?"

"I don't know."

Harvey pressed down on the bandage.

"Ow! Ow!"

"Well?"

Again, no answer.

Harvey's stomach seized. What a terrible person he'd become. But he pushed harder.

Igor yelped. "She knows too much."

"And?"

"You can guess."

"Tell me."

"Moscow will send someone to kill her."

Chapter 33

A Full Moon

Amaya wasn't at her desk when Harvey arrived at work the next morning, but her laptop was gone, which meant she was somewhere in the building. Still angry with him, she no longer worked in their shared office, but would grab her computer off her desk and head for an empty conference room. The office was quiet and lonely now. Harvey was beginning to miss his cubicle and even the racket from his golfing coworkers in the coffee room.

He set a vase of red roses on Amaya's desk, sat at his own, took out his burner phone, and called Luke. "How are Vladimir and Igor doing?"

"They'll heal okay. I found a regular FBI doc to check them out."

"I'm relieved I hadn't killed someone."

That wasn't something Harvey ever thought he would hear himself say. "What're you doing with the two?"

"We're hanging onto Vladimir. Our friends in the CIA can arrange it to look like he defected and slipped over the Canadian border."

"What about Igor?"

"We'll convince the Russians that Vladimir had killed him, and that the Boston police believe it was a mugger. We'll keep Igor for now—I don't know what we'll eventually do with him. He claims to have turned, but we're wary. By the way, you did good last night."

"Did I actually hear you compliment me?"

"Don't let it go to your head."

Harvey pocketed his phone just as Amaya stepped into the office, her laptop clamped under her arm.

He got up from his desk and took a step toward her. "Good morning."

Amaya steered around him and sat at her desk. She didn't look up.

Harvey cleared his throat. "I said 'Good morning.'"

"I heard you."

Amaya pushed the vase of roses aside and pulled a manila folder from her desk drawer.

Harvey said, "Margo has a boyfriend."

"I heard."

"Doesn't that make a difference?"

Amaya opened the folder and thumbed through the papers. "Women cheat on their boyfriends, just as men cheat on their girlfriends."

"Talk to Margo. She'll tell you nothing's going on between us."

"Of course she'll say that."

Amaya glanced up at Harvey, hesitated, then said, "Does it hurt?"

"Yes, it hurts like hell. I miss you every minute of the day."

"No, I meant your black eye."

Harvey had forgotten that Vladimir had punched him. The eye didn't hurt much, but Harvey said, "It feels like it's on fire."

"Owen said you walked into a door. Don't tell me you got into a fight?"

"I got into a fight."

Harvey closed the door, came back, and sat on the edge of Amaya's desk. He described the stabbing attack on Igor and his own battle with Vladimir, characterizing it as a deadly man-to-man duel and leaving out the part about how he'd rammed into the guy from the safety of the car. Then he spoke of Luke's arrival, the trip to the mob doctor, and Igor's decision to cooperate.

Amaya's jaw dropped. "You could have been killed."

Harvey honestly hadn't thought about it. He flashed on his mother and Kathy, side-by-side on the white couch, hugging and weeping, acting out the script penned for a cruel and alternate universe.

"But I wasn't."

Amaya bit her lower lip, picked up a rose, and sniffed it.

Was it time now to hug her? Or let her come to him? Harvey couldn't decide. "With Igor now on our side, you can relax."

Not really, but Harvey didn't want to upset Amaya. From the couch, he'd heard her shouting in her sleep the night before. He'd tried to join her in bed to comfort her, but she'd ordered him away.

Still, he wanted to be honest with her, at least in important matters. He and Brenda had lived in a swarm of lies. He'd told mostly fibs. She told whoppers. Only too late did he learn that her business was a disaster and that she was sleeping with her partner.

Harvey hesitated, rested his hand on Amaya's shoulder and said, "One more thing you should know: Igor told us that, after this business is over, the Russians have... uh... plans for you."

Harvey couldn't force himself to say *kill*.

Amaya nodded. "I expected that."

Her voice was flat.

"I won't let anything happen to you," Harvey said, his hand still on her shoulder. "I love you."

"I know."

He waited for her to say, 'And I love you.'

Instead, she lifted his hand from her shoulder, grabbed her laptop, and stood up.

Harvey held his arms out for a hug.

Amaya slipped around him and scurried to the door.

Harvey let his arms drop to his sides. "I'm going to drive to the harbor this evening, park at that spot we like, and listen to music. It's supposed to be a beautiful night with a full moon. It'll be relaxing. We both need that. Come with me, and we can talk things over."

"'Things?'"

"How we can keep you safe. There'll be a full moon."

"You already mentioned the moon."

Amaya hesitated, the door halfway open, and clutched her laptop tightly to her chest.

Was she coming back for a hug?

She wasn't.

She stepped halfway out, turned and said, "Just for an hour but no more."

*   *   *

Harvey was pacing back and forth in the hallway outside his office and struggling to think of something that would convince Amaya that he wasn't cheating on her, when he spotted Margo walking toward him. The head of finance was at her side. She said to Margo, "What's your niece going to do now that she's graduated from high school?"

"She's bumming around Europe this summer with her boyfriend. Then they're both going to the University of Maine in the fall."

Yes! Yes!

Harvey had forgotten that Margo had been out of town for the graduation.

He hurried to Margo's office. The administrative assistant was sitting behind her desk. "Yes?"

"Is she in?"

Eleanor shook her head. "She just left for a meeting."

"I wanted to talk to her about taking some extra vacation time."

"Let's see when she's free."

Eleanor reached into her top desk drawer, pulled out Margo's calendar, spread it open, wrote something in it, and slipped it back into the drawer. "You can see her at two-thirty today."

Eleanor used her computer as little as possible. No one said anything because she was sweet and motherly and liked by everyone, and Harvey felt guilty for having to steal her calendar.

Which he did when she carried a note into Margo's office.

The sticky-bun programmer walked in just as Harvey was leaving. Good. Another suspect. Harvey would return the calendar the next morning.

*   *   *

Harvey parked at the edge of the harbor, with his car facing the water.

Amaya said, "What's that big dark spot on your back seat?"

"Uh… tomato sauce. I dropped a pizza face down."

"That's a lot of tomato sauce for just one pizza."

Igor had bled a lot. "That's how Pete makes them."

Amaya pointed at the sky. "There's that full moon you advertised."

It sent a golden strip of light rippling across the water. A brightly lit dinner boat rumbled past, sending a V of waves lapping onto shore.

Harvey unwrapped a bouquet-shaped air freshener and hung it on his rearview mirror.

Amaya said, "Do we really need that?"

"Wait."

They waited.

Another boat pulled out, hurtling rock music across the water. A booze cruise, Harvey guessed.

He said, "Does that scent remind you of how I smelled when I came home that night, and you thought it was Margo's perfume?"

Amaya leaned close to the air purifier and sniffed. "Maybe some. But that doesn't really prove your case."

"This will," Harvey said. He turned on the dome light, reached into the glove compartment, and pulled out the admin assistant's calendar. He opened it, laid it across Amaya's lap, and tapped a date.

She bent down to look. "Oh."

"Margo caught a flight to Pittsburgh at 8:35 in the morning on the day I came home late," Harvey said, "and returned on the 8:10 p.m. flight a day later."

"Oh."

"Margo was attending her niece's graduation."

Amaya nodded.

Here's where Harvey had expected her to tumble into his arms, a warm bundle of sobs and tears and apologies.

Instead, Amaya didn't move. She fumbled with the handle of her purse and pushed her hair behind her ear.

Harvey waited.

Then Amaya threw her arms around him. "I'm sorry, I'm so sorry."

He hugged her. Her tears wet his neck. He felt like crying, too. He swallowed hard and stammered, "Marry me."

Amaya pulled away, stared, opened her mouth but said nothing.

"I want you to marry me," Harvey said.

She dove back into his arms. "Yes, yes. Of course, I'll marry you."

They cuddled and kissed and shed tears and talked about the little white house they'd someday own. Amaya wanted a dog, and Harvey said okay as long as she walked it and bagged the poop. He wanted an astronomical observatory for the backyard, and she said as long as it wasn't too big and one of those ugly round things. They talked about trips to India to meet her family, hiking in the New Hampshire mountains, and flowered wallpaper in the bedrooms—Harvey hated wallpaper, but she loved it—something to work out later. They planned winter jaunts to the Caribbean, summer trips to Paris, skiing, snoozing late on weekends, and hugging in front of the fireplace. A normal life lived by normal people.

They didn't discuss the Russians and Boris and how this ugly business would eventually end.

Harvey slipped the engagement ring on Amaya's finger. She held her hand up, studied the ring the dome light, and again burst into tears.

He wiped them away, kissed her on the top of her head, stroked her hair, kissed her again, and then they started home. They said nothing on the way. They had happily talked themselves out.

Bliss, Harvey thought.

He stopped the car out front of his place, and they renewed their discussion about the future, followed by a few more sniffles, and then Amaya yawned and said she was exhausted.

Harvey walked her inside and upstairs to the apartment, then returned to his car. The tank's warning light had been on for several miles, so he drove to the self-service gas station a few blocks away, floating on a puffy white cloud of happiness. What if all of life was this wonderful? If that became the norm, would people still find reasons to complain?

They would. People always managed to find something to gripe about—the heat, the cold, in-laws, and income taxes. What would his ancestors think if they could catch a glimpse into the modern world of life-saving vaccinations and automobiles, painless dentistry and flush toilets? Wouldn't they wonder how we could find anything at all to complain about?

He would have to tuck that somewhere into *Big History: The Birth and Death of Everything.*

Adrift in thought, Harvey filled the tank, climbed back into his car, closed the door, and heard a banging on the side window. He turned to look.

A man was tapping the muzzle of his pistol on the glass. "Get out!"

Chapter 34

I Don't Think I Was Smiling

Harvey looked at the man, the gun, the man again. He was tall and muscular and angry.

"Get out! Now!"

A thick Russian accent.

Drive away? No, the guy would shoot him as soon as he reached for the starter.

Harvey took his time unhooking his shoulder belt so he could slip his burner phone under the seat.

"Out!"

Is this really happening?

Harvey opened the door a crack, placed both hands firmly against it, and slammed it into the Russian.

The man stumbled backwards and dropped his pistol.

Harvey leaped out of the car, bent down, and reached for the gun. Bang!

A bullet sparked off the pavement near his hand.

Harvey jerked it back, straightened up, and swung around.

It was a short, dark-haired woman with narrow eyes and a large pistol.

She held it in both hands and waved it toward the black van parked a few feet away, its rear door open.

The man staggered to his feet and punched Harvey in the face. Harvey stumbled sideways.

The man swung again.

Harvey ducked.

"That's enough, Viktor!"

He hesitated, then picked up his gun and shoved it into his belt. He seized Harvey by the upper arm, steered him to the van, slammed him facing up against it, and emptied his pockets.

The woman handed Viktor a black scarf. He tied it around Harvey's eyes and shoved him inside and onto the floor.

Harvey heard Viktor getting in beside him and felt his gun pressed against his aching cheek.

Viktor said, "Elena, do you want me to drive?"

"No, stay back there and guard him."

Doors slammed. The van took off.

Harvey lay on the hard floor and listened for police sirens. None. Just another random shot in the night. Nothing worth reporting.

Elena drove slowly, not wanting to attract attention. A trained operative.

The calendar. Harvey remembered that the calendar was still in his car. He wouldn't be able to return it, and Margo's poor assistant would search all over. Stupid to be thinking of this now.

He counted left turns and right turns and estimated how far they'd driven from one turn to the next, but soon lost track.

The ribbed metal floor hurt Harvey with each bounce, and his cheek throbbed where Viktor had punched him.

This had to be connected to the Russian's planned cyberattack. They must have been following his car, but had waited for him to be alone. They wanted him as a hostage to keep Amaya in line.

The van slowed, took a sharp left, crept along for a few hundred feet, then stopped.

Harvey heard the front door open, then the sliding door. Viktor grabbed him by the arm and dragged him out. The air smelled of car exhaust and cat piss. A narrow alley, Harvey guessed.

Viktor pushed him inside a building, walked him down a hallway, turned him to the right, and gave him a shove.

Harvey felt carpeting underfoot. The air smelled of dust and mold. Viktor yanked off the scarf.

It wasn't the abandoned warehouse Harvey had expected from movies and television, but a spacious first-floor sitting room with dark-wood paneling and tall windows, their curtains closed.

Viktor shoved him backwards onto a wooden chair.

Dust particles floated beneath three floor lamps with glass beads dangling from their shades, casting pale yellow circles on the brown carpet. A floor-standing globe stood nearby, three feet across. It was old and yellowed and unaware of the breakup of the Soviet Union.

Portraits of the long-dead lined the walls, scowling men with mutton-chops, grim women in black dresses, all staring down and judging, horrified at what had become of their refined Boston townhouse. Harvey guessed the Russians had rented the place from the estate of a centenarian who'd dwelled here for decades with cats and fading memories.

Viktor waved his pistol in Harvey's face and said over his shoulder to Elena, "We should have just shot the guy and dumped him in the harbor."

Harvey shuddered and tried not to let it show. He couldn't let them know he understood Russian.

Viktor tapped Harvey on the forehead with the barrel of his gun. "Maybe I'll cut his balls off and shove them down his throat."

"Stop fooling around," Elena said. "Come over here and sit down."

Viktor hesitated, then joined Elena at the table next to a bow window. They rotated their chairs toward Harvey.

Viktor said, "How long are we going to hold this guy?"

"Until Boris is through with him."

Boris? Boris the poisoner? Boris the torturer? The man who'd sent a hitman to kill Igor?

"Why's this jerk so important?" Viktor asked.

"He's the guy who works for that company that writes the software for those stupid oil pumps."

Viktor turned to Harvey and grinned. "That's Lovelorn?"

"That's him."

Viktor laughed.

Elena laughed.

Harvey didn't.

Viktor said, "He's a big guy."

"That's why Boris told me we both had to guard him at the same time."

Viktor picked up his gun and sighted it at a gloomy, bearded ancestor with his thumbs looped into his vest. "I liked it better when we worked for Igor."

"Me, too."

"Too bad a mugger killed him," Viktor said.

"Life is dangerous in America."

Viktor nodded toward Harvey. "Especially for Lovelorn."

Again Viktor and Elena laughed, and again Harvey didn't.

*   *   *

Harvey recognized Boris from the photo Luke had shown him a few weeks earlier: the wrinkled face, the heavy black eyebrows, and the cranky expression. He was a stout man in an expensive blue suit, shiny gray tie, and black Nikes with thick white soles. A big eater with foot problems.

Boris dragged a wooden rocker in front of Harvey and sat down with a wheeze.

I'm not supposed to know who he is, Harvey reminded himself, so he said, "Who in hell are you, and what do you want with me?"

Boris shifted in his chair. It creaked. He said, "I ask the questions."

He spoke slow and formal English.

A line from a bad movie. Well, this was a bad movie. Harvey searched for his next line. "You have to let me go."

Boris snorted. "I will, but only after you've answered a few simple questions."

Yeah, sure. "People will come looking for me."

"No one knows where you are."

Luke might. He'd bragged that the FBI had watchers at the Russian's safe house on Nickols Street.

If this was Nickols Street.

Harvey said, "I have nothing to tell you. I'm a former college professor, divorced and living alone, close to broke, and I work as a lowly technical writer at an excruciatingly dull job I've had for only a few months. Nothing I write about is important."

"You mean that nothing that Amaya writes about is important."

Amaya, of course. They didn't expect to get much information from him but had snatched him to put pressure on her. What made them think they had to do that? Had her brother and family slipped away, or did the Russians somehow fear that Amaya was getting ready to turn? Or maybe that's just what they did with operatives they'd forced into cooperating.

"I'll admit it," Harvey said. "I'd lose my job if it weren't for Amaya. We work well together."

"And you live together."

Harvey wondered how much else they knew.

Again, he asked Boris who he was. The next line in a clichéd script.

Boris shrugged.

Harvey said, "How do you know so much about me, and why are you so interested in me?"

Boris lit a cigarette. Smoke crawled out of his nose and up his forehead. "I'm a private investigator hired by Lotus Worldwide Consultants to learn who's selling trade secrets to their competitors. Amaya is just one person on a long list of employees. If what you tell me clears her, I'll release you, leave town, and move on to the next suspect."

The cover story made little sense, but Harvey felt it best not to point that out.

"Okay," he said. "Ask your questions and let me go."

Boris glanced at his watch. "It's already three in the morning. We'll start tomorrow." He turned to Viktor and said in Russian, "Go get today's newspaper. There's a kiosk right out front."

Why a newspaper?

Boris lit another cigarette.

Harvey sweated.

Viktor returned a minute later, out of breath, and handed a copy of *The Boston Globe* to Boris.

He tossed it to Harvey.

Harvey said, "You want me to read to you?"

"Wise guy," Boris said. "Hold up the first page in front of you."

Harvey did.

Boris reached inside his suit jacket and pulled out his phone.

Just like what he'd seen captives do in movies, Harvey told himself. Except this time, he was the poor jerk holding up the paper.

Boris raised his phone. It flashed once, twice, three times. "I know you're telling yourself that Amaya will show this photo to the police, and they'll come rushing to your rescue. But no one knows where you are. And Amaya won't tell anyone that we've grabbed you because we'll make it clear to her that, if she does, the next picture of you will be a basketful of Harvey Hudson parts."

Boris laughed and shook all over.

Harvey trembled inside, but felt compelled to say, "Take another photo. I don't think I was smiling."

Boris grunted and said in Russian, "Elena, you and Viktor escort our comedian to the guest room."

Harvey leaned forward to stand up, then caught himself and eased back down. He wasn't supposed to know Russian. He had to be careful, very careful.

And figure out how to escape.

Boris stood up, eyed Harvey and smiled his awful smile. "Sleep well."

Chapter 35

Calf Raising for Fun and Profit

Harvey did not sleep well. He had his standard nightmare, with Tommy calling to him. "Save me, Harvey! Save me!" Over and over. Harvey flailed his arms in the water, getting nowhere.

Harvey jumped out of bed at dawn, turned on the light, paced, did twenty push-ups, paced again, then did twenty more push-ups.

The Russians had locked him into a third-floor room, fourteen steps in one direction and seventeen in the other, with a closet-sized bathroom. The room had a narrow bed with a scratchy purple quilt, an empty, three-drawer dresser, two plastic folding chairs, and a round wooden table with cigarette burns around the edge. Steel bars crisscrossed a single window of filthy double-layered glass that muffled the sounds from the street below, as well as any cries for help from the room's desperate occupant.

On the table lay a thick tome on molecular biology, a Russian-language hiking guide to the English Midlands, and a slim pamphlet entitled "Calf Raising for Fun and Profit." The corner of a stack of porn magazines peeked out from under the bed.

The rose-patterned wallpaper took Harvey back to when he and Tommy helped his mother plant tulips along the walkway. A world away.

What was she doing now? And Kathy, Amaya, and Margo?

Harvey climbed back into bed, dozed, then woke up with a start and felt hungry. He hoped they'd feed him. He hoped they wouldn't torture him. He hoped he could escape.

Not easy and maybe not even necessary. Amaya would ignore Boris's threats and show Luke the photo Boris had sent her. In fact, Luke would have probably already intercepted the picture of the forlorn prisoner holding up the newspaper. According to Luke, the FBI knew the location of the Russian safe house, so just be patient. Help was on the way.

What would his mother and Kathy think when he didn't answer his phone, text messages, or emails, and when his car turned up abandoned at a gas station? The poor women. If he hadn't outsourced his job, none of this would have happened, nor if he hadn't taken a high-tech job for which he was unqualified, if Middlebridge college hadn't botched their finances, nor if he'd taken a teaching job somewhere else.

Nor if this, nor if that—all reaching back to the beginning of time, back to the Big Bang.

Life was a series of bad decisions and good decisions but mostly blind chance.

A key rattled in the door. Harvey jumped to his feet.

Viktor came in first, carrying a tray. Elena followed, pointing her pistol at Harvey. Viktor set the breakfast on the table and stepped away. He and Elena backed out the door, not taking their eyes off him, not saying a word.

Harvey sat down to two slices of burned toast, a lukewarm cup of instant black coffee, and a spotted banana. There was no cutlery to turn into a weapon. The plate was paper. The coffee arrived in a cardboard cup.

Harvey lifted a slice of toast and had it halfway to his mouth, then hesitated. Poisoned? Boris had a nasty reputation for that sort of thing. Still, if they'd wanted to kill him, they wouldn't have gone to the bother of abducting him. So he took a bite. White bread, burned but nevertheless tasty. He thought of the cardboard-flavored, super-healthy loaves Kathy would bring him. He missed her. What was she doing now? He pictured her rushing—she never showed up early for anything—to a class for instructions on removing a defective spleen.

Harvey was already lonely, and he actually wished his two captors had lingered. They knew only a few words of English, and he couldn't let on that he spoke Russian, but just their presence would have been comforting. Locked up for less than half a day, and here he was, already lonesome.

He finished eating, walked to the window, and shook the bars. Easy, then harder. Then really hard. He pictured himself on the sidewalk below, scampering away.

He had to get control of himself. He'd once watched a documentary about men serving life terms without parole. They for the most part looked docile, accepting, sleepily looking forward to the next cigarette, the next meal, the next few turns in the yard.

Harvey sat on the edge of his bed, massaged the side of his face where Viktor had slugged him, and told himself there was even a slight possibility that the Russians might let him go if he promised to keep his mouth shut. But long before that, Luke and the FBI would swoop down and rescue him.

He hoped.

Harvey got up and paced. If an FBI swat team did try to save him, however, they would have to win a gun battle with Boris and his goons. Even if that didn't make the news, Moscow would lose contact with their agents and conclude that their cyberattack plans had been compromised. They'd then come up with a new scheme to wreck the U.S. economy, and the task force would be back to square one.

That meant that Luke might wait until the FBI's counter operation had concluded before launching a rescue.

By then, Harvey feared, he might be dead.

Was he overthinking this the way he overthought everything?

He gave the window bars another hard shake. He had to get the hell out.

He sat at the table and brainstormed.

He could fake an illness, then leap out of bed and overpower his two guards. But like him, they'd seen that trick too many times in movies. Also, only Viktor ever came near him. Elena always stood a safe distance away, her gun raised.

He could tie the bedsheets together and climb out the window, again just like in the movies. But his two sheets wouldn't reach the ground, and the window had bars.

He might start a fire by short-circuiting the wiring in the overhead light. But that would leave him locked in a burning room. Boris and the others would flee the building and leave him to die.

Shatter the window and use a shard of glass as a weapon? But again, Elena would shoot him before he got close enough to her.

But he could break the window and drop a note.

Harvey walked across the room and peered down. Pedestrians leaned into the wind. Pieces of paper flashed past, then a straw hat rolled down the sidewalk, a dapper man in pursuit.

A dropped note would tumble for blocks.

But not if it dangled on a string. Then someone would certainly see the note. But there was no string in the place. Tearing the dreadful rose wallpaper into strips wouldn't hold. Un-threading the quilt would take forever and not be strong enough.

What if he simply broke the window and shouted for help? But the Russians would be the first to hear.

What-Ifs weren't working for him.

Harvey paced, punched the wall, kicked the table leg, and punched the wall again. He'd come up with nothing. Add to that, he kept running his tongue across an irritating chunk of coffee-soaked toast caught in that gap between two upper-left molars.

He'd seen dental floss in the medicine cabinet.

That's it!

Now he was thinking like an international spy and no longer the mild academic. That wasn't surprising. He'd consorted with Russian operatives, a pair of FBI agents, and a swooningly gorgeous woman pressed into espionage. He'd knocked out a mugger and rammed a would-be assassin with his car. He'd been abducted and locked into a barred room.

He hurried to the bathroom and jerked open the medicine cabinet. He pushed aside a bottle of aspirin and grabbed a container labeled, 'Soothing Mint Flavor!'

Thoughtful hosts. This was probably a temporary hideout for Russian agents passing through town.

Harvey unrolled a foot of toilet paper, spread it out on the top of the tank, and pressed his left forearm against the sharp metal corner of the medicine cabinet until he bled. He took a Q-Tip from the medicine cabinet—another considerate touch by his captors—and wrote in blood on the toilet paper: *Prisoner, flr 3, get FBI.* The blood would convince the reader that this was no prank. He taped a bandage over the cut, folded the message, and tied the end of the dental floss around it. He grabbed a towel and hurried to the window, unspooling floss as he went.

He listened for sounds from the hallway, heard none, then wrapped his fist in a towel—he'd seen that done in a movie—and reached through the bars and punched the window. Nothing. Another punch, but harder. Nothing. And again and again and again. His knuckles throbbed, and his wrist ached. He stepped back. Bullet-proof glass.

Fuck!

He tore up the note, flung the towel into the bathroom, and kicked the table.

A leg flew across the room, hit the wall, and bounced back. The table tipped onto its side. Harvey picked up the leg and thumped it in his hand. Heavy, probably maple.

He heard footsteps on the stairs, probably Elena and Viktor coming back to gather up the breakfast dishes and check on him.

He hurried across the room and slammed the bathroom door as hard as he could to make them think he'd gone inside. Then he tiptoed back to the other door and positioned himself to the side so he'd be out of sight when it opened. Viktor always came in first. Harvey would let him get past. When Elena stepped inside, Harvey would slam the table leg down on her arm and make her drop the gun. He would snatch it off the floor, force the two to lie on the floor, lock the two inside the room, and get the hell away.

If Boris tried to stop him on the way out, Harvey would fire a couple of warning shots over his head. Or shoot him in the leg if he had to.

Harvey raised the table leg overhead and waited.

Viktor opened the door partway, stepped inside, and took a couple of steps. "He's in the bathroom."

Elena would be next. Harvey tightened his grip on the table leg.

But she stayed outside.

Harvey heard her breathing.

She said, "What happened to the table?"

Oh, shit!

The door swung open and slammed hard against Harvey.

He stumbled sideways.

Elena rushed into the center of the room and swung her pistol at him.

Harvey lowered the table leg.

Elena called him a son-of-a-bitch in Russian.

Viktor punched him in the stomach.

Harvey bent over and vomited chunks of toast and banana and a black stream of instant coffee.

Chapter 36

I'm Already in Big Trouble

They kept Harvey locked in the room for the next three days. Viktor removed the light bulbs as punishment, dimming the days and darkening the nights. Bad dreams propelled Harvey out of bed—he would pace in the dark, stub his toes on the three-legged table, punch the wall, and shake the window grill.

Elena and Viktor brought food twice a day, early morning and late afternoon. There was never enough. Harvey dreamed of lunches at the Middlebridge College faculty cafeteria, which had a surprisingly good chef, but in dreams, Harvey would find himself standing hungrily at the end of a long line, clutching in both hands an empty plastic tray emblazoned with the college crest of crossed olive branches, never to reach the food.

Meals in lockup were hard, green apples, a handful of unexpected Oreo cookies, and cold pizza slices. Would pizza figure in his last meal?

Just after sunup at the beginning of the fourth day, Viktor shook Harvey awake, grabbed his elbow, jerked him out of bed, and hustled him down three flights of stairs. Elena walked behind, her pistol pressed against the back of his head.

Harvey's legs shook from inactivity, and his ribs throbbed from the punches Viktor administered every day. Harvey remembered hard hits from high school football games. He wished he was back there. He wished he was anywhere but here.

His clothes reeked of sweat and vomit, his toes itched, and his clammy underwear clung to his privates.

Where Elena and Viktor were taking him, Harvey didn't know. He should be frightened but oddly wasn't. He was glad for a change of scenery and to have someone else around, even armed Russian thugs. He'd always been like that, his ex-wife had complained, always needing someone around. She was sick of it, she would tell him, and she needed her distance. She'd had a point. After Tommy had died, Harvey hated being all by himself.

Tommy had shouted to Harvey for help in a dream of the night before, while Amaya sat in the office, bent over her laptop, not touching the keys, and sobbing into her hands, and Harvey found himself dressed in sagging and sweaty jockey shorts in front of a class, his jaw hanging open, unable to speak, his students pointing and laughing.

Viktor pushed Harvey into the living room and shoved him backwards onto a wooden chair.

Elena lowered her pistol and said in Russian, "We'll wait for Boris."

Those were the first words Harvey had heard from another human being in seventy-two hours.

He looked around, relieved to be out of his room. Nothing had changed, but everything captivated him. The green marble fireplace heaped with ash was absolutely beautiful, the stained-glass front window (a Tiffany knockoff, he guessed) glowed in a rainbow of colors from the sunlight streaming through from the outside, and the hefty tan globe—still refusing to acknowledge the collapse of the Soviet Union—ached to be touched, spun, perused.

Dust coated the globe, the end tables, and the areas of hardwood flooring at the rug's perimeter.

Harvey sneezed.

Boris shuffled into the room, flicking cigarette ash on the rug.

"Don't you own a vacuum?" Harvey asked.

Boris ignored the question and settled slowly into the rocker across from him. "What did you teach?"

"History," Harvey said.

"European? American?"

"Sometimes, but my specialty was Big History."

Boris raised a bushy black eyebrow. "What's that?"

"The history of everything from the Big Bang right up to this very moment while you and I are sitting here having this swell chat."

"Sounds interesting."

Yeah, sure. Harvey recognized softball questions designed to relax him.

"Do you miss teaching?"

"Yes," Harvey said.

"What about your current job?"

"It's a mindfuck."

Boris grunted. His way of showing amusement.

"Is Amaya easy to work with?"

Finally, we're getting around to her. "She's smart and efficient."

Boris nodded. "Is she happy in the States?"

"She says so."

"Does she ever talk about flying back to India to see her family?" Boris asked, suppressing a yawn and trying to sound casual. "She must miss them."

"She does, but I haven't heard her talk of going back, even for a visit."

Was that the right thing to say? Harvey found himself at center stage without a script. Apparently, Boris wanted to find out if Amaya had warned her brother—or was ready to warn him—to take his family into hiding. Or if she herself was ready to bolt.

Viktor brought in a tray and poured a cup of tea for Boris, another for Elena, one for himself, none for Harvey.

"So, you're not happy as a technical writer?" Boris asked.

"It pays the bills."

Boris blew on his tea, then took a sip. "I've actually been told very little about the business your company is in."

Uh, huh.

"Fill me in."

Harvey did. He spoke of pumping stations and pipe pressures but said nothing that Boris couldn't learn from the company's website.

He grunted. "Does Amaya ever talk about staying in the States?"

That again.

Harvey shook his head.

"The two of you live together," Boris said. "What happens after she's finished working with you?"

"She'll go back to India."

"Won't you miss her?"

"Some, but we're not a good match. We both agree on that. Our personalities and our cultures are too far apart."

Was that the right thing to say?

Boris drowned his cigarette in the rest of his tea. "But you act like a real couple."

Harvey shook his head. "We're just fuck buddies."

It took Boris a while to understand, then he smiled. "That's an expression I'll have to remember."

Then he stopped smiling, set his cup on an end table and leaned forward. "You attempted to club Elena and Viktor with a table leg. Try something like that again, and you'll find yourself in big trouble."

"I'm already in big trouble."

*   *   *

Harvey climbed the stairs, with Elena jamming her pistol into his back and Viktor somewhere behind.

Harvey stepped into the bedroom. The door lock behind him.

He leaned against the window and stared down at the street. There wasn't a chance in hell that Boris would ever let him go.

His only hope was Luke.

The day had already begun for normal people on the street below, scurrying back and forth, off to jobs or shopping or just for bracing, early morning wake-up walks. They were free to fret over the raise they didn't get, the knock they'd heard in their car engine the day before, the Red Sox slump, and the cute guy who hadn't called back after a first date even though they'd had such a really terrific time. None of those people worried that Russian agents might kill them in their sleep.

Harvey had learned his neighbors' routines, and today was no different. Dapper Mr. X left the building across the street every morning at a little after nine, always wearing a dark suit, briefcase in hand. He would pause in the doorway and look both ways before turning right and scurrying off. Soon afterwards, Ms. Y would open her second-floor window to water a sickly geranium in a flower box. Two boys in blue school blazers—ten or eleven—would shuffle past at 9:15, unhappily on their way to summer school.

Everyone came and went as they chose. Why weren't they smiling and singing and dancing and celebrating their freedom?

Harvey wanted to become a boy again, like one of those below. Either would do, although he thought the redhead had the better chance with girls. Neither boy had a brother who'd drowned.

Harvey watched a young couple walking a small white dog that kept getting its leash tangled in their legs, a burly priest who sneezed twice, and a gaunt, tall man standing in the opening of the alley across the street, reading a newspaper, a Red Sox cap pulled low over his eyes, glancing up often.

A short man sauntered past in a tan raincoat, its collar turned up, with a black fedora covering his eyes. The two men nodded at each other.

Harvey's heart leaped.

A black van crept in from the far end of the alley. A second. A third.

Harvey wanted to cheer, to jump up and down.

The shorter man dropped his cigarette, snuffed it out underfoot, and disappeared into the alley.

Harvey waited. Five minutes, ten minutes.

Why aren't they moving?

To give other agents time to circle around behind the building, that's why.

A small drone drifted out of the alleyway, rose three floors and hovered.

No cars or trucks or pedestrians passed by on the street. It must be blocked off at both ends.

Come on, come on!

The tall man stepped from the alley, his phone to his ear.

In an hour, I'll be free, Harvey told himself. No, it'll be just minutes. He would see Amaya again, he would see his daughter and his mother again, he would walk where he wanted to walk, eat what he wanted to eat, and do what he wanted to do.

A burly man in tan slacks and a black jacket slipped out of the van in the alley. Then two more and a woman. All wore bullet-proof vests. They had 'DEA' printed on their jackets. What was the Drug Enforcement Administration doing here and not the FBI?

It didn't matter. Help had arrived.

The agents bunched up at the near end of the alley.

The woman stepped onto the sidewalk, looked left, right, then signaled for the others to follow her.

They poured onto the street.

One man lugged a metal tube the size of a bazooka. A door-breaker, Harvey guessed.

Just a few more minutes.

Harvey shook the window bars. He wanted to shout. He wanted to sing and dance.

Just a few more minutes, and he would be free!

He would thank his rescuers one by one, shake the men's hands, kiss the women.

The agents veered off to Harvey's right.

He heard three thumps, then a door breaking down.

Harvey pressed his forehead against the bars and watched the agents rush through the entrance to the building next door.

No! No! No!

Harvey ran to that side of the room and beat his fists against the wall.

"In here!" he yelled. "I'm in here!"

He pounded and swore and shouted.

More doors broke in the other building.

"I'm in here!" Harvey screamed and kicked the wall. "I'm in here!"

No response. He waited and listened. His heart thumped.

He ran back to the window and shook the bars.

A half dozen agents led two men away in handcuffs.

Another agent followed, a bulging plastic bag in each hand.

A drug bust! It was a goddamn drug bust!

Elena burst into the room. Then Viktor.

He slammed Harvey face down onto the floor and jerked his arms behind him.

Elena stuffed a rag into his mouth.

Chapter 37

Hotdogs with Mustard and Ketchup

Harvey awoke, opened one eye, then the other. His mouth was dry, and his tongue was swollen from thirst. His gut hurt, his head hurt, he tasted blood. He was slumped with his back against a wall, his legs bent up almost to his chest, and with his toes touching the other side.

The place was dark except for a thin band of light leaking from under the door. The floor was hard.

Where in hell was he?

He reached out and touched all four walls. A closet, empty except for him.

Voices came through the door. Russian voices, the words muffled.

The walls closed in. Harvey struggled to his feet and banged his fists on the door. "Let me out! Let me out!"

No response.

Now he remembered the drug raid, the sock in his mouth, the needle in his neck, getting dragged to the van, passing out.

The lock clicked. The door opened. Light flooded inside. Harvey squinted.

Viktor set a tray of food on the floor, pushed it into the closet with his toe, then stepped back. A grim-faced thug stood six feet behind him, a gun pointed at Harvey.

The door closed, and everything went dark again.

Harvey sat down, grabbed the paper cup with both hands, and drank the contents in three gulps. Pepsi, he guessed, gone flat. He felt around on the tray until he found a pair of cold hotdogs. He shoved the first one into his mouth and chewed. The bun was stale, and mustard and ketchup dripped down his shirt. Absolutely delicious. He gobbled down the second hotdog. Afterwards, he licked his fingers. They too were delicious.

Harvey thumped the door with the side of his fist. The key in the lock clicked. Viktor opened it up, bent down, and pulled the cardboard tray toward him. Again, the other goon stood by, pistol raised.

"I have to go to the bathroom," Harvey said in English.

Viktor shook his head. He didn't understand.

Harvey touched his crotch.

Viktor half turned. "Nikolai, I gotta let him out."

Nikolai nodded, lifted his pistol, and aimed it at Harvey's forehead. "We should just shoot the guy."

"And then Boris will shoot us."

Harvey pulled himself to his feet, wavered, squinted in the light, shuffled out, and grabbed the waistband of his sagging trousers.

His captors had removed his belt and shoelaces. He supposed they were afraid he'd hang himself on the clothing bar. They apparently wanted to keep him alive—at least for now.

Harvey stepped into a large, windowless room with sweating concrete walls. A basement, he guessed. A pair of brown, plaid easy chairs sat in the middle of the room and faced a torn leather couch. Three cots lined the far wall. The bathroom and kitchenette were on the near side of the room, next to the closet. Nearby were a small square table and two folding chairs. Boris sat on one and smoked. He didn't look up.

Viktor grunted something and shoved Harvey into the bathroom.

This became the routine: meals of cold hotdogs and flat Pepsis, bathroom trips, boredom, loneliness, fear, and long spells when Harvey daydreamed he was outside, loping barefoot across soft cool grass, the sun shining, birds singing, and Amaya running at his side, holding his hand and laughing.

Harvey jogged in place as best he could in the cramped closet and did deep knee bends. Push-ups were impossible—his ribs hurt too much from Viktor's blows, and, anyway, there wouldn't be enough room to stretch out.

He had to curl up to sleep, which intensified his claustrophobia and made his legs restless and itchy. He dozed but never slept properly, waking up cramped and aching and in panic. He longed for Amaya, for freedom, for his family, and for Pete's pepperoni pizzas. He played word games—how many synonyms could he come up with for *happiness, freedom, love, hotdog*? Could he name all the U.S. Presidents and in order? He couldn't. The state capitals? Most. The flavors of ice cream in the Middlebridge cafeteria? All twelve.

Boris, Viktor, and Nikolai came and went, along with Elena and two other guards whose names Harvey didn't catch. Two guards were always there to watch him around the clock. They spoke in low tones. Harvey strained to hear but could make out only snatches of Russian conversations through the closet door, mostly about cars and women.

Sometimes he heard rumbling. Trucks passing overhead? The subway? But why only some afternoons and evenings and in short bursts? Harvey thought he heard cheering, and he wondered if he was going mad.

He agonized over his mother and Kathy—were they safe? What would they make of his absence?

He knew that Amaya was painfully aware of his situation because Boris had sent the photo of him holding up a newspaper. She must be sick with worry.

He supposed she'd told his mother and Kathy that he'd been called out of town on a company emergency. Luke would probably tell Tucker the truth, but no one else. Tucker would make excuses for Harvey's absence.

Harvey's thoughts often turned to Tommy and imagined him as alive and an engineer because he was always building things. Tommy had been a creative kid who would no doubt have grown up happy, with a happy wife and two happy children. Tommy in his alternate universe.

As best he could, Harvey would nudge his thoughts toward pleasant memories: the pink birthday bike he'd given Kathy when she turned six. The next day, she unbolted the training wheels and taught herself to bike "like a big girl," resulting in a tear-filled series of scrapes and bruises. Or the birthday when he'd bought his mother a Caribbean cruise, which made her cry. Or the time he'd simply brought breakfast to Amaya in bed, with a red rose in a flute vase, a glass of freshly squeezed orange juice, scrambled eggs that were a touch dry, toast a bit burned, the delight in her eyes, her arms outstretched to hug him.

Harvey sat with his back against the wall, his knees up, and his hands folded tightly across his stomach—this somewhat suppressed his constant hunger—and he relived the good moments and some of the bad, and he entertained a string of What-Ifs.

As a boy, he'd fantasized stepping into a time-travel machine like the one he'd seen on television and watch through a tiny porthole as a woolly haired scientist with madman eyes turned cranks and threw levers as he prepared to transport his youthful passenger for a redo back to that fateful day at the beach.

Later studies of Einsteinian time and space ruined that dream.

Early afternoon of the third day—or was it the fourth?—Harvey smelled food frying and heard something sizzling in a pan. Apparently Boris was the cook, and Viktor was standing nearby. They were close enough for Harvey to make out what they were saying.

Viktor said, "This place sucks. Since it was just a drug raid, we didn't need to move the guy."

Boris said, "I thought the neighborhood would start getting too much attention after the bust."

"Yeah, I guess you're right. By the way, you should turn down the heat. You're burning the sausages."

"I like them crisp. Oh, I forgot to tell you that Moscow sent word a couple of hours ago that they've officially confirmed Igor's death, and that a mugger killed him."

"This is a dangerous place."

"Especially for the guy in the closet."

Boris laughed, and Viktor laughed, and Harvey didn't.

"What about the woman?" Viktor asked.

"She'll stay on the job as long as we have Lovelorn locked up."

"And then?"

"I think you know."

Harvey pressed his back against the closet wall and closed his eyes.

Amaya. He had to escape. He had to save her or die trying.

What if he pretended to be unconscious? When Viktor bent over to shake him, he could grab him, bang his head against the wall, then leap out of the closet, and charge the second guard. But he always stood six feet back, anticipating just such a move, and far enough away to get off a shot.

Pretend to cooperate? Would anyone believe him? Probably not, and in any case, it was unlikely they'd ever release him.

If he couldn't come up with a better idea, he'd have to pursue one of the risky ones. Succeed or die.

Harvey stood up, did a dozen knee bends, then decided to try a few pull-ups.

The wooden clothing bar was much too low, so he got on his knees, gripped the bar, and pulled himself partway up.

The bar snapped, and Harvey fell.

He listened for a reaction from outside. None. Boris and Victor were arguing over the right way to fry sausages.

The bar had broken off at the end. Harvey set it on the floor.

Then he picked it up and touched the tip. It was jagged and splintered and sharp.

Yes.

Calm washed over Harvey. Now or never.

He crouched, faced the door, rapped on it, and grasped the clothing bar in both hands, the sharp end pointing forward.

The lock clicked, and the door swung open.

Harvey leaped out and jabbed Viktor in the stomach.

He yelped and bent over.

Harvey hit him with an uppercut.

Viktor stumbled backwards and dropped to the floor.

Bang!

The bullet ricocheted off the concrete wall.

Harvey rushed at Boris, swung the clothing bar like a baseball bat, and knocked the pistol to the floor.

Boris grabbed Harvey around the waist.

They fell, rolled, grunted, punched wildly.

Boris broke free and scrambled on hands and knees for the gun.

Harvey jumped up and kicked it away.

Boris got to his feet and charged.

Harvey stepped aside, grabbed Boris by the back of his collar, and propelled him headfirst into the concrete wall.

Thud!

Boris fell face down.

Harvey picked up the gun and pointed it at Boris, then Viktor, then back at Boris. Neither stirred.

Harvey kicked Boris in the side. Hard. That was for Amaya.

Harvey kicked Viktor in the side even harder. That was for all the punches and abuse.

Harvey grabbed a potholder, then the sizzling iron frying pan, and dumped the sausages on the floor. He stood over Boris and raised the pan overhead, ready for a killing blow, trembling in anger.

His arm wavered. His thoughts wavered.

He lowered the pan and dropped it with a clank.

He grabbed a blackened sausage off the floor and bit off an end. It burned his tongue. It was delicious. He pulled out a chair and sat down.

Now what? Elena or Nikolai or one of the other goons would eventually arrive to relieve these two.

Harvey finished the sausage in two more gulps, picked up the second, and chewed.

The room shook, and he heard a roar.

He had no idea where he was, but he knew that, if he had any chance of escaping, he'd have to blend in. But not with laceless shoes, beltless trousers, and a shirt with mustard, dried blood, and puke down the front.

Boris was stout, but Viktor was about the right size.

Harvey rolled Victor onto his back, tugged off his shoes, unbuttoned his shirt, and opened his belt, all the time keeping himself positioned so he could see the door in case someone came in. He kept the pistol at arm's reach. Could he bring himself to shoot another human being if they were trying to kill him? He hoped he didn't have to find out.

Harvey struggled Viktor out of his shirt and trousers, then stripped off his own clothes and put on Viktor's. The shirt was blue, short-sleeved, and tight at the shoulders, and the tan slacks hung loose at the butt. The shoes were two sizes too big. Harvey laced them as tightly as he could.

He reached into Boris' pants pocket and pulled out a phone. It wasn't turned on. Harvey tossed it aside and took Viktor's phone from his shirt pocket. It was on but didn't get a signal underground. Harvey tucked the phone into his pants pocket.

Harvey dragged Boris to the closet, folded him inside, rolled Victor on top, then closed the door and locked it. He shoved the key under the rug and picked up the pistol. It was heavy. The handle was warm. Take it? No, it would just attract attention, and he probably couldn't bring himself to use it. He slid the gun under the sofa.

Harvey took a deep breath, stepped through the door and into the hallway. He heard the crack of a bat and the cheering of a crowd, and he knew exactly where he was.

He was in Fenway Park.

Chapter 38

Tunnel Rats

That explained the cold hotdogs and flat sodas.

The Russians had held him in the same basement room where he and Margo had delivered three sausage-and-mushroom pizzas just a few weeks earlier. Viktor and the other Russian agents were working as baseball park guards.

Harvey hurried down the long concrete hallway toward the set of stairs that led to the floor above and the exit just beyond. He remembered it from the pizza delivery.

His legs ached and wobbled and seemed detached.

But soon he'd be free. Soon he'd be in the open air. Soon he'd see Amaya and his mother and daughter.

A figure stepped into the far end of the hallway.

Damn!

It was Elena.

She showed no sign she'd recognized him in his guard's uniform.

But she soon would.

Keep going and overpower her? But was she armed? Probably.

Or go back? To where? A room with two unconscious Russian agents stacked in a closet?

Harvey slowed to a halt.

He thought back to that happy time when he and Margo had delivered the pizzas. He remembered the cranky workman who'd popped out of a side tunnel and challenged them.

Harvey turned around and tried to look casual. He walked twenty feet, opened the door to the tunnel, slipped inside, and pulled the door closed.

It clanked behind him and left him in total darkness, like the closet. He shivered. The tunnel smelled of mold and sewage and things that had died.

He groped the wall for a light switch.

None.

He waved his arms overhead, trying to find a pull cord.

No luck.

Go back and take his chances with Elena? Anything was better than this. He'd been locked in a closet for days and was going over the edge.

Then he remembered Viktor's cellphone. He pressed the flashlight icon and played the beam across the walls, the ceiling, and into the darkness ahead. He found the light switch. Turn it on? No, because anyone entering the tunnel would see him.

He walked slowly, dodging puddles and ducking under pipes. Water dripped on his head.

He'd heard somewhere that tunnels crisscrossed under Fenway Park so that plumbers, electricians, and others could move about unhindered during games. With any luck, this one led to the outside world.

He stepped carefully over piles of junk—broken wooden skids, sections of discarded water pipes, a twisted bleacher seat with '322' painted across the back, stinky puddles, and a bloated dead rat lying on its back.

His feet were heavy, and his head ached. Nothing seemed real. He was hungry and thirsty, and for days he'd suffered from sensory deprivation, and now too many sounds and sights and smells invaded his space. He was overwhelmed.

And detached. He couldn't quite believe what was happening. Was it really him, Harvey Hudson, fleeing for his life? He didn't feel that he belonged in this moment, in this body, behaving like this strange person.

A pair of tiny eyes reflected the light from the phone. A fat, black rat took a last drink from a puddle and scampered into the darkness.

Harvey moved on, stumbled over something, and fell into the puddle. He swore, got up, soaked and stinking.

A boot had tripped him. He picked it up. It must have belonged to a small person because it wasn't that much bigger than the boots Tommy had worn the morning he'd drowned. But this was a work boot. Tommy's had square toes and tooled leather.

The policewoman who'd showed up at the front door was tall and pretty. She carried Tommy's boot in a transparent plastic bag. Harvey hung a ways back. The policewoman removed the boot and held it up. It looked still wet. "Can you identify this?" she asked. Harvey's father nodded. His mother grabbed the boot, clutched it to her chest, and hurried with it to Tommy's bedroom. Harvey and his father had hugged and burst into tears.

Harvey wiped the dirt off the boot that had tripped him, then carefully positioned it upright on a nook in the wall.

He took a few more steps just as a row of dangling bare bulbs came on and lit the tunnel from end to end.

Harvey spun around to look.

Elena jerked a gun from her belt and fired.

The bullet whizzed overhead, banged off a pipe, and echoed through the tunnel.

She was a fifty feet away. A difficult shot with a handgun. But she could get lucky.

Harvey broke into a run.

Another wild shot, then another.

He turned a corner, safe for a moment.

A rat scampered over his feet. Then another.

Harvey splashed through puddles, banged his shoulder against the wall, fell down and jumped up.

He turned another corner and bumped into a door.

He grabbed the handle and hesitated.

It had to open, it had to open.

It did.

Harvey jumped through and slammed the door behind him.

A bearded, elderly man in gray coveralls stood at a workbench, screwdriver in hand, mending a stadium seat tipped on its side. A schedule of Red Sox games hung on the wall. A half-eaten meatball submarine sandwich lay on the workbench. Harvey eyed it hungrily.

The man turned to him. "Who are you?"

"Do you have a key to that door?"

"No. Why do you want one?"

"Because the tunnel's full of rats," Harvey said. He grabbed a chair and wedged it under the door handle. "I want to make sure none get out."

"Rats can open doors?"

"The big ones."

The guy looked puzzled, then shrugged and said, "What were you doing in there?"

"Checking the pipes. They're all looked good, by the way. The boss will be glad to hear that. He's worries about leaks."

Harvey wiped his hands on his trousers because he thought that's what a plumber would do right after a job.

The man lay his screwdriver on the bench. "That's what you do, check out pipes?"

"And other things."

"How come you got a guard's uniform on?"

"That's also one of my duties," Harvey said.

The man didn't look convinced.

Time to get the hell out of here. "You might want to set some rat traps in the tunnel," Harvey said, then hurried to the door across the room. "Have a nice day."

Harvey hoped it led to the outside world, to freedom, fresh air, to Amaya.

Damn!

He was standing on a ramp between the bleachers and the right-field seats.

He pulled out Viktor's phone and called Amaya.

She didn't pick up on the first try or the second or the third, no doubt wary about an unknown caller. But she answered on the fourth ring. "Yes?" Her voice was tentative.

"It's me."

"Harvey! Are you okay? Are you hurt? Have they—"

"Go into hiding right away! Call Luke and tell him I'm at Fenway Park!"

Pause. "You went to a baseball game?"

"Sort of."

"What does that mean?"

"I'll explain later. I love you. Now call Luke and tell him to get right down here and bring lots of backup. And get yourself someplace safe."

Harvey pocketed the phone, then spotted one of his Russian captors off to his left, shouting into his own phone and jogging toward him.

Harvey hesitated, then ran up the ramp, eased over the wall next to the bleacher seats, and dropped onto the playing field.

It was a Red Sox/Yankees game, fourth inning, with the Sox up by two.

Harvey looked up at the Jumbotron. He waved and saw himself waving back.

Chapter 39

The Madman in the Jumbotron

Harvey was wet and stinky, hungry and thirsty, and in great danger. But he was also ecstatic to be outside and unfettered, even though he felt light-headed and unhinged.

A bat cracked, and the crowd roared. The player dropped his bat and trotted toward first base. A homer. That put the Red Sox up five runs over the reviled Yankees.

The guard scrambled over the fence.

Harvey broke into a run.

The home plate umpire waved his arms overhead to suspend play. The batter stepped away from the plate. Other players turned to watch Harvey.

He ran past the right fielder, who bellowed, "Get the hell out of here!"

Harvey shouted over his shoulder, "Yankees suck!"

He ran past the bleacher seats. A second guard tumbled down the steps, lowered himself onto the field, and joined in the chase.

It was another of the Russians who'd guarded him.

Harvey swung left and headed in a wide circle toward home plate. He looked around. He'd expected to see more people coming at him from all directions. Why hadn't they? His guard's uniform must have confused them.

Now what?

Surrender to a police officer, that's what.

Harvey glanced around him as he ran. None in sight.

He looked over his shoulder. The two guards were gaining.

Get out of Viktor's floppy shoes.

Harvey hopped on his right foot, ripped off the left shoe, hopped on his left foot, ripped off the right shoe, and took off again.

He passed close to the stands and shouted, "Call the police! Call the FBI!"

A drink cup hit him and splashed soda down the front of his shirt.

Someone shouted "Asshole!"

A woman held up her phone, waved and smiled and took his picture.

Other people swore at him. A few clapped and cheered.

He knew he should be afraid, but he wasn't, probably from hunger and thirst, beatings, abuse, and sensory deprivation. An odd feeling. A liberating feeling.

He had grass under his feet, an open sky above, and room to run. He felt buoyant and detached from reality.

From time to time, everyone should lose control and play the clown. Something for his book.

A drink cup missed him and splashed on the grass near his feet. Another hit his knee.

Harvey glanced at the Jumbotron and saw the stocking-footed fool with two guards running behind him. Was that really him, the clown, the escapee, the grinning jester? What would Amaya think if she saw him? Or his mother or Kathy? Or former colleagues and students?

Did he really care?

It seemed to Harvey that somehow his existence had dissolved, and all that was left of him was the madman in the Jumbotron.

He swung around behind home plate.

The umpire, the batter, and the catcher stood side-by-side and shouted at him. A chorus of curses.

Harvey headed toward first base. "Call the police! Russian agents are after me!"

One guard had cut across the bases to head him off. Harvey dodged left, right, then left again. The guard leaped to tackle him but missed and landed on his stomach.

Harvey felt back on the playing field.

He ran past the stands near first base. That's where he and Tommy and their father had sat that one time they'd gone to a game together. A foul ball hit near them. A man caught it on the second bounce, gave it to Tommy, and called him a cute kid. Harvey had been jealous.

He wished he could return to that afternoon.

He looked around. Still no police.

He headed toward right field. A complete circuit.

Call 911? Of course. He reached into his rear pocket and pulled out Viktor's phone. Dead—lighting it in the tunnel had drained the battery.

Harvey's legs throbbed, and his lungs burned. He was out of shape, but he didn't slow down. He was running for his life.

Elena dropped over the fence right in front of him. The guy repairing chairs must have let her out of the tunnel.

Harvey skidded to a stop. A gun bulged under Elena's jacket.

He turned and ran back.

More park guards came from every direction.

He had to surrender. Which were Russians, and which were not?

Harvey started toward one. No! He's one of the thugs who'd been guarding him. Harvey turned back.

That one? Or him?

There!

A police officer was racing across the outfield toward him.

He ran up to her and held his arms out in front, wrists together. "I'm ready to give up!"

She was a short, sunburned blonde. She pulled a pair of metal handcuffs from a leather holder on her belt. "You're going to jail, buster."

"I'm a secret agent working for the FBI."

"All of you runners have stories."

"But mine is true. I've just escaped from Russian spies who've been holding me in a hidden underground room and feeding me hotdogs. Call the FBI and ask for Luke, although that's probably not his real name. He's my boss. I'm a part-time agent."

The policewoman jerked Harvey's hands behind his back and clamped the cuffs tightly around his wrists. "And I'm James Bond."

Chapter 40

A Better Person for It

Four Months Later

Harvey turned his coat collar up against the chilly ocean breeze.

Amaya stood to his left and his mother and Kathy to his right, all facing the water, all silent, all lost in thought. It was November, and they had the beach to themselves.

Harvey said, "Everyone's freezing. We should get back to the car."

"Not yet," his mother said. "Not yet."

She wore a gray, ankle-length coat, the hood up, and she clutched a bouquet of red roses in her gloved hands.

This was the first time any of them had returned to the beach where Tommy had drowned. The sea was rough, the waves high, and the wind strong—not unlike that awful day. Harvey recalled the soft sand underfoot, the gray sky, the seagulls squawking overhead, the boy lost to the waves.

Amaya squeezed his arm and rested her head against his shoulder. She wore the puffy blue winter coat that she and Harvey's mother had picked out. The two shopped together, went to coffee shops together, teased Harvey together.

Earlier that morning, Harvey and his mother had shown Amaya around Marblehead, ending up at the cottage the family had owned. It looked just as Harvey had remembered—the little front porch, the gray shingle siding, and the shutters now painted an unpleasant orange.

Harvey put his free arm around his mother's shoulder and drew her closer. Had she slipped into her fantasy that a ship had rescued a half-drowned boy who'd lost his memory but would someday regain it and return home? Or did she picture Tommy splashing in the waves and going down for the last time? Or was she seeing the panicked older boy who himself almost drowned trying to rescue his little brother?

No one spoke for a long time. Each in their own world.

Finally, Kathy said, "Dad, you still haven't told me why you disappeared for a couple of weeks four months ago. Amaya won't tell me, either."

It wasn't a real question, but Kathy's attempt to change the subject and lift everyone's spirits. She was good at that. She would have a great bedside manner.

"I've told you already," Harvey said. "I was on an unbelievably dangerous and secret mission as an international spy."

Kathy laughed, then turned to Amaya. "Is that true?"

"Every word of it."

"You're no better at telling the truth than he is."

"I was before I met him," Amaya said.

"Poor dear, my son's had a bad influence on you," Harvey's mother said, "and I humbly apologize for the way I raised him." She stepped free of Harvey's grasp and pulled her hood tighter around her face. "He has an uncontrollable imagination. I thought he'd get over it when he grew up, but I actually think he's gotten worse."

"That's because he hasn't quite grown up," Kathy said.

"Hey!" Harvey said.

The three women enjoyed team-teasing him.

He had told his mother and Kathy nothing about the Russians, the FBI, his incarcerations, the danger and—yes—the thrills. He didn't want them to worry after the fact. Neither woman ever went on YouTube. If they did, they might have seen him running around inside Fenway Park, waving at the Jumbotron, playing the clown, half out of his mind.

The cops had shoved Harvey into a cell, treated him like a crazy drunk, and let him sleep for twenty hours. Harvey woke up clear-headed. It took an entire day to convince the police to call the FBI.

Luke and Elliot showed up in minutes and flashed their badges. Luke leaned close to the police sergeant and whispered that Harvey had been on a dangerous secret mission, that the jaunt inside Fenway Park was a critical part of the operation against the Russians, and that Harvey was patriotic and courageous way beyond the call of duty. Did the police really want word to get out that they'd locked up a national hero? The police sergeant said he didn't.

Luke and Elliott led Harvey to their car, got in, turned to him, sniffed the air, and opened all four windows.

Amaya was waiting in front of the poultry store. She rushed forward and held out her arms. Harvey waved his hands and told her to stay away because he smelled like a sewer. Amaya flew into his arms and said she loved him no matter what, although a shower and a change of clothing would be greatly appreciated.

Harvey's mother was saying something. Harvey asked her to repeat herself.

"I said that Mary moved out from across the street not long after you returned from your mythical spying adventure. I really miss her."

Harvey had not told his mother that Mary was an FBI agent and not a true friend, who got reassigned soon after the operation ended.

The Russians knew they'd been played, but had not learned that Amaya had betrayed them, nor of Harvey's role. In cooperation with the CIA, Luke's task force convinced the Russians that a mole inside their own intelligence service had compromised their scheme to destroy U.S. petroleum pumps.

The Russians were no longer threatening to harm Amaya's brother and his family. They even gave Amaya a big bonus, along with a chilling warning never to reveal her role in the operation, and they promised they were through with her. She wasn't quite convinced. Neither was Harvey. Nightmares persisted for both.

After the FBI had captured Boris, Viktor, and the rest of the Russian guards, they nabbed Elena at Logan Airport. Luke said that eventually they'd trade the bunch for American spies. The FBI was still holding Igor but hadn't decided yet what to do with him now that he'd turned.

Luke had assured Harvey that they'd wanted to rescue him even though it would have compromised their mission, but they couldn't because they didn't know where the Russians were holding him. Harvey didn't believe that.

In all seriousness, Luke asked Harvey to join his team full time, which made him laugh.

The arrests at Fenway Park forced the task force to put their counter operation into play two weeks ahead of schedule, but it worked anyway. It saved the petroleum pumps and released malicious software bugs into a dozen Russian military networks. Oil prices hadn't risen. Vladimir Putin and his cronies had lost billions.

Harvey's mother said, "You must be very proud of Amaya."

Harvey knew where this was leading. MIT had accepted her into their PhD program in computer science.

Both she and Harvey had quit their jobs at T&M Consultants, and Tucker had hired his niece to replace them. She turned out to be as incompetent as Harvey.

He said, "You do know that I teach two nights a week at Boston University."

"But that's not a full-time position, is it?"

"I don't want one."

And he didn't. He loved teaching Big History to adult students who were eager to learn and had the maturity to absorb what he had to say. No one fell asleep, no one spent fifty minutes texting friends, and no one ever skipped class. Also, Harvey didn't have to attend staff meetings, and he'd spoken with the department chairperson only on the day she hired him and once since. He wouldn't recognize the dean if he saw him in the hallway.

Sometimes, but only rarely, did Harvey feel that he'd come down in the world. But whenever he took his turn at delivering pizzas, he felt free, unstressed, and in charge of his life.

Before Pete retired and moved to Phoenix, he sold his business to Harvey (*Harvey's Pizza Palace*). He bought the place with the money he'd extorted from the FBI in exchange for his silence. No mention was ever made of the quarter million dollars he'd used to pay off his mother's mortgage.

Amaya helped in the restaurant from time to time. She was good with the books and charming with the customers, but she had also forced Harvey to go all organic, which meant raising prices. Still, he'd started attracting health-conscious foodies and the college crowd.

In fact, business was doing well enough for Harvey to hire an assistant manager and to have time to finish *Big History: The Birth and Death of Everything.* A textbook publisher was bringing it out in December of the next year.

On a whim, Harvey had started writing an espionage novel, based loosely on his experiences. Amaya edited the text. She continually toned down the sex scenes and granted snappier lines to the hero's love interest. For a title, she'd suggested *The Accidental Spy.*

The wind picked up. Harvey said, "Let's get back to the car."

His mother handed him the roses. "First these."

He walked to the water's edge and tossed the bouquet as far as he could, then came back and joined the others.

No one spoke.

The flowers lifted and fell on the waves.

Harvey's mother took his hand. "I have a sense of calm here. We should have come long ago."

"I don't think we were ready."

The flowers drifted farther and farther away, bobbing on the waves, then finally sank out of sight.

Harvey's mother said, "He's not coming back, is he?"

Harvey glanced at Amaya and Kathy, then shook his head and patted the place over his heart. "No, he's not. But he'll always be inside us."

Harvey wanted to say more, but he'd choked up and couldn't speak.

Silence, then his mother said, "Well, let's get off this beach before we freeze our noses off." She sounded at peace.

They started toward the car.

"You're all invited back to our place to warm up," Harvey said. "We'll make you lunch."

His mother stopped, turned to him, and lifted an eyebrow. "'We?'"

"Well, Amaya will," Harvey said.

His mother started walking again. "You had me scared."

Harvey and Amaya dropped behind. She said, "It'll be fun showing them the house now that it's all fixed up."

It was a modest Cape Code in a western suburb of Boston. The exterior was a light blue and not the white that Amaya had envisioned, but Harvey promised they'd change the color with the next painting. The picket fence was white, however. Harvey had built it the second week they'd moved in. The first storm blew it over, so Harvey hired a carpenter. Nevertheless, Amaya always referred to it as "Harvey's fence."

Harvey picked up a seashell, poured out the wet sand, and let his mind drift away from the stress of the day. What if humans also went through life inside a hard shell, discarding it when it got too tight, and then growing another? Would we be better protected in car crashes and falls and be free from the arthritis that attacks our joints as we grew older? What if all creatures had shells? Maybe not the birds and insects, because that would make flight impossible. No, some beetles did have hard shells that were called *elytra*, and they could fly. So what if…"

"You look lost in thought," Amaya said. She, too, was holding a seashell and examining it.

"I was wondering what it would be like if humans went through life wearing shells."

Amaya burst out laughing.

"What?"

"Your mother's right—you are a bad influence on me."

"What makes you say that?"

Amaya took Harvey's hand, turned it palm up, laid the seashell in it, then went up on tiptoes, and kissed his cheek. "Because I was thinking the same thing you were."

Harvey laughed. "And you're a better person for it."

Acknowledgments

So many people have contributed to my writing over the years that I don't know where to begin. Their feedback, patience and encouragement have been invaluable, and I owe much of my success to them. I want to thank my sister, Laura Salazar, Bill Regan, Jane Roy Brown, Richard Bolt, Vicki Sanders, Peggy McFarland, the late Steve Gordon, Alyson Miller, Erica Harth, Arlene Kay, Kevin Symmons, Elizabeth Lyon, Judy Giger, David Gallant, Ray Anderson and especially my wife, Nancy, also a writer, who understands my need to write and understands me (as much as I'm understandable).

I would also like to thank Cynthia Brackett-Vincent and Eddie Vincent for bringing me into the family of Encircle Publications and Deirdre Wait for her clever cover designs.

About the Author

David Gardner grew up on a Wisconsin dairy farm, served in Army Special Forces and earned a Ph.D. in French from the University of Wisconsin. He has taught college and worked as a reporter and in high tech. He coauthored three programming books for Prentice Hall and wrote dozens of travel articles and many mind-numbing software manuals before happily turning to fiction.

His debut novel, *The Journalist: A Paranormal Thriller*, appeared in February, 2021, followed by *The Last Speaker of Skalwegian* in November, 2021, both published by Encircle Publications.

He lives in Massachusetts with his wife, Nancy, also a writer. He hikes, bikes, messes with astrophotography and plays the keyboard with no discernible talent whatsoever. For the latest news, follow David on Facebook and visit davidgardnerauthor.com.

If you enjoyed reading this book,
please consider writing your honest review
and sharing it with other readers.

Many of our Authors are happy to participate in
Book Club and Reader Group discussions.
For more information, contact us at info@encirclepub.com.

Thank you,
Encircle Publications

For news about more exciting new fiction, join us at:

Facebook: www.facebook.com/encirclepub

Instagram: www.instagram.com/encirclepublications

Twitter: twitter.com/encirclepub

Sign up for Encircle Publications newsletter and specials:
eepurl.com/cs8taP